FOLLOW THE BLOOD TRAIL

BEN WASSINGER

Best wishes
Ben Wassinger

FOLLOW THE BLOOD TRAIL

Editor: Carol Weber: http://carolscorrections.weebly.com/
Cover and Formatting: Blue Valley Author Services http://www.bluevalleyauthorservices.com/

ISBN-13: 978-1-5333-9579-5
ISBN-10: 1-5333-9579-9

PROLOGUE

JAMES SAT AT HIS DESK, pouring over his notes and getting more confused by the minute. He didn't like confused, he liked neat. And this was way off the chart. Thank God no one had died yet.

Forty-five miles away in Kearney, Nebraska, sweat poured off the surgeon's forehead. He asked the surgical nurse to wipe his brow. The clear plastic face mask he wore to avoid blood splatters from entering his eyes, mouth, and nose always made him sweat, but for some reason he was sweating more profusely than usual. The nurse replaced the mask and he returned his attention to the patient on the operating table.

"Jesus," the surgeon said, unable to isolate the source as the bleeding continued. "We better get this bleeding stopped or it's going to be all over." Concern had replaced his normally unflappable demeanor. They were suctioning blood off as fast as they were putting it in. *What the hell am I dealing with here?*

The surgeon had received a call from the hospital about forty-five minutes earlier. A patient had showed up at the emergency room with an abdominal bleed. Her medication list indicated she was taking Warfarin, an oral anticoagulant. The staff had given her Vitamin K, and later transfused her with red blood cells when her hemoglobin dropped to 8. Due to the extensive blood loss, and continued bleeding, the surgeon decided to open her up and try to isolate and control the source of the bleed. Prior to surgery she was given fresh frozen plasma, platelets, and packed red blood cells to maintain oxygen transport to the tissues.

1

The patient's vital signs were dropping rapidly. Carrie, the nurse anesthetist in the OR knew she was in over her head. She paged Dr. Curtis, the anesthesiologist and department head. Dr. Curtis gowned up and just as he entered the operating room, he heard Carrie say, "I'm losing her." He rushed to her side, looked at the monitors, then glanced at the patient. "Oh my God, what happened?" he said as he looked at the blood flowing freely.

"No way to stop the bleeding," the surgeon said. He watched helplessly as the patient's heart went into tachycardia and her blood pressure began to drop, depriving her vital organs of life-giving oxygen. . He announced the time of her death.

Before the week was out, similar events would happen in three neighboring communities. People were dying, and the medical community was baffled. They had to find the cause, and find it fast.

PART I

CHAPTER 1

THE SADDLE CLUB WAS PACKED. A landmark in central Nebraska, the club dated back to 1945, when a group of horsemen needed a place to board their horses. They built stables with an adjoining clubhouse which served sandwiches. A full scale restaurant followed, and after being destroyed by a tornado in 1980 it was rebuilt. The new club owed its ambience to a wall of windows overlooking beautiful Kuester Lake, and was a hot spot after the horse races.

James Wilson and his friends Curt, Rick, and Bob were celebrating their good fortune after opening day at the horse races. Grand Island was home to Fonner Park, the last live horse racing track in Nebraska.

James had a great day and agreed to buy dinner with his winnings, which totaled a little over three hundred dollars. After everyone ordered, James figured he might be lucky enough to get home with half of his money. He raised his glass in a toast to the number eight horse, Blind Alley, when his phone sounded *knock, knock, knock*: his message alert for an e-mail. James took a quick peek. It was a message from his partner. "Administrator says she wants you to meet her at Harvest Nursing Home at 7 AM tomorrow." James frowned as he got a puzzled look on his face before snapping his phone back in its holster. *I was just there two days ago. What does she want now?* James liked Jane, but she could be a real pain in the ass sometimes.

"Hey, James. What's with the serious look on your face? We're supposed to be celebrating your good fortune. Lighten up dude," Bob said, raising his hand for a high five.

James slapped Bob's hand, laughing and told him; "You're right. Find that waitress and tell her to bring another round."

The administrator of Harvest Home was at her desk when James arrived the next morning. He tried to hide his irritation at being summoned so early, but his head was still hurting from the night before, and he wasn't certain he was going to succeed. James stuck his head in the door of her well-appointed office as he rapped his knuckles on her doorsill. "Morning, Jane. What's so urgent we need to meet this early?"

Harvest Home was a new eighty-bed long-term-care nursing home. Conventional thinking now led away from the facilities built in the 1940's and 1950's; tiled floors, efficient, economical, and smelling like day-old spinach. Harvest Home embraced the new trend: large, carpeted rooms, with light streaming in from windows overlooking either the nicely landscaped lawn or the garden courtyard. Artwork tastefully selected by Bartenbach Interiors brought life and color to the hallways. The comfortably furnished family room, complete with a fireplace, made a homey environment for recovering patients and their families.

Jane Macron was in charge of this building, its staff, attending physicians, and most importantly, the welfare of *her* residents. This protective attitude was a good thing, James knew, but it put undue pressure on the staff at times.

Jane was visibly upset. In fact, she looked like hell. Her normally perfectly coiffed blonde hair hung in disarray, and her eyes were puffy. It appeared she hadn't slept the night before. "Have a seat. I want to wait for Marianne and Dr. Findley before I begin." *This can't be good.*

James took a seat. Marianne was the Director of Nursing and Dr. Findley was the medical director for the home. When together, they made a real "Mutt and Jeff" scenario. Dr. Findley was six feet four inches tall, bald as a doorknob, and slim as a whip. Not much to look at, but an excellent physician. Marianne, on the other hand, had a rag mop of jet black hair, obviously dyed, and her scrubs strained to keep her short, stocky frame contained.

James Wilson was the consultant pharmacist for Harvest Nursing Home. He and his partner, Fred Hawthorne, owned Hawthorne Pharmacy, Inc. Fred was in charge of Hawthorne Pharmacy, the retail store; James was in charge of Odyssey Solutions, the side of the business that serviced the nursing home.

Dr. Findley and Marianne walked in together and took the two empty chairs. Findley nodded at James as he sat.

"Thank you for coming," Jane began. A concerned look crossed her face. "We seem to have a problem here at the facility. Two residents were admitted to the hospital with bleeding issues in the last three weeks. Both residents had medication orders for Warfarin. Their laboratory tests were normal while at the facility, but high when they were admitted to the hospital." *Covering the facilities ass.* She paused. "I have had an occasional resident develop a bleed while on Warfarin, but never two residents this close together. I'm concerned and want to get to the bottom of the problem."

Dr. Findley took the lead. "I think it's too early to press the panic button, Jane. It's probably just a coincidence. These things happen occasionally, and sometimes we never know the cause. I assume their personal physicians have the bleeding under control." Jane nodded in assent. "At any rate, I appreciate being notified." Dr. Findley looked at James. "James, do you have an opinion?"

"I agree," James said, adding, "I just reviewed all the charts two days ago, and recall that one resident had high labs, but her physician withheld her Warfarin dose for a day. But then, it's rare a month goes by that I don't see a few charts where the labs indicate a change in Warfarin dose is needed."

"I think we should look at the two charts again," Jane stated emphatically.

"I'll get them," Marianne said as she jumped up and headed for the door. Dr. Findley seized the opportunity and rose to leave. "I have a colonoscopy scheduled for 8 AM. If you find anything, let me know." His demeanor made it obvious he thought Jane was overreacting.

There was an awkward silence until Marianne returned with the charts. They were inconclusive. James closed a three-inch thick chart,

7

shrugged, and said, "Don't know." He stood, grabbed his jacket, and headed for the door. "Let me know if anything else develops." He was anxious to find some Tylenol for his headache. *Damn, I could have gotten another hour of sleep!*

Jane looked at Marianne and said, "Well! I can't believe they just blew it off!"

"It is unusual to have two bleeds so close together, Jane," Marianne said, "but like Dr. Findley said, it may just be a coincidence. I assure you, I will personally keep tabs on the situation."

"Thank you, Marianne. It's good to have at least one person on whom I can depend. Those other two will wait until someone dies before they do anything!" Jane said, eyes flashing anger mixed with frustration.

CHAPTER 2

ONE HUNDRED THIRTY MILES AWAY Omaha was experiencing a spring snowstorm. Spring snowstorms brought heavy, wet snow coupled with high winds. This one was particularly bad because there was freezing rain the night before and the roads were already slick.

"Dad, we're going to be late!" Molly exclaimed from the back seat of the car.

"Just relax, sweetie," Sam replied. "A lot of people are going to be late today with these icy streets." Not for the first time that morning, Sam was frustrated that his Suburban was in the shop getting some minor repairs done, leaving him driving his wife's four-door sedan.

"But, Dad, I've got a perfect attendance record," Molly whined. "I've never been late before."

Her sister, Maddy, turned toward her, and moving her head side to side said mockingly, "You're going to ruin my perfect attendance record."

"Okay, that's enough, girls. I need to concentrate on my driving, not referee a shouting match." Sam noticed the tongue come out and the ugly face in return as he glanced in his rearview mirror. He smiled as his eyes returned to the traffic. *God, how I love those girls!*

Maddy was thirteen, going on twenty. She had long straight black hair, beautiful brown eyes, and was as slim as a broomstick. She had recently talked her mom into allowing her to have her ears pierced. Sam had begun noticing a reddish tint to her light brown cheeks and lip gloss. He told Iris she was too young for makeup, but Iris just smiled, shook her head, and walked off. He wasn't ready for his girls to grow up.

9

Molly had darker skin like her mother, and curly hair. She hated her hair. The nine-year-old begged her mother to let her straighten it. Iris told her straightening would ruin her hair, and the answer was "No." Molly approached Sam to intervene on her behalf. One look into those big eyes and Sam almost caved, but eventually backed Iris up. When Molly realized she was going to lose, she put her hands on her hips, tilted her head, and told Sam she was going to save her allowance and get it done herself. She turned on her heel and stomped off. Oh God, she reminded Sam of her mother. *And when did she start getting an allowance?*

Sam had the defroster and wipers on high, but the wind-driven wet snowflakes kept pelting the windshield. The blowing snow cut his vision to less than a city block.

Sam slowed almost to a stop as he approached the intersection. He saw the car coming from his left with its turn indicator light blinking in the freezing rain, and knew it was moving too fast to make the turn in these conditions. He watched the car begin to slide as the driver tried to maneuver the turn, tires losing traction on the ice. He said, "Brace yourselves, girls," and the blue sedan slid into the side of his car, making a crunching noise. It hit his door and pushed his vehicle up against the curb in slow motion, as they both slid to a stop. Sam looked in the back seat. "Are you girls all right?"

Maddy nodded her head and Molly began to cry. Satisfied there was no major injury, Sam said some soothing words to calm her down and told them he was going to check on the other driver.

"What are you doing, Dad?" Maddy asked as he tried to clamber over the console in the front seat.

"Trying to get out," Sam grunted. "That car has me sort of pinned in." He managed to work his way out and found the other driver had the same problem. The cars were parallel, pushed tightly together, and neither driver's door could be opened. The other driver was an older gentleman and assured Sam he was fine, but couldn't climb over the console, so he was stuck in his car. Sam said, "I'll call the police, but first I'm going back to my car to stay with my daughters and make sure they're fine."

The older gentlemen apologized. "It was my fault; I was going too fast. I should have been driving slower. I'm really sorry. I hope no one was hurt."

Sam realized the man felt bad. "It's okay. We all make mistakes. At least no one was hurt."

Sam checked on the girls when he got back in the car. Squabbling. That confirmed they were okay. Sam googled the Omaha Police Department phone number and placed the call. A recording told him to state the phone number this call was placed from, and a second message stated that if this was an accident report, and there were no injuries, drivers should move out of traffic, exchange insurance information, and order tow vehicles if necessary. *Must have had a million of these this morning to have the message programmed in already.*

"Why are you calling the police, Dad?" Molly said. "You *are* the police, aren't you?"

"Not this time, honey; I'm not that kind of policeman. Besides, I can't investigate my own accident."

"Yeah," Maddy chimed in, "Dad is with the FBI and they catch criminals, not investigate car accidents, stupid!"

Molly began to cry again so Sam got in the back seat between them and called a tow service. *How has Iris put up with this every day?* Sam told Molly he would call the school and explain why she was tardy, and as soon as the tow truck came, he could drive her to school.

"Okay," Molly said. "But Mom is going to be really mad when she finds out you wrecked her car!"

Ah, the wisdom of a nine-year-old!

Sam Washington was enjoying the time he was able to spend with his family after a four-year separation. Wrongly accused of stealing money during a drug raid, he'd spent two years in prison, and lost his position with the FBI. Every day he spent behind bars he renewed his vow to bring down the man who had put him there. After his release from the penitentiary, Sam had gone through two dark and angry years, abandoning his family and living on the streets. He was determined to prove the guilt of the man who had framed him before he'd go home to his family. That was when he made a friend who needed his help.

Sam redirected his anger and focus, eventually bringing his accuser to justice, and taking a bullet in the process. Iris accepted him back into their lives after the ordeal was over.

Iris had raised the girls by herself for those four years while living with the shame brought on the family by her husband's conviction. While she knew Sam was innocent, and would never be the same if he had to live with the shame of being labeled a crooked cop, that didn't mean she accepted him back unconditionally. Iris was a strong-willed woman and didn't hesitate to inform Sam that although she understood his reasons, she and the girls had suffered greatly. She was not about to put them through another day without their father, so for him to return to the FBI as a field agent indefinitely was not an option.

That was a year and half ago. Sam had agreed, and after much soul-searching, decided to apply for a position as a consultant for the FBI. He had his law degree from Loyola University and had extensive experience in corporate law. This was the age of fraud, corporate greed, identity theft, and cyber scams, and Sam's expertise made him the frontrunner for the position. Pending approval of his appointment, Sam had been reinstated as an FBI agent. Sam was anxious for change, as it would allow him more time for his family. It would also give him an opportunity to do *pro bono* legal work for the homeless, a need he'd discovered when living in a shelter those two years.

"Okay, girls, here comes the tow truck." Sam turned to Molly and said, "Sweetie, I think we need to declare this a snow day, and take this car home so I can inform your mom I wrecked her car."

Molly immediately forgot her perfect attendance record. "Yes! Yes! A snow day!" she exclaimed as she clapped her blue-mittened hands together.

The tow truck separated the two cars. Sam walked back to his car and tried to open the drivers door. He found that the collision had jammed it shut. Sam cursed, walked around to the passenger side, and struggled to get back over the console into the driver's seat. Sam groaned as his foot caught on the shift lever. He struggled, then finally pulled it free. *Whose idea was it to put the shift lever in the middle of the console?* He put on his grumpy face as Molly giggled at his efforts. Sam turned the car around and took the girls home to make some hot chocolate.

Sam noticed a maroon van parked across the street from his house as he slid down the curving street to his home. Sam almost slid past his drive, but got the car slowed in time to make the turn. He was relieved to be off the icy streets as the garage door opened. He followed the girls inside and found the Keurig K-Cups to make hot chocolate. Sam dressed the steaming drinks with mountains of whipped cream, and served his girls. After two games of *Old Maid*, the girls soon became bored and went upstairs to their rooms to watch television. Sam looked out the kitchen window and watched the large snowflakes pelting against the window and piling up in the corner. He saw the van was still across the street and he could see the driver's outline through the frost-covered window. He and Iris had moved into the home a month ago and he didn't know all the neighbors, or the kinds of cars they drove. After staring at the car another five minutes, an eerie thought crossed Sam's mind. *Could that possibly be Frankie Colter? Maybe he's just waiting for his chance to get me alone outside.*

Frankie Colter was a name from Sam's past. Dave Colter, Frankie's younger brother, was on trial for murder, and Sam testified that he had arrested Dave for killing the clerk in a convenience store robbery. Sam's testimony was based on eyewitness accounts plus ballistics which matched the bullet at the scene to the gun Dave had in his possession at the time of his arrest. Dave was sentenced to life in prison. Frankie, who was present at the trial went ballistic, jumping up, running down the aisle, and hurled himself at Sam, who was still sitting in the courtroom. A struggle ensued, and it took five sheriff's deputies to subdue Frankie. As he was forcibly removed, he pointed at Sam and shouted, "I'm going to kill that son of a bitch!"

Frankie spent thirty days in jail, and soon followed in his younger brother's footsteps, getting busted selling drugs and receiving a six-year sentence. It was no secret Frankie hated Sam. He made it known to fellow inmates, visitors, guards, and the prison psychiatrist.

This all happened before Sam was framed, and six months before he began his own prison sentence. When Frankie was released two weeks ago, Special Agent John Williams, Sam's superior, notified Sam, reminded him of the threats, and told him to keep a watchful eye.

Sam was concerned about his family and sought out the office's criminal profiler. He assured Sam that it was highly unlikely Frankie would involve Sam's family. "He's a petty thief, and may begin to escalate the level of his crimes, but he isn't likely to step up to the level of a kidnapper. In all reality, Sam, from what I read in his file, he just isn't that smart. On the other hand, you are a prime target, and I would be extremely careful if I were you."

Sam figured it was fine for the profiler to tell him not to worry about his family, but it wasn't that easy. Sam was very protective of his family, perhaps too much so.

After staring at the car for a few minutes, Sam decided maybe he should offer some assistance in case the car had stalled, or was stuck in the snow...or was watching him. Sam put on his Kevlar vest, pulled on his blue Colombia parka, gloves, and stocking hat. He took his Glock from its holster, and put it in his coat pocket. He stepped out the door with his hand on the Glock in his pocket. If it was Colter, Sam was ready. He was halfway across the street when the van started and spun its tires, throwing snow as it skidded away. Sam tried to get a license plate number, but the plate was covered with the sticky wet snow. *Damn!* All the information he had was a maroon van. Sam wished he had paid more attention to the make and model.

CHAPTER 3

S AM SPENT THE DAY WATCHING out the window for the maroon van to reappear. Late in the afternoon, he decided to shovel a path for Iris to use when she got home from work. Sam had a shovel-width path cleared when a blue sedan pulled into the drive in the deepening snow. He turned to see Iris climb out of the passenger side, thank her co-worker for the ride, and brace herself in the wind.

Iris worked in the city clerk's office and always wore dresses or skirts to work in spite of the dress code which allowed slacks. She was wearing long dangling earrings, which Sam thought were sexy, and the wind blew them along with her hair. Sam always said she looked like Oprah Winfrey, but she just laughed at the notion.

"What are you doing out here?" Iris asked Sam.

"Shoveling a path so my lady doesn't have to walk in the snow."

"Uh-huh. I didn't know you knew how to use a shovel." She smiled. "You and the girls have a good time today?"

"Long story," Sam replied. "Let's go inside. I have something to show you." He held open the door to the garage for her and Iris stepped inside, raked the snowflakes out of her hair, and stomped snow off her shoes. She walked around the back of her car and saw the damage to the driver's side. Iris gasped. "My God, Sam. You wrecked my car! How did this happen?"

Sam told her how the other car was coming too fast and slid into him at an intersection. He just had to sit there and watch it happen. Iris wasn't happy about her car, but was thankful no one was hurt. The girls heard her come in, and raced to the garage to see if she was mad at their dad. They couldn't wait to tell their versions of the accident.

Iris finally began to laugh with the girls as they described their dad clambering back and forth over the center console, mimicking his actions and grunts and groans.

They all walked in the house, still laughing. Sam took Iris aside and told her about the maroon van.

"I think Earl Atkins across the street has a maroon van," Iris said. "Was it him?"

"Don't know," Sam said. "The window was fogged over and I really never got a good look at the driver. But why would he drive off?"

"Maybe his car died, and he just got it started when you walked over? Or maybe, just maybe," she said, rocking her head back and forth and smiling, "he thought you were the Abominable Snowman with all those clothes on?"

Sam began to respond when Iris put up her hand. "You're letting your cop imagination interfere with your common sense again. Now we need to feed those girls."

Iris reached for the cupboard door, and said over her shoulder to Sam, "Make yourself useful and get some hamburger from the freezer. I'm going to make a big pot of chili. It's a chili day if ever I saw one." Sam knew she made dynamite chili, and headed back to the garage to get the hamburger. He opened the chest freezer and cursed. Just after they moved, they'd bought a new freezer and he had just tossed the frozen foods into it, intending to organize it later. Later had arrived, and he had forgotten about it. His hands were freezing by the time he found the hamburger. He hustled into the kitchen and put his hands under the cold water tap to warm them up.

Sam and Iris had purchased the house two months ago. Prior to that they had been living in the same two-bedroom house they'd had before Sam went to prison, and had outgrown it. Maddy was of an age that she really needed her own room. They searched for several months, and the realtor found a home that pleased them both. Iris had her large kitchen, Sam had a study, and the girls each had their own room. The large fireplace in the family room and the curved wooden stairway that led to the upstairs bedrooms gave it a homey feel.

Iris looked at him and said, "Glad you found the hamburger. I almost got frostbite last time I looked for anything in that freezer." When Sam didn't answer, Iris said, "Be sure and put placemats on the table. I don't want to ruin the finish on my new maple table."

"But it has a tablecloth on it," Sam said.

"And I also don't want chili on my clean tablecloth," Iris retorted.

Sam helped with the dishes and the girls went to their rooms to watch a little television before bedtime. Sam had settled on the sofa with his iPad and was scanning his emails when Iris flopped down beside him. She rested her head on Sam's shoulder, and said, "Sorry I was so bossy earlier. I guess I just got so used to doing everything my way when you were gone, and sometimes I go back to that time…" Her voice trailed off. He closed his iPad and put his arm around her shoulder. "It's been a tiring day," Sam said. "Let's go upstairs and we can unwind together."

"You are a naughty, naughty man," Iris said. "Besides, the girls will hear us."

"No, they won't. I'll turn up the volume on the basketball game, and be real quiet."

"You really are a bad man. Let's go, but no basketball game. I want your attention all on me. There's only one game going on in our bedroom."

CHAPTER 4

T HE MAN SNEEZED IN THE morning sunlight, reached into his
back pocket, and grabbed a partially used Kleenex. He twisted
it around to find an unused dry spot, and wiped his runny nose.
Damned head cold! He coughed, rolled down the window, and spit into
the snow. He was miserable. He was also nervous. *Where were they?
They should be back by now.*

He watched the massive snow blower headed his way. It was still
two blocks away, blowing the hill of snow that had been plowed to the
center of the street into a waiting dump truck. It took his mind off of
his head cold and he absentmindedly rubbed his watering eyes. *C'mon,
guys. If that blower gets to me, they're going to make me move this car.*

Before he saw any movement behind him, both back doors of the
SUV opened and Kyle said, "Let's go. Slow and easy. Just on our way
to work."

Relieved, Butch slowly pulled away from the curb. He turned left
at the next intersection, bouncing over and crunching through the
mound of snow in the street. He had previously shifted the SUV into
four wheel drive, anticipating some challenging snowdrifts. He couldn't
afford to get stuck. He took a quick look in the rearview mirror at his
passengers, still bouncing from the turn over the mound of snow. They
were silent until they had gone another eight or ten blocks.

Kyle spoke first. "Piece of cake," he said, as he ran his hands
through his full head of hair. It flopped back into its former disarray.
"No other customers around because of the storm. We just walked in,
did our business, and walked out. Looks like we're still in the clear.
Just keep driving like you're some ordinary schmuck on the way to

the office. Stay on Dodge Street. They'll be expecting us to hit the interstate and get out of town. Looks like we're catching a little traffic now so we'll blend in and nobody'll put this car at the scene."

Butch secretly wished Kyle would shut up. His mouth ran day and night, talk, talk, talk, repeating the same things over and over. Butch's head cold didn't help his disposition, but thankfully his ears were plugged so he could tune Kyle out.

The other man, Frankie, sat mute in the backseat. Frankie was a big dude, quiet and really scary looking. Butch knew better than to say anything to irritate him. Frankie was always playing with that switchblade knife he carried. Flipping it open and closed. Spinning it in his fingers. Butch had never seen him use it, but imagined he probably had. Several times. It sure explained the nickname Butch had heard of "Frankie the Knife." In Butch's mind, Frankie was a psycho, and he didn't want to say or do anything to push him over the edge.

Frankie finally spoke. "Did you see the look on that bitch's face when I handed her the note? I bet she peed her pants." He laughed and banged his fist on the back of Butch's seat. It made Butch jump.

"Yeah," Kyle chirped in. "You didn't have to hand it to her on the end of your knife, though. That kind of freaked me out too."

"Just wanted her to know we meant business," Frankie said.

"It went really smooth," Kyle said, mostly to Frankie, but also for Butch's benefit. "We handled it like pros. In and out with no collateral damage." He raised his hand toward Frankie for a high five, but got only a glare in return.

Kyle was celebrating so Butch decided to ask the big question. "So how much did we get?" Frankie's surly answer made Butch regret that he'd asked. "Do you think we had time to sit down and count it? We were putting our asses on the line while you sat in the car listening to redneck music. How much did we get? Dumb fucking question!"

Butch was wishing he had never met these guys. Down on his luck, he was in the wrong bar at the wrong time. Of course, at the time he felt he happened to be in the *right* bar at the *right* time. He overheard Frankie and Kyle talking about needing a reliable driver. Butch was desperate for money. He had boosted a few cars in his younger days, and sauntered over to their table and asked if he could join them, offering his assistance. Frankie initially told him to get lost, but Kyle let him tell his story. Now he was part of the team, and going to share in the loot.

Butch listened to the rhythm of the snow and slush drumming against the undercarriage of the Tahoe the next few miles. He arrived at the strip mall where Kyle and Frankie had left their cars, and turned into a parking slot. "Meet at my place tonight at seven," Kyle said as he grabbed the duffel bag and opened his door. "We'll split up the money then."

Sam was headed to the office. He was pleased the auto shop had dropped his Suburban off at his home the night before. It was much more safe on the slick streets. He stopped on the way to pick up some suits from the dry cleaner. He was carrying his suits to his car, sloshing through the slush when Butch pulled into the parking lot a couple of spaces away from him. Sam opened the hatch on his Suburban and leaned in to hang his suits on the hook. Through the window, he saw a man of average build, wearing a black hoodie under a black jacket, exit the Tahoe. He was carrying a good-size gym bag. *Guess he decided to jog inside at the fitness center today.*

The man got into a black Ford Explorer and drove off, throwing spray from his tires. Sam absentmindedly glanced at the license plate. SVR9... His attention shifted when another man exited the Tahoe. He was average height, broad-shouldered, probably a weight lifter. Sam could only see his profile, but the brow line and nose were enough. Frankie Colter. The ugliest man Sam had ever seen. Close -cropped dark hair, a large flat nose, and black eyebrows the size of paint brushes. Sam watched Colter walk to a late-model blue Honda Civic and begin to drive away. The license plate was obscured with snow. Sam closed the hatch, hurried around his car, and climbed in.

Sam put his key in the ignition, intending to follow the Civic. He looked over, noticed there was no driver in the Tahoe, and hesitated. Where was the driver? *Strange...I think the engine is still running.* Sam turned his gaze to the back of the car and saw the gray smoke puffing from the exhaust greet the frigid air and swirl away with the wind. *Where's the driver? I never saw him get out.* Sam felt his pulse quicken as his mind shifted into turbo drive. The maroon van flashed through his mind. Sam checked his rearview and side view mirrors, and saw no one sneaking up behind him. *What the hell is going on? Is this a hit? Was this a diversion so Colter could come back, or was he expecting me to follow him and is intending to ambush me somewhere along the way?*

Sam knew Frankie Colter wanted him dead. Sam's gut clenched. Something was going on. Sam didn't believe in coincidence. What were the odds that Colter and he would be in the same parking lot? Slim, or none at all. Unless that son of a bitch Colter had been following him. Sam looked for the driver again. No one else was in the parking lot. Sam felt his pulse racing and knew he had to get it under control. He forced himself to breathe slowly and evenly, and attempted to focus, to analyze the situation. *Think, Sam, think!*

It hit him like a ton of bricks. Unless it was a coincidence, it had to be a diversion. Colter wanted Sam to see him. He knew Sam would recognize him, even in profile. That gave the driver enough time to get under Sam's car...and do what? *Place a tracking device? Plant a bomb? Oh, shit. Is it wired to blow when I start the car? Is it on a timer? Or is Frankie parked nearby with a detonator in his hand so he can watch me blow up?* Sam threw open his door and hurled himself into the wet slush in the parking lot.

CHAPTER 5

SUSAN WILSON LEAPT OUT OF her chair when she heard the scream. She charged up the dark stairs of their Tudor style home, not feeling the pain as she tripped and fell on her knee at the landing. The yelling filled the air and she forced herself up and ran to the bedroom. By the light shining in from the hallway, she saw James in the corner banging the floor with his shoe.

"James, what are you doing?" Susan hissed in exasperation.

"I'm killing a mouse," James shot back. "The damned thing ran right up on the bed while I was on it."

"You scared the hell out of me!" Susan said. "I was afraid you were having a nightmare again."

"That damned mouse scared the hell out of me. I yelled, it ran, and I cornered it and killed it."

"Yes, you did. My hero," Susan said, head bowed, hands crossed at her heart, sarcasm dripping from her voice. "Now please get that mouse out of here and Clorox your shoe and the floor."

James gave her a look, and she left the room.

Susan wore her blonde hair cut short in a chic style. A petite woman, her cute and perky style belied how assertive she could be when needed, and her determination made her someone you wouldn't want for your enemy. Her husband, James, had disappeared two years ago, and Susan had waged a full scale campaign to alert the media and the public in an effort to find him. She also succeeded in harassing the local police department on a daily basis. James had been the victim of a vicious beating, and was suffering from amnesia when he was found, almost six months later, over a hundred miles away in a homeless shelter. Susan brought him home, and James eventually regained his memory with the help of a therapist.

For the first year, James suffered from nightmares in which he felt he was being bitten by snakes. When Susan heard the scream, her first thought was that the dreams had returned. Now, relief welled up inside her. She went back downstairs to her cold coffee and Continuing Education lesson. Susan was a nurse in the Intensive Care Unit at the local hospital and needed to keep up on her CE. She reached down and felt the rug burn on her knee when she sat down. It was turning red and was going to be sore for a couple of days.

Susan rose to get some ice from the freezer to place on her knee. Noticing the vanilla ice cream when she opened the door, she grabbed a bowl and put three scoops in, then added chocolate topping. She refreshed her coffee, went to the table, and sat with the plastic bag of ice on her knee. It felt good.

Susan picked at her ice cream and began reading the CE article. Her mind kept wandering back to James's plight.

Susan would lie awake at night, watching James toss and turn in his sleep. She would examine the scar on his face which ran from his temple to his eye. The scar, along with the nightmares, were a constant reminder of the vicious beating he had undergone.

Unable to concentrate, Susan finally gave up on the CE, took the melting ice cream, bag of ice and cold coffee to the kitchen counter, and turned off the light. She climbed the stairs, checked on James Jr., and went to check on James. It was dark, but James was still awake. Susan slipped off her clothes and crawled into bed, curling up with James.

"Did you get that mouse out of here?"

"Yep. And cleaned up the mess."

"Good...and thank you for being my hero," Susan said, kissing him. "Now, let's get some sleep.

CHAPTER 6

S AM SLID IN THE SLUSH when he hit the sloppy pavement after diving from his car, stopping just shy of the Tahoe. He scrambled to his feet, started to run, slipped, and grabbed the hood to keep his balance. He started to run again when something in the windshield caught his eye. *Is that what I think it is?* Sam pulled his service weapon and ran around the hood to the driver's door. He looked inside and saw the driver. He was slumped over in the seat, his throat slit from ear to ear. There was blood splattered on the windshield and dash, and it was pooling everywhere. *Jesus! That's why I didn't see the driver; Frankie slit his throat before getting out of the car.* Sam didn't think the man could possibly be alive, but had to check. Sam holstered his Glock, pulled his cell phone out of his soaked pocket, and dialed 911. "This is Agent Sam Washington with the FBI. I need to report a stabbing. Dispatch an ambulance and OPD unit to the strip mall on the north side of Dodge Street near eightieth."

"Please stay on the line, sir," the 911 operator replied.

"No, but I'll keep my phone on. I have to see if I can help the victim." Sam ran to his Suburban, splashing snow and slop, and grabbed the shovel he kept in the back. He ran back to the Tahoe and swung the shovel like a man possessed, smashing the rear door window on the second swing. He reached his arm in, unlocked the front door, and pulled it open. There was no place on the victim's neck to check for a pulse. Sam could see the severed windpipe and tendons in the gaping hole that had once been his neck. Sam felt the man's wrist. Nothing. He was dead.

Sam looked at the blood on his hand. As he bent to wipe the blood from his hand in the sloppy slush, the roar of a car engine caught his attention and there was a series of loud pops. Sam knew that sound. *Gunshots!* He dived to the pavement, rolling onto his back, partially under the Tahoe. Sam lifted his head as he drew his Glock, but only saw the taillights of a blue car sliding out of control in the icy slush. *He's going to do a 180 and come back at me!* By the time he could sit up and raise his weapon, the car had turned 90 degrees, recovered from the skid, and was bouncing over a curb near the exit of the lot. It raced onto Dodge Street, cutting off a white car as it skidded into the traffic.

Sam found himself shaking. *So there wasn't a bomb. Iris is right. I am paranoid. I'm also damned lucky to be alive.* Sam checked himself. No pain, other than from when he had hit his head on the Tahoe diving to the pavement. He was soaked, pants, overcoat, shirt, shoes. Sam pulled himself upright and kept his Glock in his hand.

Sam heard the wailing of sirens as the OPD cruiser flew into the lot, sliding sideways to a stop. Both officers opened their doors, pointed their weapons at Sam, using their doors as shields, and ordered him to drop his gun.

Sam didn't want to place his gun in the water, and considered asking the officer if he could just place it in the Tahoe. But then, these guys had no idea who he was, or what this situation entailed. It may be daytime, but even police calls in broad daylight sometimes took cops into dark places.

"Drop the gun!" the officer shouted again.

Sam bent and dropped his Glock in the slush. Nothing more intimidating for a police officer than to rush to a scene and be confronted with a man holding a weapon. Sam knew what dispatch calls did to a cop's brain. One minute you're driving along, talking to your partner about your kid's dance program the night before, and the next minute, dispatch comes over the radio. You listen to the faceless voice give you instructions and the dance program is compartmentalized somewhere in the back of your brain. You hit the gas as your partner hits the lights and siren, and as the car begins to race, you realize that the adrenalin in your bloodstream is already racing through your body. It's a rush of fear, excitement, and purpose, all rolled into one. And no matter if your body is shaking, you have to control the adrenalin in your brain. You have to remain calm. You're the source of reason in every scenario. It's the job. It's what you were trained to do.

Sam asked permission to retrieve his credentials from his inside coat pocket, as the officer cautiously approached. No answer. Sam heard the siren and saw the lights of a second cruiser entering the parking lot. The sirens in the distance signaled that the ambulance wasn't far behind.

"Keep me covered, Sean," the officer said as he approached Sam, keeping a good line of sight for his partner. Sam looked at the officer's name tag. It read "Garrity."

"Officer Garrity, may I reach in my pocket for my credentials?"

Garrity stood about four feet from Sam, his weapon trained on him. "Yes, but go very slow and easy. I want you to open your coat, and I want to see your hand at all times."

Sam complied. He reached into his inside coat pocket, and pulled his credentials, keeping his other hand in the air.

Officer Garrity made sure Sean, his partner, was keeping Sam in his gun sights, and reached for Sam's credentials. He quickly read them, and said, "Okay, Sean, he's who he says he is." Sean stepped out from the door of the cruiser, holstering his weapon.

Sam said, "Too bad you didn't get here two minutes earlier." He pointed at the bullet holes in the Tahoe. "You could have taken down the scumbag that did this."

"The victim was shot?" Garrity asked. "Dispatch said it was a stabbing."

"Yeah," Sam said, "it started out that way." It was then that Sam noticed the placement of the two bullet holes in the Tahoe. *If I hadn't stooped over to wash my hand...* Sam trembled. He quickly regained his composure. "The victim was stabbed. Shots were fired at me after I found the victim. I called it in as a stabbing because I didn't know how to describe *that*," he said, pointing at the open door of the Tahoe.

Sean walked over and looked in the car. "Jesus Christ!" He managed to get a few steps away from the Tahoe before he sank to the pavement, alternating between vomiting and the dry heaves. When he finally stopped, Garrity helped get him up, and walked him back to his cruiser to sit down. Meanwhile, the other two OPD officers were busy sealing off the crime scene with orange cones and yellow tape.

The ambulance had arrived and the paramedics were rushing to the Tahoe. "No need to hurry, guys," Garrity called. "Victim just about had his head cut off. Worst mess I've ever seen."

Sam explained the scenario to Garrity. When Sam described the two men who had exited the Tahoe, Garrity said, "Shit! Sean, get over here!"

CHAPTER 7

SEAN, RECOVERED NOW, RAN OVER when he heard the urgency in Officer Garrity's voice. "The description Agent Washington gave matches the description of the suspects involved in that bank robbery this morning. Same physical description, same clothing. And, Agent Washington got a partial plate from a black Ford Explorer: SVR 9-something. Other vehicle was a late-model blue Honda Civic. Driver of the Honda returned to the scene, and fired shots at Agent Washington. Washington identifies the perp as a Frank Colter. He was released from prison a couple of months ago. Get an APB on the radio now! And find out who Colter's parole officer is, and get an address on Colter."

Detectives arrived on the scene. Sam was glad to see Chance Murray was one of them. They had worked together in the past, and Sam liked Murray. Short and stocky, with graying hair, he was always making jokes. Underneath that jovial attitude, however, was an excellent analytic mind. His demeanor was relaxing to suspects, but Murray's keen senses were always on high alert.

Murray came over, stomping his feet to get the slush off, then looked at his wet shoes, as if thinking, *This pair is toast.* Murray shook Sam's hand. "Hell of a morning, huh?" Murray saw that Sam was soaked and said, "Let's go to my car. I'll turn the heater up and you can dry a little." Sam filled Murray in on Frankie Colter, aka "Frankie the Knife," and Frankie's vow to kill him after leaving prison.

"We have an APB out on both vehicles, and should have a name on the driver of the Explorer," Murray said. "Can't be too many black Explorers with that prefix. Good work, Sam."

"I'd prefer to be sitting at my desk," Sam said.

"We'll get Colter, Sam. At very least on a parole violation." Murray laughed at his own joke.

Sam filled Murray in on the mornings events and told him he was going to go home and change. He would be in the office if Murray needed him. Sam exited Murray's car and Garrity waved him over. Sam sloshed across the lot in his soaked shoes.

"I imagine you want your Glock back," Garrity said. "If you had discharged it, the gun would have to stay here as evidence, but since it hasn't been fired, here," he said handing it to Sam.

"Thanks," Sam said. "I was just going to retrieve it."

"Hope you don't mind," Garrity said, "but Sean disassembled it, wiped it dry, and reassembled it. I know you may not want other people messing with your weapon, but it was a mess..."

Sam took his gun, worked the slide, and chambered a round. "Works fine. Just hope I don't need to use it. Tell Sean thanks."

Sam began to walk back to his car, but Garrity said, "Detective Murray said you're the agent that took Nathan Landry and his drug cartel down."

Sam turned, smiled, and said, "Sometimes it's better to be lucky than good." Sam turned back toward his car, waving over his shoulder as he walked to the Suburban.

After driving home and changing into dry clothes, Sam finally got to the office. First thing he did was knock on the door of Special Agent in Charge of the Omaha Division, John Williams.

Williams was on his way out,, and didn't bother to move the conversation into his office. He already knew about the morning's incident. "What the hell is it with you, Washington?" his boss growled. "Why is it whenever there's trouble you seem to be in the middle of it?"

Sam shrugged. "Guess maybe I need to change dry cleaners."

Sam had to admit that he often wondered how he had ended up in unforeseen situations. His ability to see beyond his own case, and tie seemingly unrelated events together, made Sam a formidable adversary for lawbreakers. Sam had solved a good many crimes, or given information to other agents to help them solve their crimes. A team player, Sam never wanted sole credit for anything; he was simply happy to take criminals off the street, and content for the entire office to have the acclaim.

Williams had never liked Sam. It was possible Sam's law degree intimidated Williams. He had worked his way up through the ranks. Twenty-five years with the bureau. Capable, but with a chip on his shoulder.

"Washington, you know you will need to see a department counselor. You were involved in a shooting, and its policy. In addition, you need to turn in your weapon until you are cleared."

"I know the policy, sir. I wasn't involved in a shooting. I drew my weapon after the fact, and it was never fired. Technically, I was just an innocent bystander and managed to duck in time."

"See a counselor," Williams snapped, and walked off.

As Sam walked to his office, he couldn't repress a small pleasure in seeing Special Agent John Williams stew. John had never been the first on the scene for anything. Well, that wasn't entirely true. He was always first on the scene when the press or cameras were involved. John spent his time behind his desk, and accepted the acclamations of his superiors in Washington, occasionally giving one of his agents a pat on the back.

Sam settled at his desk, called Iris to let her know what happened before she heard it on the news, and got a busy signal. "He fiddled with some paperwork. He couldn't get Frankie Colter out of his mind. Or the maroon van. *Could the van driver have been Colter? Or maybe Colter's partner from this morning?* Sam realized his hand was trembling. *Maybe I need to see Kim.*

Kim was the therapist who had helped Sam's friend James Wilson regain his memory. After Sam was shot, he needed help getting back to a normal life so he also saw Kim professionally. While there was a therapist on staff for the Division, Sam was allowed to continue seeing her when needed, and this was a time he needed to talk. He called her, and she made arrangements to see him after lunch.

Sam called Iris. "Hey, hon. Just checking in with you…Yeah, everything is fine. Still a little shook up. Not to mention still chilled to the bone…I'm going to see Kim right after lunch. Think it would be good to talk about this."

Iris offered to skip her birthday dinner with the other office workers that evening to be home for Sam. Sam said, "No need. Go out and have fun. Colter's not going to show his ugly face for a while. Every cop in the city is looking for him. I'll leave work early and take my girls out for pizza."

"Sam, promise me you'll be careful," Iris said.

"I will be careful, promise. Love you."

"Love you, too," Iris said, concern in her voice.

CHAPTER 8

F RANKIE HAD SLIT BUTCH'S THROAT, and he would be the first to tell you it was a work of art. *Pat Butch on the left shoulder and when he turned his head, whip the blade around from the right with lightning speed. Then slash back to sever muscle, tendons, windpipe, arteries, and anything else that got in the way. He was so fast, he hardly got any blood on his knife.* Frankie didn't have time to admire his own work. When he looked to make sure no one had seen him, Frankie saw Sam watching Kyle walk to his car and drive off. He hastily exited the Tahoe while Sam watched Kyle, and hurried to his own vehicle.

Overwhelmed with hate, Frankie had gone about two blocks when he decided to kill Sam Washington today. This was the day. He made a right turn, sliding around the corner, drove to Cass Street, and doubled back to the strip mall. He would come in the east entrance behind Sam, and do a drive by. Frankie knew Sam would be standing by the Tahoe, still shocked at seeing Butch's mutilated body. Frankie stopped around the corner from the mall. He reached under the seat and pulled out the Beretta 9mm handgun. Frankie didn't need to check to make sure there was a shell in the chamber. He always kept it loaded.

Frankie lowered the passenger side window and slowly approached and turned into the lot. There Sam was, standing beside the Tahoe, thirty yards away. It was just as he had imagined. Frankie slowly drove about ten yards and then hit the gas. The car leapt forward. Frankie aimed and fired at Sam, his arm extended toward the open window. The sound from the burst of shots rang loudly in Frankie's ears as smoke and the smell of gunpowder filled the car. *Take that, you son of a bitch!*

Just about that time, the tires lost traction in the icy slush, and Frankie's car started to slide. He had to grab the wheel with both hands, taking his eye off of Sam, and dropping his gun in the process. The car slid sideways, but Frankie cramped the wheel and got the car straightened out. He glanced in the mirror, and saw Sam sitting upright beside the Tahoe, a weapon in his hand. Frankie hit the gas, not noticing the concrete barrier at the exit of the lot. His car jumped up, scraped the barrier, then bounced down when it cleared it. Frankie was jostled around inside the car and had to swerve to miss the traffic on the street. Horns honked, but Frankie hit the gas again and was gone.

Frankie slammed his palm into the steering wheel. *Damn! Damn! Damn! Why didn't I just do it when I first saw him! It was perfect. His back was turned and he was watching Kyle. He never would have known what happened until his blood was melting the snow beside his body.* Frankie banged the steering wheel again. *I never should have risked going back. I never was any good with a gun.* He took a deep breath.

Frankie hated Sam more than he had ever hated anyone in his life. That included his father who beat him unmercifully, and his mother, who stood by and allowed it to happen. If Frankie didn't like you, God have mercy on your soul. Frankie didn't take prisoners. He liked to think he released them from their earthly bonds. In short, Frankie was a head case.

Frankie had never actually met Sam. He first saw Sam in court at his brother's trial. Frankie sat in his seat, scowling at the highly polished wood in the courtroom. He seethed at all the pomp and circumstance when the judge strode in wearing that ceremonial robe. It pissed him off that the FBI agent wearing the nice suit and tie could convince the judge to put his brother in jail. In Frankie's warped mind, Dave was just down on his luck. The shooting was self- defense. *Hell, the clerk was reaching for a gun under the counter when Davey shot him.*

The verdict was announced and that was when he snapped. He rushed at Sam Washington. It took five deputies to stop him from choking Sam to death. Too bad he couldn't have brought his knife into the courtroom, or he would have had his revenge right there.

Frankie was soon to follow his brother Dave. He got busted dealing drugs and received his own six year sentence. This gave Frankie time to think, and his already warped mind blamed FBI agent Sam Washington for all of his own troubles. He sat in his six-by-eight concrete box, stared at the walls and planned his revenge. When the news that his brother had hanged himself in his cell arrived, Frankie went totally berserk. He was uncontrollable, and spent the next few months heavily sedated in a cell in the prison infirmary.

The rage and psychosis subsided, and obsession took over. Frankie had a Swastika tattooed on his left bicep, with the word "HATE" below it. On his right bicep, the tattoo read "DAVE". Below the name was Dave's birthdate and below that, the word "LOVE." Frankie took a vow that when he got out he was going to get that son of a bitch Sam Washington. After all, it was Washington's fault his brother had gone to prison. He was the one responsible for his death! He had lots of time to imagine how it would go down. He had been out of prison a mere two months when he and Kyle robbed the first bank. Today was the second. Frankie was going to do one more. That would give him enough money to move on with his plans. *Then I had to go blow it today!*

That's okay. I want this to be very painful, so Washington can suffer like I did. Davie was watching over me today. He made me miss with the gun. He wants me to do something very special to Washington.

Frankie drove on, satisfied fate had intervened in his favor. It was a very good day, especially now that he and Kyle only had to split the money two ways. *Or, maybe, just maybe, we won't have to split it at all? Kyle will never miss it if he's dead.* Frankie laughed out loud.

CHAPTER 9

J AMES BOLTED UPRIGHT AT THE sound. He tried to open his eyes, but they wouldn't cooperate. The sound came again...and again. He finally forced himself awake and found his phone on the nightstand.

"James," he mumbled.

"James, we need you here now!"

"Jane?" James asked, a little groggy.

"Yes," the nearly hysterical voice said. "We've had another incident, and I need you here as soon as possible."

James didn't ask any questions, he just hung up and rubbed his eyes. *Jesus, my head hurts. What is it with that woman? This better be good.*

A voice startled him. "Hey, you're finally awake. Sorry it had to be the phone. Who was it?" Susan asked as she walked into the room and sat on the edge of the bed.

"Jane from Harvest Home," James said. "What time is it?"

"A little after ten," Susan replied. "I let you sleep in."

"I ought to be at work," James said.

"I called the pharmacy and told them you would be late," Susan said as she rubbed his bare back with her hand. "You better sit here for a bit and wake up."

"Jane wants me at the nursing home as soon as I can get there. Says they have another problem."

"You told me she was over-reacting last time."

"I know, but she sounded pretty rattled this morning." James let out an exasperated groan. "I better catch a quick shower and get over

35

there." He slid out of bed and headed to the bathroom. He looked back and said, "If my phone rings again, don't answer it."

James made the shower quick. He pulled on a pair of jeans, a white dress shirt, and black leather jacket. It took just eight minutes to reach the nursing home. He was walking in the door to Harvest Nursing Home when the ambulance drove by and pulled up to the West entrance. James entered the building, turned left, said hello to the receptionist, and walked past her to Jane's office. It was empty. A *clickity-clack* of heels resonated behind him. It was the receptionist.

"Jane's down in Room 204. A patient is being transferred to the hospital," she said in rapid bursts, her voice trembling. A shock went through James's body. Gwen Eyelor was the mother of Kathy Mason, a friend of his from his college days at the University of Nebraska. Kathy practiced law in Colorado Springs, and James saw her occasionally when she came to visit her mother.

"Thank you," James replied. "I'll go to the room." He could see the receptionist was shaking. She was new to the facility. "I'm James Wilson, the—" he began to say, but she interrupted him.

"I know. Jane said you would be coming in, and to send you to Gwen's room." Wondering why she let him walk past her, James noticed she was pale as the victim in a vampire movie. Poor thing was shaken up.

James said, "Walk with me. The break room is on the way. I'll see Jane sends someone to watch the desk." Side-stepping residents with walkers or manipulating wheelchairs through the hall, they met Linda, one of the nurses, on the way. James turned the receptionist over to the nurse. The nurse nodded and said, "I'll take care of her and get someone to watch the front desk."

James found Jane, Marianne, and two other staff members in Gwen's room. They were deep in conversation. Jane looked up at James, gave him a glare, and resumed her conversation. After a moment, James tired of waiting, and turned to leave the room.

"Where do you think you're going?" Jane's irritated voice boomed out.

"I'll wait in your office," James replied, not turning or breaking stride.

The sound of the heels coming down the hall were not being made by the receptionist. "Where have you been all morning?" Jane demanded.

"Whoa! What's going on?" James was angry with her attitude. "You called me and told me there was an incident, and you needed me to come as soon as I could. By my watch that was only thirty minutes ago."

James waited as Jane gave him another glare as she walked around her desk and sat down. "We just took Gwen to the hospital. She just returned from breakfast and the medication aide found her on the floor. She was groggy and confused, then lapsed into unconsciousness. We called the ambulance immediately. I looked at her chart and she is on Warfarin, like the others."

"Okay," James said as he sighed. "But we really don't know if the Warfarin is responsible for a bleed, or if it's a totally different problem. Jane, what is your fixation with Warfarin?"

"This is the third patient, James. What don't you get about it?" Exasperation from both of them filled the room like a balloon about to burst. "I am the administrator of this facility, and responsible for that resident! I am the one who will answer to her family, not you."

"I understand that, and I don't envy your position. You know I will do everything I can to help, but I need some concrete evidence there is a problem. You have, what...twenty patients on Warfarin in the facility? If there is a problem with the drug, why have only two—or three, if Gwen's problem turns out to be a bleed—had any problems? Wouldn't every patient have problems? You and Marianne had her chart in the room. When were her last labs and what was her INR?"

"Five days ago, and her INR was 2.3."

"Right where it should be for atrial fibrillation," James said. James knew that a patient's INR could vary from day to day and month to month. Hence the reason the doctor ordered a monthly blood draw for all patients on Warfarin. The name for the test is a PT/INR. PT stands for prothrombin time and measures how long it takes blood to clot. INR, the International Normalized Ratio, also measures how long it takes blood to clot, and is used to monitor the effects of the patient's current Warfarin dose. The physician adjusts the Warfarin dose based on the INR results, and attempts to keep the clotting time in a desired range, usually between 2 and 3. If the INR is less than 2, a dose increase may be necessary to prevent clots, and if above 3, a dose reduction may be necessary to prevent bleeding.

James stood and said. "Call me when you hear from the hospital."

"You think I'm panicking over nothing, don't you?" Jane's defiant glare didn't waver.

"No, I think you're concerned. Just like me. But I don't set out mouse traps unless I'm pretty sure there's one in the house. Let's wait and see." Thinking back to last night, James wondered if he shouldn't consider it. James left Harvest Home with a strange feeling in his gut. *What the hell IS happening here?*

CHAPTER 10

J AMES'S CELL RANG, STARTLING HIM. His screen said the caller was Curt. "Hey, buddy, what's up?

"Got a trip planned. Be at my office at noon."

"What time is it now?" James asked.

"I don't know, 11:30 or so. Anyway, I'll have lunch ready. Just be here."

Curt was always coming up with a hunting or fishing trip. James had been playing golf with Curt, Rick, and Bob last summer when Curt had lined up a deer hunt. James had never shot anything bigger than a pheasant, so he was the tenderfoot of the group; the rest of them were seasoned hunters. James earned his merit badge, bagging a small buck. A photo of James with his deer hung in his office. *Wonder what he's dreamed up now?*

James headed for Curt's office and found Rick and Bob already there at a card table set in the corner. Curt saw James enter the office and waved him over. "Grab some pizza. What can I get you to drink?"

"Diet Pepsi," James said as he grabbed a slice of supreme.

Rick was already on his third piece of pizza. He waved at James between bites. He appeared to be in shadow, but it was just a three- or four-day growth of beard beneath his curly hair. Rick was the joker in the group. When things got serious, Rick was always on hand with some ridiculous joke.

Bob, on the other hand, was the quiet one. Bob was a thinker, and was the one who offered sage advice when the conversation escalated out of control. His reply to a question was more likely to be a shrug of his shoulders than a glib reply.

James was the newbie in the group. The other guys had been friends for years, and he was just accustoming himself to the dynamics involved in their relationship. He had to admit they kept his life interesting.

The pizza was almost gone when Curt rose and took the floor.

"Okay boys, here it is!" Curt said as he produced a newspaper article and tossed it on the table with a flourish.

"Here's what?" James asked. The article was about a local man who had shot a bear in Canada. They all read the article while Curt stood over them, watching, and grinning like he had just won the lottery.

"Here is what I'm going to put on that bare wall over there," Curt stated, still grinning and pointing at the picture of the bear.

"So you're going to buy his bear and hang it on your wall?" Bob asked behind his sly smile.

"Wise ass," Curt said. "I'm going to shoot my own bear to hang on that wall. And you guys can all do the same."

"I called this guy in the article," Curt said. He said he would meet us at his home about one o'clock and show us his bear."

You could cut the silence with a knife.

Rick spoke first. "Are you really thinking about this? I mean, we're talking about a bear here!" After that, the questions came fast and furious. *Where? Is it dangerous? How much does it cost? Can we take guns across the Canadian border?*

"Let's just save the questions for Jason," Curt said. They all piled into Curt's truck and headed over to Jason's house.

Jason Dupree was about the same age as the four of them. James was expecting someone built more like a bear, hands the size of hams, and a heavy beard. Jason was none of those things. He was slight of build, short, thinning hair, and sported a blonde, wimpy mustache.

Everyone shook hands, and Jason took them to the basement to see his bearskin rug. He explained, "My wife won't let me keep it upstairs." Everyone looked at it and nodded approval. Rick got down and examined it closely with obvious admiration. "Pretty cool," Rick said, looking up. "How much did this one weigh?"

"Only about two hundred pounds," Jason said. "I got a larger one this year, close to three hundred. I'm having another rug made to replace this one, but I won't have it for a couple of months."

The questions flew. Jason had all the answers.

James looked at Bob. "Are we seriously thinking about hunting bear?"

"Looks like it," Bob said.

"So what time of year do you hunt bears?" Rick asked.

"Jason is going to be there most of June," Curt replied. "He hunts the first week, then helps as a guide for two more weeks. He can guide us, and we pay him instead of one of the locals…Anyway, he's going to check on availability and get back to me in a day or so."

Curt said, "Check your passports, boys. Make sure they're up to date."

James climbed in his pickup, his mind still numb from the morning visit with Jane at Harvest Home. Discussing the prospect of a bear hunt had buoyed his spirits, but now he had to get back to the pharmacy and address his Warfarin problem.

CHAPTER 11

S AM MET KIM RIGHT AFTER lunch and they discussed the events of the morning. Kim's assessment of Sam's mental state was that, although shaken up a little, he was fit to perform his duties. She said a report would be sent to Agent in Charge Williams. She also suggested Sam take the rest of the day off.

"I'll do that," Sam said, surprising Kim, who thought there was no way he would comply. Sam was too stubborn. "Iris has a dinner tonight and I'm going to take my girls out to Pizza Hut."

Iris had arranged for Amy Hansen, one of their new neighbors, to bring Maddy and Molly home from school. Her daughter, Sierra, was in Maddy's class. The girls had strict orders to call when they got home, lock the door, and stay in the house until Sam or Iris came home.

Sam entered the house, expecting to be greeted with hugs. Or complaints about school, if one of the girls had a bad day or had gotten a bad grade. The house was quiet when Sam came into the mud room from the garage. Sam took off his black wool topcoat, hung it on the hook, and loosened his tie as he opened the door to the kitchen.

"Hey girls, I'm home!" Sam shouted. He didn't get an answer. *Better see what they're up to.* Sam walked to living room and headed up the stairs to check on them. He looked in Molly's room. Empty, her backpack on her bed. Sam heard the television coming from Maddy's room as he continued down the hall. Empty, the television on. Sam walked in and looked for the remote to turn it off. He finally found it on top of some clothes in the corner. It was broken, so he turned the TV off manually. He called out, "Maddy, Molly, where are you?"

Sam checked his and Iris's bedroom, then headed downstairs. He called out again. No answer. *Hmm...Maybe they went to the Hansens'.* Teetering on the edge of panic, Sam called Iris.

"Hey, hon, I'm sorry to call you at work. Were the girls going over to the Hansens' after school?"

"Weren't supposed to. Unless Amy asked them over...why, aren't they there?"

"No, I've checked the whole house. Molly's backpack is on her bed and the TV was on in Maddy's room."

"Are you sure they aren't outside?"

"I'm sure."

"Well they know they're not to leave the house until one of us gets home," Iris said with an edge in her voice.

"Do you have the Hansens' phone number?" Sam asked, trying to mask his concern.

"It's in my purse. Wait a sec and I'll get it for you."

Colter? Oh God, this can't be happening. Real fear began to grip him. *Kill me, but not my family, you bastard!*

"Sam. Are you there?"

"Yes. Give me the number."

"Sam...Is everything okay?"

"I'm sure it is. I'll call you right back after I talk to Mrs. Hansen." *Got to calm down. Probably just at the Hansens'.*

Sam had been in many tense situations. First, in the service. He was an Army Ranger. Then twelve years as an FBI agent. He had been in every scenario one could imagine. He was trained to remain calm. At one time he thrived on danger. Yes, he had been afraid. Only a fool wouldn't be afraid, and Sam was no fool. He knew fear was his friend; it helped him focus. Clear your mind and focus on the task at hand. He couldn't let the situation get inside his head. But these were his girls! This was different.

Sam's hand trembled as he keyed Amy Hansen's number.

"Hey," the voice answered.

The young voice threw Sam for an instant. He had been expecting an adult. "I need to speak to Amy Hansen."

"Mom, it's for you!"

"Mrs. Hansen, this is Sam Washington. I'm Maddy and Molly's father."

Before he could continue, Mrs. Hansen interjected, "Please, call me Amy."

This time Sam butted in. "Amy, did you bring the girls home from school today?"

"Yes. They're here now. Would you like to speak to them?"

"No, I'll come and pick them up. You live three doors down, is that right?"

"Yes. I'm eager to meet you, Sam!"

Sam's emotions took over as he ended the call. He put his head back and took a deep breath, exhaling to relieve the tension. He had been sure his daughters had been abducted. *Sam, get a hold on your emotions. The girls are safe.* It was then that the anger took over. They broke the rules and there was going to be hell to pay!

Sam called Iris, still angry, and told her that the girls were at the Hansens'. Iris said, "Thank heavens. I could sense the fear in your voice, Sam. They've never done this before. They've always called."

"Well they didn't call this time, and they scared the hell out of me."

"Sam, calm down. You probably still have this morning on your mind. Just pick them up and give them a good talking to. No need to make a major case out of this."

"But Iris—-"

"No buts, Sam. A stern talking from you will do the trick. Now, I've got a dinner party to attend."

Sam looked at the dead phone dumbfounded. *Maybe she's right. And I'm supposed to be the one who stands up under pressure. Well, better get over to the Hansens'.*

Sam's cell rang as he got into his car. "Sam Washington," he answered. Sam listened as John Williams relayed the information that the partial plate Sam had given the police led to the home of one of the men who allegedly robbed the bank. His name was Kyle Anderson. He had no prior convictions. A team was sent to the address and the Ford

Explorer was parked in the drive. They entered the house and found Anderson lying in a pool of blood, dead, a stab wound in the chest. There was no duffel bag or money found, but a black stocking cap was discovered lying on the front seat of the Explorer.

"The local PD is grateful for your information, Sam. Wanted you to know." Sam could sense the forced thank you.

"What about Colter?" Sam asked.

"They checked his last known address. No one living there."

"Damn!" Sam said, banging his fist on the dash.

"Don't worry, Sam," Williams said. "Every cop in the city has his picture. He's got nowhere to go."

"Right. See you tomorrow." Sam hesitated, then added, "I saw the shrink today. She's sending you a report." Sam clicked off. He started the car and headed three doors down the street. It seemed silly to drive, but he didn't want to expose his girls in the open with Frankie Colter around.

The house was brick, two story, very similar to his own. Sam noticed the curved walk to the front door was constructed of pavers. Nice touch. He also noticed for the first time that most of the snow had melted during the day. Typical spring snowstorm. Here today, gone tomorrow.

Sam rang the bell and the door opened almost immediately. The smell of something good being baked wafted past his nostrils.

"Hi, I'm Amy Hansen, you must be Agent Washington," the woman said, holding out her hand. She was tall, close to six feet, and her sweatshirt had flour dust on it that she made no attempt to brush off.

Sam took her hand. "Please, call me Sam."

With mousy brown hair in need of styling, and freckles all over her face, she was not the yuppie soccer mom he was expecting, but he suddenly liked Amy Hansen. Sam was always skeptical of strangers, but Amy Hansen had broken through his shell immediately. He felt safe with his girls here.

"I'm so glad to meet you. Maddy and Molly have told me all about you."

"That can't be all good," Sam replied.

Amy laughed, turned her head and called, "Maddy, your dad is here." She looked at Sam for a moment, sensing his mood. "Is everything all right?"

"Sorry," Sam replied. "The girls are supposed to call when they get home, and not to leave the house. They didn't call."

"I'm sorry," Amy said. "I dropped them off and made sure they got in the house. We drove home and Sierra asked if they could come over. I told her to call Maddy and see if it was okay with her mom. Maddy called back and said it was okay with her mom, so I went and picked them up,"

"It wasn't your fault," Sam said. "I just get a little edgy sometimes. Guess it goes with the job. My family..." He trailed off. Sam put his head in his hand for a minute, then regained his composure. "It's just been a bad day. And when I got home and they weren't there...I assumed the worst." *Why am I pouring out my troubles to a stranger?* Sam was normally very guarded about his personal life or feelings.

"I'm so sorry, Sam. Would you like to come in and sit for a minute?"

"No, that won't be necessary. I'll have a talk with my girls. Maddy was lying. You couldn't know that. I appreciate your taking the girls home," Sam said, "It's nice to meet you. Iris and I will have to have you over soon." The girls bounced into the entryway about that time, completely oblivious to the speech they were going to endure in a few minutes.

Sam took them home, and amid the laughter and chatter on the way, his heart began to melt. Sam gave them a stern warning about calling him or Iris when they got home, and a very stern lecture about lying to Mrs. Hansen. He sent them to their rooms.

Sam had been planning on pizza, so there was nothing out for supper. He decided he made his point with the girls, and after an hour of solitude in their rooms with no television or games, he gathered them up and told them they were going out for pizza. They begged to take Sierra along, so Sam called Mrs. Hansen and invited Sierra. The events of the day were left behind for Sam and the three giggling girls. After taking Sierra home and tucking in his girls for the night, he sat alone in his recliner, trying to erase his fears about Frankie Colter. But, try as he might, the horrific image of the dead man in the Tahoe kept surfacing.

CHAPTER 12

"**H**ey, James," Marcia said as he entered the pharmacy. Marcia was one of the pharmacists employed at the pharmacy.

"Hi, Marcia," James said absentmindedly, as he walked past her.

Marcia followed him. "Hey, are you in there?"

"Sorry," James said, turning back around. "I've got my mind on Gwen Eyelor at Harvest Home. She was taken to the hospital this morning; they found her unconscious. Of course, Jane is on her Warfarin kick again."

"Is Gwen okay?" Marcia asked.

"I don't know," James answered. "She's the third one this month." Concern and exasperation fought for dominance in his voice.

"Strange," Marcia said. "I'm on call this week. The night before last I had to come down and send some Mephyton out to Charter House."

Mephyton, also known as Phytonadione, or Vitamin K, was used to counteract the anti-coagulant effect of Warfarin. That meant they had one more incident this month…at another nursing home.

"Shit!" James's blood ran cold. "Maybe Jane isn't over-reacting." He stood deep in thought. He finally raised his head.

"Marcia, can you pull records on all the patients with orders for Warfarin, and then print out their PT/INR records?" It wasn't a question.

"What then?" Marcia asked.

"Then we are going to see if we can find a pattern. Anything that jumps out at us. This is starting to bug me."

James was beginning to suspect that something wasn't right, but he didn't have a clue what it could be. He mulled over all the scenarios in his head, but none of them made sense. He needed those printouts. *C'mon, Marcia; what's taking you so long?*

Marcia finally had the printouts ready. James sat down at his desk. He reviewed the four patients who had suffered bleeds. Their INR values varied for the last year, but no more so than any other resident. He decided to review more residents. Their labs revealed no secrets. When he found INR values out of the desired range, dosage changes to their Warfarin brought the INR back into the desired range. The more he studied the printout, the more puzzled he became. Finally, James decided to call it a day. His head was beginning to hurt, and he knew no more than when he started. Other than the fact they had four patients with bleeds in less than a month, that is. He headed for home, a beer, and some supper. He would come back to it tomorrow when his mind was fresh.

"Washington, my office."

The voice of his boss John Williams, the Agent in Charge of the Omaha Division, interrupted Sam's concentration. Sam was deep into the financials of Omba Corporation, a multi-level giant under investigation for fraud. Omba's holdings included realty services, mortgage origination firms, and a chain of small banks. They had first come under scrutiny during the mortgage lending scandal in the early 2000s. Sam marked his place in the pile of papers, stood, stretched his back, and walked to Williams's office.

"Sit," Williams said, not looking up. Sam took a seat and waited patiently. Special Agent Williams was not noted for his tact.

"So how are you coming with Omba?" Williams asked.

"Slow," Sam replied. "That company is the size of an aircraft carrier and has more moving parts."

"So, is it fair to say that you're making little progress?"

"Yeah," Sam said, "that's a fair assessment."

"I want you to take a break from Omba, Sam. We have a more pressing problem, and I want you and Johansson to work on it."

"What's that?" Sam asked.

"Drugs. Illegal or counterfeit pharmaceuticals. They've had problems on both coasts, and it looks like they're moving into the Midwest. We're getting a visit from the agents in the Newark office tomorrow. They'll fill us in on their findings. Meanwhile, button up Omba for a while. It can wait."

Sam nodded. The change of pace appealed to him. Too much time behind a desk dulled your senses, as well as your reflexes. He had come to that realization when his instincts had failed him the day before with the Tahoe in the parking lot. He should have just reacted. Sam was at his best when he reacted on instinct. In a critical situation, one could lose valuable time trying to think everything through. It could mean the difference between life and death. *Time to get back on the street.* Sam went back to his office to put the printouts in a cardboard box.

CHAPTER 13

MARCIA FOUND JAMES ALREADY AT the pharmacy when she arrived at work the next day. She was sleepy, having gotten up from a deep slumber to dispense a prescription for Vitamin K the night before.

"You're here early," Marcia said.

"Yeah," James said. "Couldn't sleep. I figured I may as well be doing something useful instead of lying there wondering why I couldn't sleep."

"I had another one," Marcia said.

"Another what?" James asked.

"Vitamin K order," Marcia said.

"Jesus, who for this time?"

"Anna Kolechek at Gateway."

"That settles it," James said. "Two is a coincidence. Three is a stretch. But five? That's a pattern."

"So what do you think the problem is?" Marcia asked.

"I wish I knew," James said, exasperation expressed in his voice. "Say, is Jennifer in yet?"

"Yeah, I saw her car when I parked," Marcia said.

"Let's bring her in on this. I'm going to get a little more data from my records. Tell her to save some time around eleven so we can pool our ideas."

James went over his records yet again. *Looks like I may be calling Jane at Harvest Home with an apology.*

Marcia and Jennifer arrived at James's office promptly at 11:00. The light was blinking on Jennifer's headset and she was still talking to someone. James waited until she clicked off her headset, then went over the events of the past week. Five residents with bruises or signs of internal bleeding. Normal labs prior to the event. After the event, labs were found to be high, indicating a lack of ability to clot.

"Okay, we have the end result in five cases," James said. "Now, we have to discuss possible scenarios, and hopefully determine the cause. Ideas?"

Jennifer led off. "Interactions with other medications, especially short-term medications."

Marcia chimed in. "Diet. There are foods that can interact with Warfarin. We need to talk to dietary for any recent changes in food offering."

"Good thought," James said.

Other possibilities were discussed. Medication errors from the pharmacy. Medication administration errors at the nursing home. Contaminated lab testing equipment giving false test results. Wrong labels on the Warfarin bottles.

"One thing we haven't discussed," James said. "If it was a medication error at the nursing home, was it accidental or intentional?"

Marcia and Jennifer shared an incredulous look.

Seeing the look, James nodded and said, "I know it's a stretch, but we can't leave any stone unturned. I'm going to check the three facilities and see if any nurses or medication aides works at more than one home. Perhaps a temp." He paused and thought for a minute, then said, "Okay, let's each work on different segments. We'll meet at the same time tomorrow." James made the assignments. "In the meantime, I'm going to call Jane Macron at Harvest Home, and eat some humble pie. I'm also going to call Dr. Findley, the medical director and ask him to send a fax to physicians suggesting an order for a PT/INR *weekly* instead of monthly."

"Won't that send up a red flag?" Jennifer asked.

"We'll find a way to temper the note," James said. "I would imagine most of the physicians are aware of the problem by now. You know how rumors spread in a hospital. Besides, maybe a red flag is just what we need. "Right now, let's call Medical Associates, our wholesaler, and change the brand of Warfarin we use. I don't care if it costs more, we need to change brands. When it's delivered tomorrow, I want all the existing Warfarin in the pharmacy and in the nursing homes replaced. We'll send all of our existing inventory and the medication at the nursing home in for testing."

Sam walked into the conference room and joined Agent in Charge John Williams, Agent Katie Johansson, and the two agents from New Jersey. After introductions, Williams turned the meeting over to the agents from the Newark branch, Agent Kopeck and Agent Leeds.

"Thank you for allowing us to visit with you," Kopeck began. "We've been investigating the manufacture of counterfeit pharmaceuticals on the East Coast. We first became aware of it about eighteen months ago. We've had two teams on this for the last year, and believe me, we were close to breaking the case."

Sam noticed Kopeck seemed to be directing his conversation at Agent Johansson. No surprise. She was about thirty-five, blonde and tall, typical Norwegian features with a strong nose. Not overly pretty, but attractive.

"We found their laboratory and had it under surveillance 24/7. We had the entire operation figured out, from the chemicals purchased, to the manufacturing, packaging and labeling. All we were waiting for was the man at the top. Our team had rented an apartment in a nearby building where we could see both entrances to the lab, and monitor anyone entering or leaving. We identified all of the suspects working in the lab, but never had eyes on the man or organization behind the operation."

Agent Leeds took over. "Then the strangest thing happened. We were pulled from the operation."

Sam asked, "You mean you were assigned to another case?"

"Well, yes," Agent Leeds said, "but the Bureau never re-assigned anyone to the pharmaceutical case."

Kopek added, "You see, Agent Washington, I think someone with a lot of clout got the FBI to drop the case. We turned in our case files, surveillance tapes, and that was the last we heard of it. Whoever is behind this operation has friends in very high places. I went back to the building that held the laboratory a week later and it was cleaned out. The chemicals and equipment were all gone. No sign the building had ever been occupied."

Agent Johansson spoke for the first time. "I'm more than a little puzzled. Did someone actually bribe, or perhaps I should say, *influence*, the Bureau, or is this just speculation on your part? And, if they did, why did the Bureau authorize you to reopen the case here?"

"That's the catch," Agent Kopeck said. "Officially, we are not here. Leeds and I came on our own."

Sam looked hard at Williams. "And you're okay with this, John?"

"Yes, Sam. You see, this is a personal favor to Mark," Williams said, nodding at Agent Kopeck. "We went to the academy together and have been friends ever since. Mark visited with me about the case, and also the probability the operation has been moved to the Midwest. They spent eighteen months on this, Sam, only to have the rug pulled out from under them. All that time and effort, and some bureaucrat in Washington gives the person behind this a God damned 'Get out of Jail' card. I told Mark we would look into it." Williams sounded emphatic in his conviction to push forward, but Sam sensed he felt ill at ease and was mentally wringing his hands, so to speak.

"Is the Bureau all right with this?" Johansson asked, concerned about her future. "Personally, I wish you hadn't told us the entire story. Now we have to work with a cloud over our head."

"Actually, you don't," Williams said. "I have the authority to assign cases in my division as I see fit. We operate on informant tips all the time. This time the informants happen to be in our own Bureau. The worst case scenario is that the higher-ups will also pull us off the case. Hopefully, we can make arrests before that happens."

"Why me?" Sam asked. "You know I've put in to be a consultant to the Bureau, and am just waiting for an opening. Or is it something to do with our shaky relationship?" It wasn't Sam's nature to be so

FOLLOW THE BLOOD TRAIL

confrontational, but he was unwilling to work on this case unless all the cards were on the table.

"Sam, I know we have had our differences, but I respect you. You are the best agent we have."

Agent Kopeck interjected. "I asked for you, Agent Washington. I'm aware of your history, and no one in his right mind would endure what you did to prove your innocence. Plus, you not only proved your innocence, you took a huge drug ring down in the process. We need someone with that kind of dedication."

"And what about me?" Agent Johansson asked.

Williams took that question. "I picked you, Katie, because you are like a hound dog on the scent. You have a tenacity that's lacking in some of the other agents. You have talent, and I think Sam can teach you to hone your instincts and become even better. Consider him your mentor."

"Flattery will get you anywhere? Is that what you're attempting to do here?" Katie asked with an edge to her voice. Sam put his head down, smiled, and shot her an approving look. He got a slight nod in return.

Kopeck interjected again, perhaps in an effort to thwart the sparring. "Let us show you some footage and share our information with you. If you decide you are not interested, we'll get on the bird back to Newark, no hard feelings. Okay?"

Sam looked at Katie. Her lips were pursed. Then she raised her hands in a "whatever" gesture, and said, "It's your dog and pony show."

Leeds hit a key on his laptop and the projector came to life. The slide show was finally over and Sam and Katie had seen pictures of the lab, three men coming and going, and various vehicles entering and leaving the premises.

"Why didn't you bust the lab?" Katie asked.

"We had to sit on it because we couldn't figure how they were getting the product distributed to the wholesale drug houses. Plus, we wanted the big fish."

"So how much of the Midwest are we expected to cover?" Johansson asked, then added, "And what makes you think they're in the Omaha area?"

Agent Leeds was expecting the question. He nodded at Kopeck, who put up a slide on the screen. It was a map of the Midwest, with Nebraska in the middle.

"Look at this map," Leeds said. "Interstate 80 runs east and west, through Nebraska, coast to coast. Interstate 29 heads south to Kansas City, and north all the way to Canada. Go a little further west to York, Nebraska, and Highway 81 goes north to Canada, and connects south to Interstate 35 all the way to the tip of Texas."

"So you're saying Omaha may be at the center of a distribution system throughout the Midwest?" Johansson asked.

"Yes, it's a good possibility."

Sam said, "How did you discover this illicit lab?"

"Good question," Agent Kopeck said. "A homeless man told one of the beat cops he knew of the whereabouts of a drug lab…he was looking for a little cash to buy booze, probably. Anyway, the PD followed up on it, and sure enough, it led not to a meth lab as expected, but to a sophisticated illicit manufacturing laboratory.

"We got involved at the request of the FDA as it's their responsibility to assure the purity and safety of all pharmaceuticals." He shook his head. "The problem is, the counterfeiters have no equipment to test the strength or purity after making the tablets. If they make an error and put too much or too little drug in each tablet, lives could be lost."

"So we're looking at a time bomb," Sam said. "It's just a matter of time before someone makes a mistake, and innocent people suffer the consequences."

"Exactly," Agent Kopeck answered. "All we had to do eighteen months ago was sit on the operation and eventually we would have found the people at the top. But thanks to someone high up interfering with our investigation, we're back to ground zero. Unofficially, we've narrowed the search to Omaha, and we're counting on Agent Johansson and you, Sam."

Sam raised his eyebrows pursed his lips, and let out a sigh. He sat in thought for a minute, bumped his fist against his chin. He raised his eyes, and finally said, "I'm reluctant, but I'll help you out." He turned to Kopeck. "Have the file put together and on my desk, and we'll start tomorrow. Will that work for you Katie?" She nodded assent.

Fifteen minutes after the meeting broke up, Sam heard a knock and looked up to find Johansson already in his office.

"May I come in?" she asked.

"Looks like you already are," Sam said. "What's up?"

"I just want to make sure you're okay working with me," Katie said.

"Why wouldn't I be?"

"I don't know," she said. "John told me you preferred to work alone, but he was assigning me to the case also."

Sam studied her face for a minute, then looked her in the eye. "Assigned you as a baby-sitter, informant, or partner?"

"Partner," she said, sincerity in her voice.

Sam extended his hand. "See you tomorrow then, partner."

Sam left the office wondering just what the hell had happened. The whole counterfeit drug thing was thrown at them on a moment's notice. On the one hand, he was anxious to get back on the street again. On the other hand, he preferred cases that touched on areas where he had some prior experience. And the cloud of someone in Washington pulling the strings haunted him. On top of everything, Sam didn't trust Special Agent John Williams. He had the feeling that William's jealousy of him might be a motivating factor to set him up for failure. Or worse yet, bring the wrath of some senator or congressman down upon him, costing him his job. *Time to be careful, Sam. Watch your back. Hope Johansson is on the up and up, and not Williams's ally.* She seemed genuine enough, and Sam knew her to be a good investigator, although lacking experience. He finally decided to accept her at face value for now, and take everything day to day.

CHAPTER 14

J AMES MET WITH MARCIA AND Jennifer the next morning. They had their game plans outlined, and each discussed the respective areas they would cover. Their approach was a process of elimination that required them to explore every facet of the drug distribution and administration system until they found a flaw. In addition, the drug interactions with other drugs and foods had to be explored. It was going to involve a great deal of research, and place demands on time they didn't have to spare.

Marcia made phone calls to the nursing homes involved, and asked permission to interview the nurses, medication aides, and observe nurses and medication aides while they passed medications. . She hoped to see a failure in the medication administration process that could precipitate an error and would explain the bleeding problem.

The pharmacy used a Medication Dispensing System, a robot, which selected pills from a storage bank, and placed them into containers for each individual patient. In addition, it scanned both the barcode and the pills themselves to ensure against dispensing errors. It was 99.99% accurate, and there had never been an error attributed to the robot in the pharmacy. Nonetheless, Jennifer called the manufacturer and asked for a technician to "stress test" the machine. He would be there first thing in the morning.

James was on the phone with the College of Pharmacy at the University of Nebraska Medical Center. He needed research on drug and food interactions with Warfarin, and any recent reports of unusual bleeding in patients ingesting Warfarin tablets. After he set the wheels in motion, he contacted Jane at Harvest Home to inform her of his efforts. She told James that Gwen Eyelor was in critical condition. She had a subdural hematoma and the bleeding was continuing. In the prior day she had been given Vitamin K and transfused with red blood cells when her hemoglobin dropped to 7. Her heart rate jumped up over 100, and her systolic blood pressure dropped below 90. The doctors gave her plasma and packed red blood cells to help keep her vital organs functioning and were life-flighting her to University Hospital in Omaha as they spoke.

James kept digging into the problem the rest of the morning. At quarter after twelve he remembered he had a lunch meeting with Curt, Rick, and Bob. They were meeting with Jason at Lee's Restaurant to hear the details about the bear hunt. Lee's was a mom and pop restaurant which served all-around good food. James decided he might as well take a break and go for lunch.

The guys were already pumped when James arrived. Jason had brought brochures with pictures of hunters with their bears, fishermen displaying huge Northern Pike, and a new log cabin in a wooded setting. To a man, the pictures were ignored and the brochures opened to the page listing the prices. The guys were relieved to see it looked affordable! Nods and smiles were shared all around.

James had to ask the question. "Is killing a bear for a rug really ethical?"

Jason spoke up. "Yes. The black bear population in the area has escalated to the point that the habitat won't support them. They raid garbage cans, dumpsites, campgrounds, and anywhere they can find food. This is the governments answer to help control the bear population in the area. Plus, it brings income into the Saskatchewan Province while solving the problem." James nodded, feeling better about the trip.

Jason had taken the liberty to have four slots held for them in mid-June pending their approval. He walked through the steps they needed to take in order to carry guns and ammunition into Canada. By the time lunch was over, it was a done deal. They were going!

Lunch had been a good break. James dreaded going back to the pharmacy. The clock was ticking, and at least one patient was in critical condition.

James walked into the pharmacy debating how he was going to break the news to Susan that he was going bear hunting for a week. *Maybe I should just tell her it's a fishing trip? After all, we are on a lake and can fish during the day.* His thoughts were interrupted by Marcia.

"James!"

"Hi, Marcia."

"You need to call this number right away! It's Gwen Eyelor's daughter and she's pretty upset." She handed James a sticky note.

"Yeah, I know her. Kathy. We went to college together. I'll call her right away."

James dialed the number.

"James, what the hell is going on?"

That's Kathy; right to the point. "I assume you heard about your mother's condition."

"Yes, they're Life Flighting her to Omaha. Last I heard she was doing okay. What happened?"

"Apparently they can't control her bleeding. There will be specialists there who may be able to get a handle on the problem." It was a stretch, but James didn't know what else to say.

"How can this happen, James? I saw her a month ago and she was fine. Now I'm sitting in the airport in Denver waiting for a flight to Omaha. My God, James, she may die!"

James wasn't sure what to say. He had to be guarded because Kathy was an attorney. It seemed strange James couldn't treat her as just another friend because she was an attorney. James was savvy enough to know you never worried about suits from patients; it was their children or siblings who filed the suits. James had been through this before. A patient had mixed up his medications at home, leading to an overdose and subsequent hospitalization. When a lawsuit was filed against the pharmacy, James could prove the medications were dispensed on different days, as the pharmacy was out of stock on one of them, and therefore the pharmacy could not have been responsible. The patient told James the lawsuit was instigated by his children, against his wishes. He and James both knew why the man had taken the wrong medicine at the wrong time. The man was a miser, and counted his pills to make sure he wasn't being cheated. He mixed up the pills when he put them back in the bottles. This had been confirmed by the admitting physician at the emergency room. James had intended to fight the lawsuit, but the insurance company insisted he settle. It grated him that he had to admit to a false claim, but decided the alleged error would make the front page of the newspaper, and the court verdict would be on page ten in small type. He finally gave in and settled. It still stuck in his craw.

James had to decide with whom he was dealing: a college friend, or the attorney daughter of patient Gwen Eyelor. He finally decided. Ten years ago she was a college friend; today she was a distraught daughter and an attorney.

"I'm so sorry, Kathy," James said. "All I know is that she suffered a massive bleed, and I'm not aware of the cause. These are questions you need to discuss with her doctor. I went to the nursing home as soon as I found out, but she had already been taken to the hospital. If there's anything I can do, please let me know. I'll keep both of you in my prayers."

"Thank you, James. I'm…just beside myself, I guess. I'll let you know when I hear any news."

"I'd appreciate that, Kathy." The phone went dead.

James put his head in his hands. He chastised himself for being vague with Kathy, but deep down he knew where this would end up: in court. He wasn't concerned about wrongdoing, but if he had acted sooner, could he have prevented it? After giving it several minutes of thought, James came to the conclusion that he would handle it the same way again. He could see now that something was amiss, but it wasn't reflected in any studies, nor did he suspect that Jennifer or Marcia would find fault with the nursing home or the pharmacy.

Marcia, Jennifer, and James had ruled out every possible scenario that had been discussed. His only conclusion was that it must somehow be the drug. *Could it have been tampered with?*

James had notified the FDA's Medwatch Adverse Event Reporting Program just in case there were more problems elsewhere. James wasn't sure what the outcome would be, but hoped they would take note since he was reporting *five* incidents.

In other areas of the country, patients were getting uneasy. They were afraid to take their Warfarin. Their physician soon took second place to social media as the patients' new source of information. Social media was filled with graphic photos of people showing large bruises, vomited blood, and even dark, tarry stools; all attributed to Warfarin. Although many of the Warfarin users were elderly, their children saw the posts and called their parents with concerns. The posts indicated there was a new drug on the market to prevent clots, and the bloggers were touting it as the answer to Warfarin's woes. Phone calls from patients to physician offices triggered thousands of requests to get them off of Warfarin.

Unaware of the social media hailstorm, James had to make a decision. It was one of two things: the medication itself, or someone intentionally overdosing the patients. It was time to notify the authorities.

CHAPTER 15

FRANKIE COLTER PACED THE FLOOR. *Where in the hell is she?* Frankie had sent his girlfriend of one week, Savana, (pronounced Sa-*vahn*-a, according to her) to the store to buy groceries. He had given her a hundred dollars, and she had been gone for over an hour. The store was only five blocks away. *If that fucking bitch spent the money on drugs...* Frankie knew she was an addict, but there was no one else he could trust right now.

He went into the bedroom and checked to make sure the duffel bag containing the money was still there. His paranoia was starting to take over his mind. He thought about Kyle, and started to laugh. *What a dumb shit! Thinking he was smarter than me.*

After he had bungled the hit on Sam, Frankie decided not to wait to meet Kyle at his house that evening, and headed directly there. Kyle was shocked when Frankie showed up thirty minutes after he did and pushed his way in the door.

Frankie could see the incredulous look on Kyle's face. Kyle said, "What the hell, Frankie? We had a deal."

Frankie said, menace in his voice, "The deal has just changed. I want my half now, not tonight."

"What about Butch?" Kyle asked, starting to get angry.

"What about Butch?" Frankie said mockingly. He repeated it, still mocking. "Butch is dead, and if you don't get that bag right now, so are you!"

Kyle just stood there, trying to get his mind wrapped around what Frankie had just said. He saw the knife in Frankie's hand, but was too stunned to react. The last thing Kyle saw was Frankie walking past him with the bag of money. The image began to blur, and Kyle's head rolled over into the pool of his own blood.

Where is that bitch? Wait 'till she gets back. I'll teach her a lesson she won't forget. Frankie paced for another few minutes, slamming his fist into the wall. In a fit of rage, he gave the coffee table a kick and it flew across the room, breaking a leg.

He finally turned on the television to calm himself down. He flipped through the channels, suddenly stopped, and backed up the channel. He was looking at a picture of himself! *Son of a bitch! They know who I am and my picture is all over the television. Shit! Everybody in the country will see my picture. I better stay here—can't afford to be seen on the street…Where in the hell is she?*

Frankie was paranoid and it suddenly dawned on him. *She saw the picture on television. She called the police and kept the money. That bitch!* Frankie went to the bedroom, grabbed the bag and headed for the front door. It opened just as he reached it, and Savana was there with a bag of groceries in her arms.

"What the hell, Frankie. Are you leaving?"

"Where the fuck have you been so long?" Frankie shouted.

"At the fucking grocery store!"

"For two God-damned hours?"

"All right! I needed a hit. It takes a while to come down sometimes."

"Have you been watching the television?" Frankie said, his eyes narrowing and his hand on his knife.

"I've been stoned, Frankie. I'm still a little stoned. Who cares about the God-damned television! That piece of crap over there doesn't work half the time anyway," Savana said, pointing at the television. She also noticed the overturned and broken table, and a sudden fear gripped her.

Frankie had to be sure. He grabbed Savana by the hair. The grocery sack fell to the floor. Savana heard glass breaking and started to cuss at Frankie. She stopped in mid-sentence when she saw the knife. "I'm going to ask you one time, and one time only," Frankie growled. "Did you watch the television while you were out?"

"I told you, *no*," she whimpered, the fear stealing the volume from her voice. She felt the tip of the knife cutting into her throat.

"You better be telling the truth. If I so much as hear a cop car even a mile away, I will cut your throat from ear to ear." Savana saw the evil look in Frankie's eyes. She had never been this frightened in her life. Frankie let go of her hair, her knees wobbled, and she dropped to the floor. Frankie looked at her with scorn, and said, "Now get that mess cleaned up and fix me something to eat!" Savana noticed he said "me" not "us."

Frankie scarfed down the miserable meal Savana had made for him. Two burned hamburgers, beans, and instant mashed potatoes. He washed it down with the only beer he found in the refrigerator.

It had been an hour and no cops yet. She was probably telling the truth, Frankie thought. He desperately needed a place to lie low for a while, and junkies didn't have friends, only suppliers. Plus, she could supply him with other needs while he was there. He decided to cut a deal.

"Savana?" Frankie said.

"It's Sa*vahn*a," she retorted.

"Okay, whatever. Here's the deal. I need a place to lay low for a couple of weeks. You apparently told me the truth. I like people who tell me the truth. You let me stay here until the heat's off, and I'll make it worth your while. We'll forget about the money you stole from me to buy drugs. You cooperate with me and when I leave, I'll give you five hundred dollars to keep your mouth shut. Deal?"

"How do I know you won't just kill me and leave?" Savana snapped.

"You don't," Frankie said, a smirk on his face. "But I just told you I like people who tell me the truth. And I may need to find a safe place again, so why would I kill you?"

Savana nodded, mostly out of fear. She knew she had nowhere to go.

The next morning Sam and Katie were in Sam's office reviewing the New Jersey case files. Katie interrupted their conversation to compliment Sam on his information leading to the discovery of the bank robbery suspect.

Sam said, "William thinks it would be nice if just once I could produce a live suspect instead of a dead one."

Katie asked, "So how are you dealing with being shot at? I imagine I would be a basket case. I've never fired my weapon on duty, and certainly never had someone shoot at me."

Sam fingered his right ear. The earlobe was missing from a gunshot a couple of years earlier. "I should have been expecting it. Frankie Colter has an obsession with killing me. He's dumb as a wall, psychotic, and won't stop until one of us is dead. Frankie thinks no more of killing a human being than swatting a fly. He's murdered two in the last twenty-four hours. Williams offered me administrative leave, but I'd rather stay on the job. It keeps my mind off Frankie, plus I have you to watch my back." Sam winked at her and reached for the next file. "Back to work."

After an hour, she slapped the file on the desk, looked at Sam, and said, "Okay, we looked at their case files. That was in Newark. Here in Omaha, we have no knowledge that a crime has been or is going to be committed, no suspects, no leads, no nothing. All we have is a hunch from Williams's buddy, Kopeck. If they have moved to the Midwest, and I say *if*, where do we begin? We can't run all over Omaha looking for a warehouse with a sign that says "Illegal drugs manufactured here." She threw her hands in the air in frustration. "I've got a good notion to tell Williams where to put this case."

Sam was beginning to like Katie Johansson. "I've told him that before. The man just doesn't get it."

CHAPTER 16

"**M**ORNING, LARRY," JAMES SAID TO Detective Larry Malone. "Where's Max?"

"Cleaning out the car, I hope." Both men laughed. Max Worthy was Larry's partner, and was notorious for leaving food wrappers and other assorted trash in their unmarked car. "Makes a hell of an undercover car," Larry used to joke. "People think it's a MacDonald's Dumpster."

"So, I don't imagine you called to serve me coffee and donuts."

"No, sit down."

Larry settled his six foot frame into the uncomfortable plastic chair opposite James's desk.

"I really don't know where to begin..." James said. He hesitated before taking a deep breath and plowing ahead. "In fact, I don't even know that I should be talking to you, but something is terribly wrong and I can't figure out what it is." James related the events of the past week. As he was getting to the meat of his theory, Marcia knocked on the door.

James could see her through the small window. "C'mon in, Marcia." Marcia came in the office and James introduced her to Detective Malone.

"James, I thought you should know. Gwen Eyelor died this morning."

James sat mute for a moment, feeling the shock. "Do you know any details?" James asked.

"No," Marcia said. "We got a fax from Harvest Home that said she was deceased." It dawned on James how impersonal a faxed communication really was. A human life had been lost, and all of a sudden the patient's humanness was gone, and they became a statistic. It had always been done that way, he thought, and until now he just accepted it. He knew protocol dictated the fax be sent by the nursing home to inform the pharmacy not to send more medications. Regulations required facilities to document everything. No mention that spouses, children, grandchildren, and friends were in mourning; no mention that the loss reflected an end to a special life. Ironic, how a person had importance, and then they died. Life went on. Basically, it sucked. James made a mental note to call Kathy Mason, Gwen Eyelor's daughter, as soon as he was finished with Malone.

James thanked Marcia for informing him. As she left his office, he looked at Malone and said, "I hope what I'm thinking can't possibly be true."

James explained his research and the conclusion that only one of three possibilities existed: 1) There was a problem with the medication in the manufacturing process, or 2) It had been tampered with, or 3) It was an intentional act on the part of person or persons unknown.

Malone stared at James for a minute. He leaned forward with his hands on James's desk. "James, you understand, unless it was number one, you're talking about a possible murder here. That's one hell of an accusation."

"I know, Larry," James sighed, "but there's no other explanation. The FDA confirms that the lot numbers of the tablets we dispensed were tested and the drug and strength were correct. That only leaves option two or three."

"So let's assume option two," Detective Malone said. "Where was it tampered with?"

"Could have been the wholesale distribution center, the pharmacy, or the nursing home."

"So what do you think?"

James frowned in thought. "I think it's all about confidence . It's no different than a computer in some respects. All you care is that the computer works. You don't give a damn where it's made, how it's made, or how it gets shipped to the store. You expect to turn it on, see the Windows or Mac logo on the screen, and bring up your friends on Facebook.

"Medications are the same way. We expect them to work. Every individual metabolizes them a little differently, so we adjust doses or change medications until we find the right medication and the right strength for each individual patient. We know it takes a certain level of drug in the body to exert its effect, and in the case of the drug we are discussing, we can measure that level. The puzzling thing is that the levels were normal just prior to the incidents. When the bleeds occurred, however, the levels were off the chart. We need to restore our confidence as well as the patient's to trust their medication.

"That's fine, James, but how can I help?" Malone had to bite his tongue to repress a glib *Thanks for the pharmacology lesson, James.*

"I just wanted to give you a heads up in case we do find some suspected criminal activity," James said.

" Okay, I'll make some calls," Detective Malone said, standing to go. "I have contacts in several larger cities. Maybe someone else has run into the same problem." He shook hands with James and left.

James decided to be proactive. He still had Kathy Mason's number in his phone. He hit the button.

"Kathy, James Wilson. I just heard about Gwen. I'm so sorry."

"Thank you, James," she replied. "I just can't believe she's gone... this is horrible. I can't imagine what she went through. The doctors said there was nothing more they could have done... James, the doctor just stepped in. I'll call you later." His phone went silent.

James just sat in his desk chair, thoughts racing through his head. *What in the hell is going on? What have we missed?* He leaned back in his chair and let out an exasperated sigh. The phone jarred him from his trance.

He answered. "Hey, Suz...Just sitting here trying to figure out what's going on with the Warfarin thing. Found out Gwen Eyelor died today." Susan said she'd heard as well, and expressed her sorrow. Susan said, "You remembered that you are to pick up JJ today, right?" Their son was the joy of their lives, had been walking for several months now and was even learning a few words. Susan had begun to call James Jr. "JJ" to avoid confusion as he got older.

"Glad you called," James said. "I had forgotten with all that's happened today. So why can't you pick him up?"

"You've been so preoccupied lately, James," Susan said. "I told you last night that I had a meeting after work, and you needed to pick him up."

"Yeah, sorry," James said. "I remember now. I'll be there at four. That's the time you said, right?"

"Right. See you tonight."

James took out his phone and set the alarm for 3:45 P.M.

CHAPTER 17

J AMES TOOK JJ HOME AND began to fix supper. James always fixed the same thing; either hamburgers or steaks on the grill, cheesy scalloped potatoes, and beans. The snow had melted and the temperature was in the fifties, making it perfect grilling temperature, although he could also be seen at the grill in the dead of winter. He always figured it was easier than cleaning pots and pans..

The phone interrupted James as he was seasoning the steaks. . "Hey, Sam. What's happening?" Sam Washington and James had remained friends since Sam had helped James when he was suffering from amnesia. James owed his life to Sam, and he and Susan had been honored when Sam agreed to be JJ's godfather.

"The usual. Work, church, and sleep," Sam said, "and, of course, the weekly gun battles with the bad guys." He gave a hollow laugh.

"I thought you were sitting behind a desk now," James said.

"You know me," Sam said. "Can't keep my behind bolted to a chair. Got to get out and get some action…So, how's my boy?"

"JJ's great," James said. "Wait until you see him. He's starting to talk now."

"Well, teach him to say "Sam," all right?

"So what's wrong with "dada" or "mama?" James replied.

"Borrrring…Hey, you guys are still coming to Omaha on Friday, right?" Iris had tickets to the ballet at the Orpheum Theatre for herself and Susan. Sam and James were going to supervise the girls when they babysat JJ.

"Oh yeah! Not going to miss that. Are the girls ready to do some serious baby-sitting?"

"They're ready. In fact, they are out with Iris finding some new toys for JJ."

"They don't need to do that."

"Yes they do. Nothing's too good for my godson. Hey, can you get off early on Friday? Iris and I would like to take you out to eat at Charleston's."

"Sure, but let Susan and me buy. You're giving us babysitting services and a place to stay. The least we can do is buy dinner."

"We'll argue later. I'll make reservations for five-thirty."

"Great. Looking forward to seeing you guys and your new home."

"And we get to do dinner, but don't have to do the ballet!" Sam said. James chuckled along with Sam as they said goodbye.

Susan walked in shortly after he hung up. JJ toddled to her and grabbed her leg. James said, "Hey, Suz."

"Hey, yourself. What's for supper? Could it be hamburgers on the grill...again?" she asked, her head turned and eyebrows raised, looking at him out of the corner of her eye. The impish smile belied her sarcasm.

"Why don't you change out of those bloody clothes and..."

Susan instinctively looked at her scrubs. No blood. "You turkey!" she said, giving James a whack on his arm.

"Gotcha!" James said, a grin spreading from ear to ear. "Now, change and I'll get some wine. We're having steaks tonight. Oh yeah, Sam called. He and Iris want to take us to dinner Friday before the performance. Can you get out of there on time?"

"I don't work Friday, so the answer is yes. You're the one who's usually late."

"Not Friday. I'm leaving no matter what."

Susan turned and headed up the stairs, rolling her eyes.

James put the seasoning on the steaks and poured the wine. All he could think of was poor Gwen Eyelor when he looked at the blood oozing from the raw steaks.

Frankie was still angry with himself for botching the hit on Sam Washington. He had settled into a routine at Savana's place. Savana seemed to tolerate him and hadn't attempted to call the cops. No doubt because he allowed her to have some drugs delivered to her house. She had taken several "hits" over the past couple of days, and it kept her mellow. They were out of food, but he could afford to order pizza delivery. Thank God Pizza Hut had items besides pizza. He always had Savana answer the door, not knowing if his face was in the papers or the television. So far, so good. He just had to stay in control for a few more days, then he would decide what to do with Savana. The trouble was, he was beginning to like her, junkie that she was. Or maybe it was just the sex? Oh well. Everyone is disposable. He obsessed a while longer about Sam Washington. He desperately needed to do some reconnaissance, and Savana's car was his only transportation.

Frankie glanced at the time. It was quarter to eight. The days were beginning to stay light longer, and it was just starting to get dark. He would act soon, because darkness was his friend. If he waited too long, he might miss his chance. He was not going to let that happen.

Frankie had two problems. He couldn't take a chance driving in the daytime for fear of being recognized, and he couldn't afford to let Savana drive if she was under the influence of drugs. That left only one option: Get her stoned and steal her car. It would be risky...*But hell, everything is risky, right?*

PART II

CHAPTER 18

S AM AND AGENT JOHANSSON SPENT their days visiting area pharmacies and alerting pharmacists to report any suspected counterfeit pharmaceuticals, especially Warfarin. It raised a lot of eyebrows, like, *You've got to be kidding me.* Some were downright defensive, thinking they were being accused of knowingly buying illicit drugs. Sam and Katie had agreed that this was step one, but were still at a loss to figure out what step two would be. In fact, they didn't know if they could go much beyond step one with so little information.

Sam thought about the cop television shows and the excitement they generated about investigative work. The reality was that it was tedious, tiring, and basically boring. It was just like anything else: You had to keep at it until you got results, and maintain your sanity waiting for that day to arrive. But when it did—that's when your hard work paid off...and the adrenalin rush pushed you into the next phase of tedious, tiring, and boring investigative work. Work; success. More work; more success. And on and on.

Friday couldn't come soon enough for Sam. He hadn't seen James's family for several months and was looking forward to spending the weekend with them. He and James had forged a bond starting with that fateful day Sam had found James lying in the alley. James was beaten nearly to death, and Sam fled the scene, only to summon help soon after. Sam denied there was any bond for a long time, but it kept coming back. The psychologist had warned Sam that it might not last. But she was wrong. It was more than a casual bonding of two homeless people. It was much stronger than that. Sam knew both he and James would ensure the relationship would endure.

One more day of pounding the pavement, so to speak, and he could relax for the weekend. Sam and Katie decided to call it quits about noon on Friday, and come back fresh on Monday morning.

"Okay, girls," Sam said, "I think JJ's mom said this was the time to get him ready for bed." He tuned out the protests, and James came to the rescue.

"C'mon, girls," James said to Maddy and Molly, "you two get to give this little guy a bath and get his pajamas on him. I don't know who had more fun with his new toys, JJ or you girls, but you'll see that bath time is even more fun!"

While James was supervising the girls and JJ, Sam decided to take a look around the yard. He was still spooked about Colter. Sam stepped out of the house and walked around the lawn, checking every bush and shrub. He finally walked over to the surveillance vehicle parked across the street. The driver's window slid down, and Sam leaned on the sill and asked if they needed some coffee. The men both declined, saying their shift was up in an hour, and they needed to get some sleep. Sam apologized for the inconvenience of having to babysit him, and thanked them for their protection. He walked back across the street, and as he started up his front steps he heard a car door open, and the sound of someone running. He spun around, and saw the two agents chasing a man down the opposite sidewalk. They tackled him and cuffed him. Sam ran over and heard them reading him his rights. They put him in the back seat of their car, calling for a unit to come pick him up.

Sam asked them what had happened. They told him the man came from between two houses across the street from Sam's house. When they opened their door to question him, he started to run.

"What's his story?" Sam asked.

"Same as all the rest," the agent replied, "'Hey man, I ain't done nothin"...I'll bet he's up to no good. Doesn't belong in this neighborhood, and sure didn't stick around when he saw our badges.

We'll let the OPD sort it out...You better get back into the house. You're a target out here."

Sam headed back to his house. He decided not to tell Iris. No sense having her worry. He and James would wait up for Iris and Susan, and a nightcap would settle his nerves while they waited for the women to get home.

James finally asked Sam, "What's going on with you, Sam? You're a nervous twit, pacing back and forth, looking out the windows. Is something wrong?"

Sam hesitated, but decided to be forthcoming, and he told James about Frankie Colter, the threat on his life, and the recent attempt. Sam explained he was afraid Colter might attempt to hurt his family if he couldn't get to Sam.

"Is that why that car is parked down the street with the two guys in it?" James asked.

"Yep," Sam said. "Pretty obvious, isn't it? But then, the idea is to deter him, not necessarily apprehend him."

"Geez, Sam," James said. A concerned look crossed his face. "How do you live with this every day?"

"Let's talk about something else. In fact, my neighbor brought over a bottle of Scotch for a housewarming gift. Let's crack it open and enjoy the evening."

James and Susan awakened to the smell of pancakes and sausage. Maddy and Molly were helping Sam cook breakfast and set the table. Sam figured he better get some work out of them before JJ came downstairs. Their attention would turn immediately to JJ.

The night before, James had shared his suspicions with Sam regarding the unusual bleeding events. Sam listened intently, not saying anything to James about his current investigation, but wondering if the deaths James was describing could have anything to do with the counterfeit drugs. If the lab was in the Omaha area, there was a good chance the drugs were making their way to Grand Island.

The rest of the evening was spent talking about JJ and the girls, work, and James's upcoming bear hunt.

"Why in the world do you want to go on a bear hunt?" Sam asked.

"I don't know. Maybe it's because my uncle took me to a cabin near a lake on vacation after my parents were killed. There was a bearskin rug in the living room and I would go out and lie on it when I couldn't sleep. It gave me solace in a terrible time, and I rather imagine its nostalgia."

"Okay, I can live with that," Sam said nodding his head.

He asked Sam not to mention it to Susan, as he hadn't told her yet.

Sam grinned, a twinkle in his eye. "Maybe I should break the news to Susan. Take the heat off of you."

James and Susan packed up the car after Sunday church. "Keep me up to speed on your findings," Sam told James. "I'll check into it on my end." Sam wished he could share more information with James, but thought that would be crossing the line. Best to wait and see how things played out in Omaha.

James returned to Grand Island, and found no further incidents. This continued for another month, and James assumed the problems were over. But why? He couldn't figure out why the Warfarin overdoses had come to such an abrupt stop, and was troubled at how it all made no sense. He wondered if it was that the original tablets were mislabeled.

Still looking for answers, James called the FDA. "Where are the test results on the Warfarin tablets I sent you from the nursing home? I know it takes time...Yes, I understand. But do you understand we have had a death due to possible errors in manufacturing? The tests on those tablets may be the key to saving more lives."

After further assurances that they were doing their best, which was another way of saying nothing was going to happen fast, James finally ended the call. *Damn, I should have used a private laboratory. But no, I had to follow protocol and notify the FDA. Serves me right for trusting the Federal Government.*

With no more bleeds occurring, James decided to go on his bear hunt. He was still apprehensive about leaving, but he knew all he could do was wait for the lab tests to come back. He had no control over the past.

"Hey, Suz, let's take a road trip."

"And just where would we go?"

"I need to run to Kearney and pick up some things at Cabela's for my trip."

"You really know how to excite a woman, you know."

"Yeah, one of my greater talents."

"Hey, maybe we can get JJ a rubber bow and arrow."

James stood in his basement, carefully packing his gear. The clothes, at least, didn't take much thought: camo, camo, and more camo. Susan was less than enthusiastic about the hunt. She came to the basement with an armload of freshly washed underwear, still wishing he would change his mind.

"What if you get mauled by a bear, or eaten?"

"Then I won't need all this underwear," James said with a laugh.

"James, this isn't funny. I'm going to worry about you all week."

"I know." He put his arms around Susan and kissed her on the forehead. "Bigger chance I would fall out of a tree," James said, immediately regretting the statement as Susan pulled back and glared at him.

CHAPTER 19

T HEY WERE GASSING UP THE rented van in Saskatchewan, Canada. Rick and Bob were arguing over the difference between an imperial gallon and a US gallon of gasoline.

James was finally beginning to relax for the first time in two months. He smiled at the guys arguing. It wasn't until now that he realized how badly he needed a guy trip to get revitalized.

"Where's the nearest liquor store?" Curt asked the convenience store clerk, ending the argument between Bob and Rick.

"About a half kilometer down the road, but it won't do you no good. It's Sunday. Government run, you know," The clerk answered. They piled in the van, and as Rick drove past the liquor store, Curt said, "Wait a minute, stop!"

"You heard what the guy said, no liquor sales on Sunday," Rick replied as he drove on past.

"Stop the car and go back," Curt said with authority.

Rick pulled the car to the curb and made a U-turn, grumbling to himself. He pulled into the lot of the liquor store. Curt got out and said, "Wait here."

Rick, James, and Bob waited in the van as Curt walked around the back of the building.

Three sets of eyes opened wide ten minutes later when Curt came around the corner pushing a hand cart loaded with six cases of Labatt Blue beer. "Let's get her loaded fast, guys. I promised the owner we would get out of his lot pronto."

We were back on the road in record time.

"So what happened back there?" James asked, still a little dumbfounded..

"I noticed the side door of the store was open," Curt said. "That meant someone was inside."

"Yeah, but it's Sunday," Rick insisted.

"Yep. I flashed some bills in front of him and he swore it was Monday," Curt said, laughing. "Money speaks its own language."

Two hours later they saw the sign: WALLEYE LANDING. It was a nondescript sign, hand painted. Rick turned off the paved road onto a hard clay path.

The road narrowed and darkened as it wound through about two hundred yards of thick pines. Streaks of sunlight danced across the van as it emerged into a small clearing. A narrow two-track road meandered toward a cabin.

A small sign identified the cabin as the office. They later found out it was also the grocery/sporting goods store as well as skinning shed. A big man in his early fifties emerged from the doorway, his belly pushing against his flannel shirt. A flannel shirt wasn't normally out of place in a hunting camp, but it was at least eighty degrees outside. His wispy, shoulder-length sandy hair blew in the warm breeze. As the man drew closer, James's attention was drawn to the right side of his face. A jagged scar ran from his eyebrow to his cheekbone. The eye was in a perpetual squint— hiding between the lids. *Encounter with a bear, perhaps?* No one dared ask. James instinctively ran his fingers over his own scar.

"You must be the guys from Nebraska," he said with a crooked grin, pulling a toothpick from his lips. "I'm Dutch." He stuck out his hand.

Ever the clown, Rick took his hand, saying, "I thought you would be Canadian," laughing at his attempt of a joke.

Dutch shook his head. "It's going to be a long week. Let's get you boys checked in. We leave at 7 p.m. for the stands."

They checked in and Dutch led them to their cabin. The camp looked like a Kansas tornado had dropped cabins at random among the trees. No roads connected them, just paths, and there was no orientation as to which of the cabins' two doors was the front. They wound around a couple of cabins and arrived at their own. Their cabin had only one door, so it was logical to assume it was the front door. The interior was a typical hunting cabin: plywood partitions separating the bedrooms, curtains for doors, gas lamps, a stove and sink. The best thing, however, was that the cabin was clean. That was reassuring to James. They may have been hunting bears, but nothing frightened James more than a mouse.

Dutch, Jason Dupree, their friend from Grand Island, and a man named Richard showed up just before seven. Richard was a native Indian, or a member of the First Nation, as they were called in Canada. Dutch unpinned a map from the wall and showed them the layout of the lake and surrounding structures. There were arrows marking each stand on the map. Dutch pointed to the stands they would use that evening, saying, "Be sure to take coats and rain gear, the stands aren't protected from the weather." Curt and Bob would be hunting along the south shore of the lake, James near the swamp behind the camp, and Jason was taking Rick across to the north shore. Dutch explained they would be dropped off at the stands, and picked up after dark. They were to stay in the stands until they heard the boat return, or in James's case, the four-wheeler.

"What if we wound a bear?" Curt asked.

"Good question," Dutch said. "Stay in your stand. Your guide will go down and check. He will follow the blood trail and dispatch the animal."

Follow the blood trail? My God, that's exactly what I've been doing the last two months! It sent a shiver down James's spine when he thought of the irony.

Dutch went on to tell them they had access to the lake during the day for fishing, but cautioned them about rocks hidden just under the surface by the unusually high water He also warned them that the abandoned nickel mine across the lake to the north was private property, and they were to stay away from it.

A few hours after dark James held on for dear life after Richard had picked him up from his stand. The four-wheeler gained speed as the raindrops began to fall. It was pitch black and the headlight flickered on and off at will, making the trees appear eerie. James couldn't see the bumps or hills, he only felt them, almost getting jostled off several times. The wind had picked up and it was beginning to rain hard. James held on, getting soaked to the skin as the four-wheeler sped through the downpour. He wanted to get off and kiss the ground when he saw the lights of the cabin. *Maybe the mosquitoes weren't so bad?* James hopped off, unstrapped his pack and rifle, and ran for the shelter of the cabin. He watched the lights of the four-wheeler cut through the torrent of raindrops as Richard roared back to the office.

CHAPTER 20

CURT AND BOB SAT IN the cabin drinking beers when James dragged his soaked body and equipment through the door. "Hey, guys! Any bears tonight?" James asked, his spirits raising up.

"Nope," Bob replied. He chuckled at James, his clothes soaked and covered in mud. "You better get out of those wet clothes, then sit down and have a beer. Didn't you ever hear of Gore-tex?

"Yeah, but I didn't think Richard was about to stop the four-wheeler and let me put it on," James replied as he began to shed wet clothes. Ten minutes later, dry and warm, James joined the others. "Where's Rick?

Bob answered. "That's why I wanted you to sit down. He and Jason are still across the lake...we hope. The waves were three feet high, and Dutch said he couldn't make it across to look for them. Which means Jason and Rick can't make it back across, either. We're just hoping they didn't try and make a run for it."

"You know Rick," James said. "He doesn't like water. I can't imagine he would get near the lake with those waves."

"Yeah, we know," Curt said. "But we don't know what Jason will do. He's kind of a cowboy."

The next two hours were spent worrying about Rick. The three guys finally settled in and slept a few hours.

James, Bob and Curt were outside with cups of coffee when Dutch stopped over to tell them he was headed out to look for Rick and Jason. As he turned to head for the dock, the roar of an outboard motor thundered in the cool morning air. Rick and Jason raced back across the now-still water.

Tired and hungry, they told their story between bites of ravenously eaten food. They heard the storm approaching and soon saw the waves were too high for their small boat, and decided to stay across the lake. Jason remembered seeing an abandoned trapper's shack on prior trips. They located the shack and weathered the storm inside. James shivered when Rick talked about the mice.

They wouldn't hunt again until the evening, so that left all day to fish. Lunch was fresh Walleye and Northern Pike, breaded and fried in grease over a campfire. A real man's lunch with no wives around to worry about their cholesterol. That evening Curt shot his bear from the boat as it walked along the shore, and James shot his from the security of his stand. James was glad it was a clean shot, and the bear died instantly. The bear had been standing on its hind legs, mad and growling, swatting at some berry bushes when James shot. It fell in a heap. James thought it looked just a little too human, and it bothered him a little.

The next day, Curt and James stayed in the camp. Dutch instructed them how to skin the bears for rugs, and after they finished he took the meat to the First Nation village nearby. Bob and Rick headed to the stands early and Bob filled his permit with a three hundred pound plus bear. Bob and Rick told the story about trying to get the huge bear in the boat.

"We would get the head and shoulders in the boat, and when we tried to push the hind quarters in, the boat would capsize." Everyone laughed until their sides hurt listening to Bob tell how they were exhausted after six or seven tries. They finally had to pull the boat up onto the shore to load the bear. They were still soaked from righting the boat and finally getting the huge bear into it.

James realized he was totally relaxed as he listened to the story. The Warfarin problem was erased from his mind for the time being.

The next day brought crisp, cool air, and a heavy fog engulfed the camp. Bob was up early and already skinning his bear with Dutch's coaching when James, Rick, and Curt sauntered over, their boots wet from the heavy dew on the grass. Dutch was watching Bob skin the bear, impressed with its size, and the length of its claws. "Claws look more like a grizzly's." Dutch rubbed his chin with his thumb and forefinger, and finally said, "You know, I've been thinking...these storms have probably disrupted the bears' normal patterns. Maybe you should be in your stands around noon."

Curt looked at Rick with raised eyebrows, gave a quick nod and said, "Get your gear ready. We're heading out right now."

Bob and James decided to take a leisurely cruise and fish their way around the west end of the lake.

It was close to noon when the structures appeared out of the fog. The sun was breaking through the clouds, and the warmth of the sun's rays pushed the haze upward. They were looking at an electrical power station, surrounded by five or six buildings. Most of the shoreline was rocky, but there was a stretch of shore where it resembled a sandy beach. Bob and James jumped out of the boat and pulled it onto the sandy patch. They both knew where they were: the abandoned nickel mine. It was surrounded by a six-foot-high chain link fence plastered with NO TRESPASSING signs. There was no lock on the gate. After a lot of discussion as to whether they should slip inside and look around, they decided to eat lunch on the beach. The sun was warm, they were tired, and as the beer and the food settled, they both stretched out on the warm sand. The gentle sound of the waves lapping at the boat soon lulled them to sleep.

James felt a hand on his shoulder. He woke up and started to ask Bob what was going on. Bob put his finger to his lips and whispered, "Stay down, I heard voices." There was a small berm between the beach and the fence that hid them from the buildings. James and Bob peered over the top of the berm.

Three men emerged from the woods where Bob had heard the voices. The man in front was older, had gray hair, and wore a blue suit. He was short, but walked with a gait that indicated he was definitely in charge. The other two were younger, both dressed in jeans, and one was carrying an automatic weapon. James and Bob exchanged looks. They were both stunned.

The three men went into the building nearest the fence.

"Holy shit," Bob said. "Did you see that?"

"Yeah," James said. "I thought this place was abandoned."

"You better tell those guys," Bob said, nodding at the building.

"Let's get out of here," James said, urgency in his voice.

"We can't," Bob said. "They'll hear the boat motor. We have to wait until they leave."

A half hour later, or close to an eternity, the door opened and the men exited the building. Mr. Muscle slung the rifle over his shoulder, and the men stood and talked a couple of minutes. The nerdy guy reached in his pocket and pulled out a pack of cigarettes. "Those damned things are goin' to kill you, Lenny," the weight-lifter guy said.

Lenny stepped toward the fence, turned his back to the breeze, and lit the cigarette. James and Bob froze as he took half a dozen steps in their direction. He stopped, and flicked the match away. He sucked on the cigarette, inhaling the smoke deeply, and letting it out with obvious satisfaction. He was looking right at Bob and James. They ducked their heads, and James started to crawl backwards toward the boat. Bob grabbed him, shook his head, mouthing, "Don't move."

The other two men walked on and were entering the path into the woods. One yelled, "C'mon, Lenny, let's go." Lenny took one last drag, and flicked the unfinished cigarette in Bob and James's direction. They both breathed a sigh of relief as Lenny disappeared into the woods. They waited fifteen minutes by Bob's watch before they dared crawl back to the boat. They walked the boat along the shore for a good hundred yards before they pushed it into deeper water and started the engine. They shifted the motor into reverse and threw their fishing lines out. If the men came back, Bob figured they would just assume they were two fishermen trolling past the mine.

It was silent in the boat. Neither man spoke until they were well out of sight of the mine. They couldn't see the far shore, so James pulled out his handheld GPS, locked it on the cabin directly across the lake, cranked the motor up to full throttle and they raced toward the cabin.

The ride continued in silence as the boat bounced its way through the waves. The roar of the outboard would drown out any attempt at conversation, but the shock factor still held Bob and James in a stupor.

Four choppy miles later they docked the boat at the camp. Bob and James went directly to the cabin, relaxed, popped a beer, and let the adrenalin wear off.

Speculation ran amok the rest of the afternoon. Were they criminals? What was so important in the mine that one of them was armed? And with an automatic weapon, no less. Guns were rare in Canada, unlike the United States. Maybe they were arms dealers?

"Is nickel worth anything?" Bob asked.

"How would I know?" James said. "Besides, Dutch said the mine was abandoned."

Rick and Curt returned about ten. They were hungry, tired, and downright irritable. They didn't even offer a "thank you" for the grilled steaks Bob and James had cooked for them. They mostly sipped their beer and complained that they didn't see one damned bear all day. "Guess maybe Dutch was wrong when he said their patterns changed due to the weather," Rick grumbled.

James and Bob couldn't wait to tell their story. Rick was mesmerized. All Curt said was, "It's none of your business and we were told to stay away from the mine. What part of 'no trespassing' don't you understand?"

Rick was eager to go to the mine and see for himself, and blurted out, "Hey, let's check out that mine in the morning, and we can still go hunting in the—"

Curt cut him short. "If these two want to get blasted in half by an automatic weapon, that's their business. We're here to shoot a bear, not *get* shot!" Rick reluctantly agreed, still wishing he were going to the mine. It sounded like more adventure than sitting in a stand all day getting eaten by mosquitoes.

CHAPTER 21

I T WAS ANOTHER COOL MORNING. The sky had a gray cast to it, and storm clouds were building in the south. James stood on the porch sipping coffee from a chipped cup, watching Rick and Curt idle the boat past the point and head toward the west end of the lake. He watched until the boat was a speck, turned, and opened the sagging screen door. The smell of bacon and eggs still hung in the cabin air, and Bob was finishing the dishes.

"Ready to go, partner?" James asked.

"Let's do it!" Bob said, tossing the towel aside.

Bob and James picked up their packs and rifles. They were wishing they had taken the guns yesterday when the men showed up at the mine. Today, they were taking no chances.

James stowed their gear away in the sixteen foot Lund outboard as Bob began to back the boat away from the dock. James counted eight boats tied to the dock, meaning none of the other hunters had left yet.

"Straight across?" Bob asked.

"No, better not," James replied. "Let's head east and work the shoreline around the lake. We don't want to set off any alarms. We can pull the boat up on the same stretch of beach as yesterday. It'll be hidden from the mine there."

An hour later the boat was secure on the sand, and the gate was still unlocked.

They waited a half hour before opening the gate and heading for the door to the building the men had entered the day before.

"Why are we creeping along?" Bob asked. "Why don't we just stand up and walk?"

"Good question," James replied, as he stood upright. "Guess we're still a little freaked out from seeing those guys yesterday."

"Maybe Curt was right," Bob said. "We should just head back. This is crazy. What if we get arrested for trespassing? After all, this is a foreign country."

"Yeah, but it's Canada, not Mexico," James said. "I doubt if they put you in jail and throw away the keys here. Besides, where's your sense of adventure?"

"Call me Mr. Conservative," Bob said, "but remember, they have guns."

"Who has guns? I don't see anyone else here," James said, laughing.

James tried the door. It was unlocked. He turned to Bob. "Fifteen minutes and then we're out of here." James opened the door.

Bob followed him into a darkened room about ten feet by ten feet. As their eyes adjusted to the darkness, they could see it contained a small desk, two metal straight-backed chairs, and a lot of dust. The dark wood paneling didn't help with the lighting. There was a steel door at the back of the room. James walked along the path where footsteps had brushed the dust away and read the sign as his eyes adjusted to the dark. It read: RESTRICTED ACCESS in large red letters. The door was unlocked. James pulled the knob and opened the door. It was black as pitch. He stepped in and stood on a small landing, jumping when Bob brushed his shoulder.

"Jeez, you scared the hell out of me!" James said.

Bob continued to reach over James's shoulder and pulled a string hanging from a light socket on the concrete wall. The dim light flicked on, revealing a narrow concrete stairway. James started down, feeling the cool and pocked concrete walls as he went. He reached the bottom and groped for a light switch. James felt the switch with his hand and turned the lights on.

The room was large, thirty feet wide and sixty feet long, solid concrete floors, ceiling, and walls. There were twenty gallon drums stacked along the wall to James's right, and six machines lined the wall to his left. A conveyer belt lined the wall behind the machines and extended to the far corner. A fine layer of dust coated the floor.

"Holy shit!" James exclaimed.

"What is all this stuff?" Bob exclaimed, looking around. "It doesn't look heavy duty enough for mining ore."

"It isn't," James explained. This stuff is all drug manufacturing equipment. They're making drugs in here."

"Why in the hell would they make drugs in here?" Rick asked, dumbfounded.

"Counterfeit drugs," James said.

"Let's get out of here!" Bob exclaimed.

"No, not yet," James said. "I want to see what they're making first."

"Well, hurry up. Have you forgotten the guy with the gun?"

James examined the tableting machines, noting that they seemed to be relatively new, digitally controlled, and meticulously clean considering the room around them. He looked over the "V" blenders where the powders were mixed with inert chemicals to get the correct amount of drug in each tablet, as well as helping the powder flow evenly. The blended powder was poured in the funnel on top of the tablet press, and as the blended powder flowed into the dies, it was hydraulically pressed into tablets. There was even a film coating machine. It looked like a home front-load clothes dryer with the door removed. The drum would rotate slowly, and as the tablets rolled over each other, the nozzles would spray a fine colored film coat on them.

James was in awe. This was a state of the art operation.

Notwithstanding protests from Bob, James went over to the stacks of drums and began to read the labels. Sodium Bicarbonate, Lactose, Warfarin...*Warfarin—what the hell is that doing here?*

Bob headed for the stairs. "Look all you want. I'm getting the hell out of here."

"Five more minutes," James said. "I just want to see what else is in here. This may be the source of the counterfeit drugs Sam Washington told me about."

Bob stopped at the foot of the stairway and groaned. "Okay, five more minutes, then I'm going to get in the boat and get the hell away from here. With you or without you!"

James continued to look at labels on the drums, letting out a "wow" or muttering some chemical name Bob couldn't understand. Bob was beginning to sweat, in spite of the cool temperature in the cellar. He glanced at his watch every ten seconds or so, willing time to go faster. The second hand just continued to move agonizingly slow.

Bob finally said, "That's it. I'm leaving right now," as he started up the stairs.

James was looking at the last of the drums when Bob hurtled down the stairs and hit the light switch, turning off the basement lights.

"What are you doing?" James almost shouted.

"Shhh!" Bob said softly. "I heard voices. There's someone upstairs."

"C'mon," James said, "You're just paranoid."

"Shut up and hide behind the barrels!" Bob said as he moved deep into the stacks of drums.

James started to laugh at him when the door above the landing opened.

The lights flicked on.

James watched the first set of boots descend the stairs backlit by the dim light emitted from the bulb in the landing above. He crouched and duck-walked to the back of the barrels.

James could feel the sweat marks spreading under his arms as the two men walked by. He was afraid to even breathe, lest he emit any sound. James heard a door slide open at the back of the room they were in. He hadn't seen the door. It was probably hidden by the barrels. James felt his leg start to cramp. *Not now, not now…* James forced his leg to relax, and the cramp finally began to subside. He had lost track of the men, when a motorized cart whined to life, and began to move through the doorway back into the room toward the stairs. When it reached the stairway, James lifted his head and ventured a glance. Just then one of the men turned around. James ducked. *Had he seen him, or had he ducked his head in time?* Sweat poured off his face, droplets pooling and falling to the powder-covered floor, making small craters.

The other man walked past James. Heavy, clomping footsteps. James froze. The man was so close he could smell the cigarette stench from his clothes. The man closed the sliding door and joined the man in the motorized cart.

"Let's get these boxes unloaded and get out of here." It was the nerdy man they had called Lenny yesterday.

"All this high-priced equipment, you'd think they could put in an elevator or something," the other man grumbled.

"Shut up and work, Abe," Lenny said. "For what you get paid, you can lift a few boxes."

They have names now, Abe and Lenny. Good to know; perhaps this will be enough to help the authorities capture them. The physical proximity of Abe and Lenny made James nervous, and he said a silent prayer. *Lord, get us out of this mess alive.* James had a painful flashback to the last time he was accosted by strangers.

After what seemed like an eternity plus three days, the cart was unloaded, and the boxes taken up the stairs. Abe said, "I'll run the cart back." As he drove past, James studied him through the crack between two barrels. He was at least six feet two, had a three-day growth of beard to match his short-cropped brown hair, and a hawk-like nose. It was obvious he had spent time lifting some serious weights. *Yeah, like dead bodies.* James could see the bulge under his jacket and was willing to bet it wasn't all muscle. Not exactly a good time to stand up and say, "Hi, Abe, what's happening, man?" James gave a rueful smile at how his sense of humor could surface while he looked death in the face.

Lenny called to Abe to stop, and asked him what he was doing near the machines.

"I wasn't near the machines, Len," Abe replied. That's when James turned to stare at Bob in horror. The footprints in the powder were all over the damned floor around the machines! James motioned to Bob to get deeper in the barrels—quietly. Not that it mattered. They knew someone else was here.

The men reached into their jackets and their faces became blurs; all James could focus on were the guns in their hands.

CHAPTER 22

S AVANA HAD BEEN DOING SOME thinking. Frankie was good to her, in spite of their shaky beginning. He appeared to trust her, didn't complain about her shitty cooking anymore, and bought the drugs she needed so desperately.

Savana grew up the daughter of a coal miner and an alcoholic mother. Her dad was hard-working, liked to go to the bar with his friends after work, but was a good man. She remembered his hands, calloused and rough, but soothing when he would take her hand in his and they would go for a walk. Or when he would soothe her after one of her mother's drunken outbursts.

Her dad and mom fought all the time, mostly about her mother's drinking. She would sit with her hands over her ears to muffle the harsh words between them.

When she was nine, her dad didn't come home from work one day. She went to bed that night and found a note on her pillow. "I'm sorry, Savana. I just can't take this life any more. I'm leaving your mother. I would take you with me, but I ain't fit to raise a daughter. I will always love you, sweetie. Love, Dad." She ran outside in her pajamas all the way to the mine office, a mile away. The mine manager was kind enough to take her home, and she never saw her daddy after that.

Things with her mom got worse after her dad left. She would go to the bars and come home drunk, or not at all. Worse yet, sometimes she would bring a man home with her, and the drinking and carousing would keep Savana awake at night. Her mom spent her welfare check on alcohol, and Savana wore second-hand clothes she found at the Salvation Army. The house needed paint, the lawn was a weed patch, and the curtains and carpet were filthy. Savana did most of the cleaning and cooking because her mother was either gone or immersed halfway into a bottle of gin.

High school was a nightmare. She was teased and never invited to parties. She knew she was attractive, even pretty, and maturing ahead of the other girls. That made the boys notice her. She found a way to get accepted, or at least get invited to the parties. That was okay with her. At least she felt like a person. She knew the boys took her out for only one reason, and that was fine with her. She wasn't lonely any more.

She allowed the boys to use her, and soon she was seeing older guys, and got introduced to drugs. At first, she shied away from them, especially when she thought about what alcohol had done to her family. But then came Bobby. Sweet, shy, caring Bobby. He was nice to her, treated her like someone special, and she thought it was the real thing. She wanted to please him, started using, and ended up losing her job when she failed a drug test. Out of money, desperate for a fix, Bobby started to beat her and forced her to take to the streets in order to feed his habit. She was doing what she had done since high school, but was getting paid for it. As soon as she was able to save some money for herself, she left Bobby and fled to Omaha.

Savana thought about Frankie. He could be nice. She knew why he was wanted by the police, but hey, they could move far away from Omaha where no one knew who he was. He had a lot of money from that robbery, and that meant drugs for her whenever she needed. Then again, perhaps she could shake her habit. Either way, it would be a new life. Maybe, just maybe, if she did something really special for Frankie, he would take her away with him.

The manhunt started to slow as the days passed. Sam returned to his usual routine, although he remained acutely aware of his surroundings. He knew Frankie Colter was still out there, and one day he would make his move. Sam actually hoped it would be soon so he could end the threat once and for all. He was still trying to grasp the fact that Frankie had come after him right after slashing his partner's throat. His unpredictability made the situation even more scary..

The daily meetings between Sam and Agent Johannsen became a chore and were totally nonproductive. Sam knew he had to keep her interest level high or she would never give her best effort. At the same time, he still had his suspicions that she was assigned to the case by Special Agent Williams only to watch him. His distrust was fueled when he showed up for work early a few times and she was in Williams's office. Nobody went to Williams's office unless summoned.

Sam decided rather than worry about the situation, it might be better to bring her over to his side. He was ready to change tactics anyway, and decided it was time to become a mentor as well as a partner.

"Let's go for a ride," Sam said one morning.

"Anything," Katie said, "as long as I don't have to visit another pharmacy and have the pharmacist look at me like I'm hallucinating."

Sam fired up the Suburban and headed for Council Bluffs, a town separated from Omaha by a silver ribbon known as the Missouri River.

"Why are we going to Council Bluffs?" Katie asked.

"Because I spent two years of my life there trying to figure things out. It was slow, methodical, and painful, but it worked. Everything eventually fell into place and I solved the puzzle. I imagine after two years the meth labs have returned."

"Maybe," Kate said, "but why do you care about meth?" Sam could sense her resentment.

"I don't, but drug lords are entrepreneurs. Not the dealers, but the people at the top. They know the market, the competition, and are constantly searching for new ways to corner more of the market, such as adding heroin to marihuana to make it more addicting. They consider themselves businessmen, not criminals. and we won't get near them. We start with the bottom feeders and hope we get a lucky break."

"Oh, shit," Katie said, "I'm not going to live in a homeless shelter!"

Sam laughed. "No, but I learned many homeless people are as smart as you or I. They're people who have been beaten down, have beaten themselves down, or just don't give a damn. They also see things, just like you and me. But sometimes they see things you or I never would. You see, they are invisible."

It was Katie's turn to laugh, and she gave him a smart ass grin. "You mean all those coats they wear are like the invisibility cloak Harry Potter wears?"

Sam ignored her sarcasm. "Not quite," Sam said. "The homeless people are always there. But eventually they become like the tree in your back yard. It's there, part of the scenery, but you're so used to it, you don't notice it anymore."

Katie gave him a quizzical look as she thought about his words. "Wait a minute. You're telling me that homeless people notice everything that goes on around them, but since they can't do anything about it, or don't care, it essentially goes unnoticed."

"Now you're getting the idea," Sam said. "And add to the equation, since the homeless aren't noticed, people may do or say things in their presence that they ordinarily wouldn't do in front of others."

Sam glanced at her. "As I recall, you're from a small town near Minneapolis…Loretto, is it? When you go home for a visit, what do you see? Where do you visit? Do places and people jar loose memories stored in the back of your mind?"

"How did you know I was from Loretto?" Katie asked, astonished.

"Do your homework, girl. Right after we were assigned together, I researched your file. I may know you better than you know yourself. Two brothers, dad was a teacher, and mom worked at the county treasurer's office. You graduated from the University of Minnesota, went to law school, dropped out after a year, and joined the FBI. Should I go on?"

"I'll be damned. You checked up on me," she said with indignation.

"Yep. And I will be disappointed if you didn't do the same with me. Everybody knows this job is finding who you are looking for in the criminal element. But you can do your job better if you understand and work with your partner. Get to know what makes them tick. What you can expect, and more importantly, what you can't expect."

"And…" Katie said.

"Let's leave it where it's at," Sam said. "We're at our destination; let's go. And remember, Agent Johansson, it was a homeless man who blew the whistle on the illicit laboratory in New Jersey. Maybe, just maybe, someone here has seen something similar, and we'll get lucky."

Sam got out of the Suburban, his feet crunching on the gravel parking lot of the homeless shelter. Katie followed Sam with more than a little apprehension.

CHAPTER 23

THE FIRST THING KATIE NOTICED was the smell of the shelter. It hit her as soon as Sam opened the door. She could live with the appearance—painted concrete block walls, scuffed and dirty, chipped metal door frames—but she hated the smell of unbathed humans. She swallowed, holding back the bile in her throat, and forced herself to breathe through her mouth. Deep breaths.

Sam noticed her discomfort. "Just hang on a minute, you'll adjust to it quickly."

"You actually lived here?" She choked out the words.

"Actually, I spent a lot of my time sleeping in the park."

"Wow," Katie said, "that's comforting."

He spoke to four or five residents, introducing Agent Johansson as his partner. He asked about drug labs in the area, along with several other questions, but got no helpful response.

After about five minutes—five hours by Johansson's clock—Sam said, "Let's go."

"Thank God," Katie said as she filled her lungs with the fresh outside air.

"Yeah, the former manager insisted on clean clothes and at least weekly baths. This guy doesn't seem to care."

"So it was a waste of time," Katie said.

"Maybe, maybe not," Sam replied. "Let's get a bite and snoop around downtown."

Katie wasn't sure she had the stomach for food right now, but she needed something to wash the stench out of her mouth and nostrils.

Duncan's café proved to be just what she needed. A bustling, rather large diner-type restaurant, it was jammed with people from all walks of life, and the smell of the food rejuvenated Katie's appetite. A couple of the diners spoke to Sam, and the waitress came up and gave him a big hug, saying, "You're a right handsome man when you clean up, Sam."

Sam introduced Katie to Jo. She was a large woman, black, had silver edged hair, and wore a bright Kwanza-style top. Her smile was disarming. She left menus and went to get their drinks.

Sam explained that he knew Jo when he lived on the streets. "I could always count on her for a cup of coffee or a piece of pie when I was broke," Sam said. "I tried to come back and repay her, but she wouldn't hear of it. I expect you to leave her a very generous tip."

"Does that mean I'm paying?" she asked.

"Yep," Sam said, with a twinkle in his eye. "And I'm serious about the tip."

Agent Johansson looked at him with a bewildered expression on her face, and finally said, "Okay, twenty percent."

"Nope," Sam replied, "twenty dollars."

"You've got to be kidding!" Katie said, her jaw hanging open.

"Nope," Sam said.

After listening to Katie tell him for the third time how good the meat loaf was, Sam grinned and said that was why he always ordered the daily special. When Jo brought the ticket, Sam asked where he could find out about the drug culture in Council Bluffs. Jo laughed and said, "You're asking the wrong person, but it's good to see you, Sam," as she walked away.

Katie paid the bill at the register as requested, including the twenty dollar tip. "Here's your copy, honey," the cashier said, handing her a handwritten ticket. Katie thanked her and hustled out the door to catch Sam who was already at the car.

"Gotta beat the meter maid," Sam said, nodding at the expired parking meter. "She takes her job seriously."

Katie got in, folded the ticket to put it in her purse, and noticed something written on the back. It said, SEE MORE. She opened the ticket and saw no writing on it other than a listing of the food charges.

"Sam, look at the back of the ticket," Katie said.

"Yep, not a dead end after all."

"I don't get it. What's it mean?"

"You'll see," Sam said pulling away from the curb.

They passed a mixture of old buildings, the new library, more old buildings, and the modern newspaper building.

"Wow, this town is old," Katie said.

"Yep."

"Would you please tell me what the hell is going on?" Katie said with indignation.

"Just look for a middle-aged guy in a brown overcoat, possibly wearing a black garbage bag over it."

"It's a beautiful spring day. Why would he be wearing an overcoat and a garbage bag?"

"Don't know," Sam said as he turned a corner and searched the sidewalks. "He always wears the overcoat 'cause it's all he owns. Maybe the garbage bag is to keep it dry, or clean."

"That doesn't make sense," Katie said.

"Not to you or me," Sam said. "There he is. Brown overcoat, no garbage bag. Same corner he always hangs around. Let's go have a chat."

Sam drove the Suburban around the corner and parked a block away.

"Why are we parking here?"

"Because," Sam said, taking off his suit coat and tie, and rolling up his sleeves, "if he sees this car he won't talk to us."

"But he knows you're with the FBI, doesn't he?"

"Yeah, but Maurie is a strange guy. Hates cops. He might talk to me, might not. Put your badge in your pocket."

Maurie was pacing the sidewalk with his head down. His hair was brown and beginning to gray around the temples. It was matted and greasy. He was mumbling something to himself, over and over.

"Hi, Maurie," Sam said.

Maurie looked up. Kate noticed the blank look in his eyes. His head went down again and he started to mumble and walk away. She started to follow, but Sam grabbed her arm. She watched Maurie walk about ten paces, stop, and turn around. He walked past them, turned around and came back.

"Sam," he said, sounding like a child.

"Long time, Maurie," Sam said.

"Not since you killed that guy," Maurie said, a sly grin spread across his face, then the glazed look returned to his eyes.

"I didn't kill anyone," Sam said. He let Maurie digest that, then said, "You still guarding the street?"

Maurie nodded.

"Watching the drug dealers? Keeping them away from the kids?"

Maurie nodded his head again.

"Maybe I can help you? You know, work together or something?"

"Like, I could be an FBI agent?"

"Sorta like that," Sam said. "I would want you to stay undercover, though. Just keep on doing what you do. Guard the streets."

Maurie gave Sam that strange grin as he turned and began to walk again. This time Sam caught up with him. Kate followed but lagged behind. They stopped and Maurie said something to Sam. He was mumbling and his speech was difficult to understand. The conversation lasted a couple of minutes, and Kate saw Sam hand him a twenty.

Maurie got a crooked grin on his face, and said, "I know more." He walked a few steps, and mumbled again, "I know more."

Sam just stood there, waiting for more information. Finally, Maurie said, "That man you killed. I see his wife. She comes to the house sometimes. She's a bad woman, Sam. Sells drugs. You should kill her too."

Sam started to ask a question, but Maurie turned away, head down, and walked off.

"Okay, let's go," Sam said.

"What in the hell was that?" Katie asked, exasperated.

"That was Maurie. Remember the note you got from Jo? She was telling us to see Maurie, not "more." She didn't want to spell his name. She lives here; people trust her. You wouldn't believe the things people tell their waitresses. Invisible, they see a lot of things, too. They go home after work and have a soap opera of stories to tell their husbands. Probably not Jo, however; she's discreet."

"So you're saying waitresses are like homeless people?"

"Only in that they are invisible, and very observant."

"That Maurie guy. He was creepy. How can you believe anything a retarded homeless man tells you?"

"Oh, he's not retarded. He was a college professor. Has a doctorate in American History. He just has physical and mental issues. He's as smart as you or I, and just as sane."

Katie looked skeptical.. "So what did this genius college professor tell you?"

"Let's get back in the car before someone else recognizes me. We sort of stand out in this neighborhood."

That brought a smile to Kate's face. "Yeah. Tall, good looking blonde with a middle-aged black man."

"*Good-looking* middle-aged black man," Sam said with a laugh. "Let's check out Maurie's information."

"And just who did you kill?" Katie asked as they climbed in the car.

"No one," Sam said. "Someone killed a man named Landry after Landry shot me. They never found out who did it. It made all the papers at the time. The widow's name is Audrey Landry. Maurie says she's running his old drug business,"

"So what are you going to do about that?"

"Nothing," Sam said. "Not our case. I was hoping Maurie had seen some strange midnight drug deliveries to the hospital. He sleeps on their lawn many a night and knows what goes on there, inside and out."

"But he didn't help us."

"Yes, he did. He told me Audrey Landry goes to her dead husband's old meth lab and is running the business.

"So what?" Katie said.

"Remember, I said drug lords are entrepreneurs. Audrey Landry may be manufacturing more than meth. Audrey Landry is big in Omaha society and has some contacts in very high places."

"You think she may be involved in the illicit prescription drug business?" Katie asked.

I have no idea, but I think I should call the Council Bluffs Chief of Police and ask him to watch her closely." Sam yawned, "Let's call it a day and meet in the morning. Oh, and thanks for lunch."

"You're welcome. Now I can go home with a full stomach and a confused mind," Katie said.

"Welcome to my world," Sam said.

CHAPTER 24

JAMES SAT WRITHING IN HIS chair, waiting for his eyes to adjust to the dark. He was worried about Bob, but couldn't see him in the darkened room. Both had their hands bound behind their back with plastic ties, hooked through the chair back. Their ankles were bound as well. Abe and Lenny had decided to leave them both in the room at the top of the stairs. After securing them both, they had just left, turning out the light behind them.

As his eyes finally adjusted to the darkness, James saw that Bob was motionless in his chair, head slumped down on his chest. He was still unconscious.

When Lenny and Abe started to search behind the barrels, they found Bob first. Abe lifted Bob by his shirt, and slapped him across the face with his gun. James was afraid he was going to shoot Bob, so he jumped up with his hands in the air. Abe walked over to him, and James cringed, expecting a blow to the head. Instead, Abe grabbed him and threw him down. As he went down, he hit his face hard on the edge of a drum. Abe motioned him over to Bob's prone body, and told him to carry him upstairs. James did as he was told, half dragging Bob up the concrete stairs.

Abe and Lenny discussed what they should do with them. "Let's just kill them and get it over with," Abe said.

"I think we better call the boss," Lenny said.

"We'll have to walk all the way back to the truck to get cell service," Abe said.

"We have to wheel the boxes back to the truck anyway," Lenny said, lighting a cigarette. He blew out a cloud of smoke, and said,

"Sort of kill two birds with one stone." He laughed at his own joke as they turned off the light and closed the door.

The plastic ties were cutting James's wrists with the slightest movement. He winced at the pain, finally stopped struggling, and tried to make out Bob in the dark. As his eyes adjusted, he could see Bob still half hanging out of his chair. *God. Abe must really be strong to hit him that hard.* He tried to ascertain the extent of Bob's injuries, but didn't see much blood on his face or in his hair. *That's good. Unless the injuries are mostly internal and he has a concussion...or worse.*

James turned his attention to himself. His lip was swollen, and he had a metallic taste in his mouth. It was his own blood. Abe had slapped him around a little, but he didn't appear to have any serious injuries.

He tried to find a way to free his hands, But the ties cut deeper into his wrists. They had bound his feet above his boot tops. He tried to work his feet around in his boots, but they were double-knotted, so there was no give.

Bob began to stir. James's hopes began to rise. But then Bob's head dropped to his chest, and his raspy breathing started again.

James began to understand the hopelessness of the situation. Abe and Lenny were going to get word from their boss to kill both him and Bob. Why not? Just make it look like a hunting accident. Their bodies might never be found in this desolate wilderness. James began to shake with fear.

Will I ever see Susan again? What about JJ? Will he grow up without a father because I just had to come back and check out this damned mine? Why didn't I listen to Curt?

Half filled with rage at himself, James strained with all his might, but couldn't free himself from his bonds. He felt the throbbing pressure in his head as he struggled, half afraid his head would burst. He twisted and jerked at the chair, stopping only as it began to tumble over. *Got to settle down. Relax. Think.*

James felt his heart stop pounding and his breathing return to normal after a minute or two. It was then that James remembered the knife in his pants pocket. It only had a three-inch blade, but it was razor sharp and tough. The good news was that it had a simple push-button mechanism to open it. The bad news was that it had a sliding button to lock it and prevent it from opening. He hoped he hadn't engaged that lock the last time he used it. With his hands tied behind his back, and hooked to the chair, however, there was no way to reach his pocket. His mind went into overdrive. *How can I get it out of my pants pocket so I can use it? Maybe if I start by getting it open?*

Knowing he had to try, he considered his options from every angle. *If I can get my legs under the desk, maybe I can raise myself up enough to press the release pin against the desk. Once it's open, perhaps I can maneuver it out of my pocket.*

James rocked the chair to slide one leg then the other toward the desk. It was painstakingly slow, and the ties were cutting deep into his legs. He was groaning in pain and grunting out loud in effort the entire time, "Ooh…Aar!…shit…*SHIT!*"

He kept it up for almost fifteen minutes, finally getting his legs beneath the desk. James was attempting to stand, raising his lap to touch the desk, and hit the release button of the knife, when Bob moaned. His voice was sleepy as he spoke. "Where are we?"

"Thank God you're awake!" James exclaimed. His spirits suddenly raised, but fell just as quickly as Bob's head dropped to his chest again. James went back to work on the knife. Several tries later, he caught the button on the bottom of the desk, and felt the knife blade release. It wasn't completely open, so he continued to try and snag it on the desk.

He had to stop for a minute. His left calf was cramping up from the exertion. Bob continued to stir in the background, emitting unintelligible sounds.

James let the cramp subside, and went back to work. After about five minutes, he had twisted and worked the blade completely open. The knife had an automatic lock mechanism that prevented the blade from closing once it was open. Now the trick was to get the knife out of his pocket and into his hand.

James tried to explore all the possibilities. He concluded there was no way he could work the knife out and get it into his hands without dropping it. *If it drops, I can just tip my chair over. Of course, that will hurt like hell! But I've got to try it!* James used the table as leverage and tried to push the knife point out of his pocket and through his pant leg. His legs kept cramping and the desk top wanted to just slide over the top of the knife. *Got to find a way to hook it onto the knife, so I can push.*

"She's going to kill me!" The slurred voice startled James. He let his chair drop and turned his head around. Bob was sitting upright, and shaking his head.

Puzzled, James asked "Who's going to kill you?"

"Doris," Bob said. "She told me I had no business going on a bear hunt. I should have listened to her. Look at the mess we're in."

"This is no time to worry about your wife. We need to worry about those two goons out there. Abe and Lenny are going to kill us as soon as they get back. Your wife will never get the chance...Can you stay awake now?"

Bob shook his head to clear it. "I guess so."

"Good. Now I'm going to crab-walk my chair over to you, so you can reach my knife." James wiggled and lifted his chair legs, scooting and bouncing to get his chair turned sideways behind Bob's back. Winded, he had to rest twice before he finally got into position. Bob's hands were touching the outer part of James's left thigh. "Okay, now I want you to feel the knife in my pants pocket. Try and pull it toward you and get the blade out."

Bob worked on the knife. He couldn't see and had to go by feel. He finally got the outline and orientation of the knife, and struggled to get his hands placed to pull on the knife. "This hurts like hell!" he said.

"Not as much as a bullet in the head. Now keep working and stop worrying about the ties cutting your wrists!"

Bob continued to work, pushing on the handle and pulling on the blade. James saw the knife point penetrate his pants. "Keep going, you're getting it."

At last, the knife blade was almost completely out of James pants. "Now, we need to make a larger hole so the handle will pass through the cut in my pants." The knife was a single blade, the handle was steel and relatively thin, enabling it to slide easily. "Try and wiggle the blade to cut my pants."

James watched the hole widen in his pants, large enough for the knife handle to pass through.

"Okay, now pull the knife out slowly. And keep a grip on the blade. Whatever you do, don't drop it." James could see the blade held tightly between Bob's thumb and index finger. They both let out sighs of relief and joy when Bob had the knife in his hands, out of James's pocket.

James explained his intention to turn his chair back to back with Bob's, grab the handle of the knife, and saw through Bob's zip ties. Bob nodded, and James turned, backed up—and bumped the knife in the process. It clattered to the floor.

CHAPTER 25

H E LAY ON HIS SIDE, still tied to the metal chair. The pain in his forearm was excruciating. He willed his mind to compartmentalize his agony. James had decided the only way he could get the fallen knife was to fall on his side still tied to the metal chair. It hurt like hell, but he had the knife in his hand. No way was he going to let himself be shot by Abe and Lenny!

James shook off the pain. "Okay, Bob, your turn, but I have a suggestion: fall forward and turn on your side. That should ease your fall."

Bob started rocking, and finally went forward to his knees, then rolled onto his side. "Thanks for the advice. What do we do now?" Bob asked, still winded.

"We get back to back and I'll use the knife to cut your ties and get your hands free."

Bob and James bucked and bounced around until their hands were both near the knife. James finally got a grip on it, and began to work on Bob's tied hands. It was painstaking work, but James finally got a good grip and Bob hooked his zip tie over the knife edge.

"Pull your hands so I don't cut your wrists," James said. The knife sliced through the ties.

Bob freed his hands and took the knife from James. Bob cut James's bonds.

"We've got to get out of here!" James said, still a little shaky, as soon as they'd cut their ankle ties. He and Bob limped toward the door, both forcing their legs to keep them upright. The sunlight blinded them for a few seconds.

"Let's get to the boat," Bob said. Hearts pounding both with exertion and with fear, they staggered up over the berm. As they cleared it, they heard voices and threw themselves down out of sight.

"As soon as they get inside, start the motor, and push the boat into the lake," James whispered.

"We need to get inside it first," Bob insisted.

"We'll be sitting ducks," James said. "They'll cut us in half with those guns. This will be a diversion. Start it and let's head for the woods!"

Bob pushed the "start" button. Nothing. On the second push the motor sputtered, gasped, then leveled out into a slow purr. Bob spotted a roll of duct tape under the seat, grabbed it, and taped the throttle wide open. The motor roared as the boat lurched onto the lake.

Inside the door, Abe and Lenny roared in fury to see the overturned and empty chairs. At that moment, they heard the boat motor start. "Check downstairs, Lenny, and make sure they didn't do any damage down there; I'll get the boat," Abe yelled, racing out the door. As he got to the top of the berm, Abe saw the boat racing away from the shore. He leveled his rifle and opened fire, only then realizing the boat was empty.

James had gotten just beyond the tree line, and looked back to see Bob still in the clearing, limping to catch up with him. "Hurry!" James hissed motioning Bob on with his arm.

"Let me catch my breath!" Bob gasped.

"No, we go or die," James said, grabbing Bob's arm and pulling him along.

Bob and James were running for their lives in the thick woods, ignoring the branches and fallen limbs trying to slow their progress. They heard the burst of shots from automatic weapons. They ran on, twigs and branches slapping them and cutting their faces. Another burst of gunfire. Finally, silence.

"Keep going," James whispered, "I think they're separating out to cover more area and find us."

Bob stopped, leaning over, panting, his hands resting on his knees. "I've got to rest. I can't make it much further."

"Come on, Bob, I've got an idea," James said. "They know we came this way. Let's go north about 400 yards, and then double back. They'll never expect that."

"Whatever way will let me get my breath back," Bob panted.

They headed north and then began to slowly and quietly make their way back west toward the mine. They had gone about a half mile when James stopped. "I hear voices," he murmured. "They're south of us, probably headed east. Let's get hidden over by those fallen logs and let them go by." They laid down behind a rotting fallen tree trunk about two feet in diameter. James tried to ignore the centipedes and other critters hiding under the log along with them. He felt them moving from his shoulder to his neck, and resisted the urge to spit or blow them off with his breath. He felt the sawdust droppings from the worm holes stick to the sweat on his face. *Please, God, don't let there be any snakes in here!*

The voices were closer now. They were almost due south of James and Bob when they stopped. The silence lasted for an eternity.

"Why did you stop? Hear something?"

"Naw, I need a cigarette."

"We can't stop now. They already have a good head start.".."

"So who gives a shit?

James froze. It sounded as if they were walking towards them. A minute later, they could hear twigs snapping as the pair pushed through the brush. They were no more than ten feet away. *Shit, they know we are here. Can't run, they have those damn automatics.*

Abe and Lenny walked up to the log and sat down, both panting from the exertion. James could smell the cigarette smoke. *Can't move. Can't make a sound. Breathe slow and easy. Stay still, Bob, don't make a sound.*

"Put that damned smoke out. We're wasting too much time.'

"Fuck you, I'll put it out when I'm done."

One of the men stood and started to walk off. James guessed it was Abe. The other one stood, cursed, and flipped the cigarette into the woods behind the log.

As Lenny walked away, James finally exhaled. He had no idea how long he had been holding his breath. They waited almost five minutes before James dared raise his head to look in their direction. No one in sight. He could still hear them moving away from them to the east. He tapped Bob and mouthed, "Let's go. Slow and quiet."

James led the way, then realized Bob wasn't behind him. He looked back to see him looking for something. Bob twisted his foot on the ground, and headed his way.

"What were you doing?" James asked.

"Stomping out that cigarette. Didn't want it to start a fire."

James forced himself to keep his thoughts to himself, but finally said, "Personally, I prefer a fire between them and us. Let's move!" They headed back toward the mine. It took almost thirty minutes to find it. The woods were thick, and it was difficult to keep going in one direction. Every fallen log attempted to throw them off track. They were both exhausted from fighting fallen trees, getting slapped from branches, and being scraped by twigs.

"Now what?" Bob asked as the building, with the berm beyond it, came into view.

"We keep going," James said. "They're eventually going to come back here, so we need to get as far away as we can."

"I need water," Bob said, exhaustion coloring his voice

"Later," James said. "We need to move."

"How far do you think it is back to our cabin?" Bob asked.

"Maybe seven miles. After a mile or so, I think we can go back down near the water, and then the walking will be easier. Let's get going. That sun is almost at two o'clock, and it's going to be cold when it gets dark."

CHAPTER 26

FOUR MILES ACROSS THE LAKE and four miles east, Curt and Rick were sitting in their stand. It was a double wide, designed to hold two people, a hunter and his guide. "I've got to get down and stretch my legs," Curt said. He threw a leg over the edge and started down the ladder.

"What if a bear comes along?" Rick asked.

"I reckon you ought to shoot it," Curt said, laughing at the ridiculous question. "In fact, I'm counting on it," he said, and continued down the ladder.

Rick watched Curt disappear into the woods. *Probably needs to take a dump.*

Ten minutes later Curt was coming back up the ladder. "Did you hear that?" Curt said.

"Hear what?" Rick asked.

"Those shots," Curt said.

"I didn't hear any shots," Rick said.

"Strange," Curt said, squinting his eyes and furrowing his brow. "They came from across the lake, but I didn't think anyone was over there today. But the really weird thing...I don't think it was a hunter firing the shots.

"Why not?" Rick asked.

"Too many shots. Rapid and evenly spaced. It sounded like an automatic weapon, or something."

"Could just be an echo," Rick said. "The lake does strange things with sound."

"Yeah, probably right."

A noise in the brush stopped the conversation. A bear cub entered the clearing and mom was close behind. Mom was a big bear. Rick's eyes got wide.

"Wow! Look at the size of those paws!"

"Yeah, wow. You're not thinking of shooting the mother, are you?"

"Well, I was thinking about it. She's a big bear. Make a nice rug."

"Not on my watch, you're not. We're not leaving a cub motherless. Besides, it's only three hours until dusk and that's the time we're most likely to see a big one."

They watched the cub and mother amble around for a while, and walk out of sight. The woods grew silent again and they returned to their vigil, making occasional chit chat to while away the day.

"We're gonna be in deep shit," Lenny said.

"Yeah, well, it's your fault. If you hadn't called the boss, we could have just killed them and been done with it. Now we have a couple of loose ends running around."

"How the hell did we lose them?" Lenny asked,

"Probably doubled back or hid somewhere. Those woods are a bitch. I've got cuts and scratches all over my hands and face," Abe said.

"Not to mention the egg on your face when we tell the boss."

"No, the egg will be on *your* face! But we may not have to tell him. We know where they're going. Back to the safety of the camp. We'll just head over there and take them for a little ride."

"Good idea. Let's get the rest of the stuff loaded and get out of here. But first—"

"I know, I know. You have to have another damned cigarette."

Lenny flicked his lighter and smiled as he blew out the smoke.

"How much farther" Bob asked.

"Maybe another mile," James said.

"I hope so," Bob said. "Look at the sun. It's dropping fast. It's not too long before it'll drop behind the trees. And I need water bad."

"Hang in there, my friend. Hey, smell that? I think it's food cooking. The sun sun is just over the treetops, and someone is cooking. It can't be far away. I need to get on the phone and notify the authorities about that drug lab."

Filled with renewed energy, they headed along the shore of the lake. Twenty minutes later they were on the perimeter of the camp. James paused for a moment, taking in the cool breeze gently moving the trees and bushes, thankful to have made it back safely. Bob headed for their cabin to get his long-awaited drink of water. He flung open the door and stopped dead in his tracks. Lenny was sitting in a chair smoking a cigarette, and had a gun pointed in his direction. Bob stood there in dumb disbelief. James reached the door just as Bob said to Lenny, "I'm getting a drink of water. I don't care if you shoot me," and walked toward the refrigerator. "And by the way, this is a no smoking cabin!" he said as he grabbed a glass and began to fill it.

"You make me laugh," Lenny said, blowing a smoke ring. "Whatcha gonna do about it?"

"This!" and Bob threw the glass of water at Lenny's cigarette.

James about shit, but then seized the opportunity, and ran at Lenny while he sat there, still shocked at having the water thrown on his cigarette. It turned out to be a bad move. Lenny caught him in the side of the head with a hard left, knocking him to the floor.

James lay on the floor holding his head, and Bob drank his water, turning to fill a second glass.

"You boys are starting to piss me off," Lenny growled. "But not for long. Now get your miserable butt up off the floor and both of you out the door." They complied, hands raised over their heads.

"Smells like somebody was smoking in here."

"Yeah, but none of us smoke," Rick said.

"And where are Bob and James?" Curt said. "Not to mention no supper."

"Probably got to drinking," Rick said, shrugging his shoulders.

"I'll go over to the office and see if Dutch knows where they are," Curt said with disgust.

Curt went out the door and walked toward the office. He heard Bob's voice. "Go ahead. I'm so damned tired I don't care what you do." Curt walked in the direction of the voice, realizing it was coming from an abandoned shed about twenty feet from their cabin. They hadn't paid any attention to it earlier as it was partially hidden by trees and brush. He poked around the side of the shed, just in time to see Bob and James get ushered inside the shed by a man.

"What the hell is going on here?" Curt demanded.

He started toward the men. A voice from behind stopped him.

"One more step and you die right here."

Curt turned his head back and looked into the barrel of a gun.

"Get in the shed with the other two."

With a wary eye over his shoulder, Curt complied.

"Hands behind your back," the first man said, plastic ties ready in his hands. "Go get the other guy, Abe," he ordered. "We may as well tie up these loose ends all at once." He laughed at his joke, picked up his weapon, and jabbed Curt with it. "Get it? Tie up loose ends."

Curt ignored him and looked at James and Bob. "You just had to go to that damned mine, didn't you." It was not a question, and was full of anger. The fear had yet to set in.

"It's my fault," James said. "I talked Bob into it."

Curt's eyes adjusted to the dark and he noticed they were bruised and had cuts on their faces and wrists. Bob had a large swollen egg under his left eye. Curt's observations tempered his disgust.

A few minutes later, Rick could be heard protesting. He stumbled into the shed, Abe following with a gun in his back. "Jesus!" Rick said at the sight of his friends. "What the hell?" James lifted a shoulder in apology.

"What now, Abe?" Lenny asked.

"Let's get them secured, then we'll drive the truck across the border and be back for these guys before first light. There will be an accident in their cabin. Darn propane stoves are dangerous."

"I don't get you, Abe; earlier, you were so eager to shoot them right away. What gives? Why can't we just shoot them now and burn down the shed?"

"Because those drugs need to get delivered, and we're already late. Besides, it has to look like an accident. The fire will burn their ties and gags, but it won't hide bullet holes. So let's get this guy tied up. And, Lenny? Take their belts and check their pockets for knives. We won't make the same mistake twice."

While Abe held his gun on the men, Lenny tied Rick's hands behind him and removed all four belts. He found two knives, one in a pocket and the other hooked on Rick's belt, and patted them down all the way to their boot tops. "They're clean," he said.

"Good; let's get their ankles secured now," Abe said.

"All four of you, down on your knees," Lenny said.

Kneeling wasn't easy with arms bound behind their backs. Rick fell onto his side. Lenny took ties and bound their ankles. While he worked, he said over his shoulder, "Abe go grab some towels from the cabin."

Abe returned with the towels, waving the keys to the van. "Look what I found on the kitchen table. I figure it can't hurt to take the keys."

"Good idea," Lenny said. "Cut those towels up into strips and wad a piece into their mouth: I'll tie a strip around their heads to hold the gags in place."

Curt twisted and resisted, but all he did was earn a gun butt on the side of his head.

Satisfied the four friends were secured and not going anywhere, both men walked out of the shed. Lenny replaced the two by four between the latches to lock the door behind them.

Abe and Lenny were walking out of the camp when Dutch strolled out of the office. He stopped short at the sight of the two men. "What are you guys doing here?" he demanded.

"You got a problem with us being here?" Abe asked, malice in his voice.

"Yeah. The deal was that you guys weren't supposed to be in my camp."

"Your camp? Since when did this become *your* camp? I believe we both know who owns this property."

"I don't care," Dutch said. "You can't go walking around here carrying those weapons. It'll scare my clients. Get the hell out of my camp!"

Abe took two steps toward Dutch and shoved his automatic weapon under his chin, forcing his head up. "Shut up! We'll do as we please. You do as we say or I'm going to pull this trigger and blow your brains out! Then I'm going to burn this camp to the ground. Understand?"

Dutch was a big man, but was no match for Abe, especially not when Abe had a weapon in his hand. Dutch nodded.

"Where's your Indian sidekick? We need him to watch the shed for us," Abe said.

"Back at the village, I reckon," Dutch said, resentment clear in his voice. "He went to check the boats about an hour ago and he usually leaves after that."

CHAPTER 27

ALL FOUR HUNTERS WERE ATTEMPTING to work their gags loose. It was difficult to breathe through one's nose. At least there was no complaining, as they couldn't speak. When Curt rolled around and pushed his head into Rick's butt, it took a moment for Rick to figure what Curt was doing. *The gag. He wants me to try and remove the towel around his head, and get the gag out of his mouth.*

Rick groped and finally got his fingers around the towel and Curt struggled and finally pulled his head from the towel strip. He pushed his head back toward Rick's fingers and after groping around, Rick finally caught a piece of the gag. After two tries, Curt managed to pull himself free, leaving the wet gag in Rick's fingers.

"Thanks," Curt said. Rick nodded his head and grunted something indiscernible. Rick kept shaking his head and grunting but Curt just started to yell. "Help! Help!" He figured almost two hours had passed, so it was safe to yell.

A scraping noise startled the four. Someone was lifting the bar across the door. All of them cringed as a figure appeared in the darkness.

The figure said, "Look at the trouble you caused. Hold still." James could tell it was a man from the deep voice, but still didn't know who it was or what his intentions were. He closed his eyes when he saw the glint of steel on the open knife coming toward him. With swift motions, the man grabbed him, turned him over, and cut his ties.

James sat up and removed the towel holding in the gag. He started flexing his arms and legs as Richard proceeded to cut them all loose. Not a word was spoken.

"What the hell?"

"They are dangerous men," Richard said in an even tone. "Dutch has been good to me, and does not deserve this mess." He gave them a stern look and said, "You are stupid, and you have caused real trouble. But Dutch asked me to help."

Abe and Lenny were nearing the Canada-United States border. Most of the border guards has seen them cross several times, however they had never crossed at night, and were a little apprehensive. Luckily the guard on duty just waved them through.

"Luck is on our side," Abe said.

"If luck was on our side, we wouldn't be in this mess," Lenny said. "We should have killed them back at the mine."

"No sweat," Abe said. "We'll be back by early morning and the camp will have a propane explosion for a wake-up call."

After Richard untied all the hunters, he was careful to pick up the zip ties and all the rags from the gags. He walked to the cabin, and dropped them on the floor, throwing the towel pieces on the floor and chairs. Overwhelmed by the mounting fear, and not sure what was going to happen next, the men were silent until Richard said, "Have to make this look good," as he went outside and threw himself through the screen door, knocking it to the floor. "Get your passports," he ordered, then disappeared into the dark.

Everyone gathered their passports and the two rifles which were left. Bob and James had lost their rifles in the lake when the boat sank.

They heard banging and boards breaking, and soon Richard returned. "What's going on?" James asked.

"Had to make it look like you kicked out boards and crawled your way out," Richard said. "Come with me."

Where are we going?" James asked.

"We are walking to my village," Richard said. "It is a safe place."

"That's over a mile away," Rick moaned.

Richard gave him a long look. "Stay here and die, then," he walked off.

The village was much like the camp. No straight roads. Houses placed at random. It was in a miserable state of disrepair. James wondered how bad it must look in the daytime.

Richard introduced them to one of the elders of the tribe. Richard called him "Wallabanne" or some similar name. He had long gray hair braided into a ponytail, and dark, leathery wrinkled skin. If it weren't for his alert brown eyes, James would have guessed he was at least a hundred years old. He wore faded jeans and a faded plaid flannel shirt, which was probably red and black fifteen years ago.

The elder looked them over, as he said, "You can call me 'Wally.' Richard feels he has to use my proper name as a sign of respect, but I am just an old man." He stood assessing the four white men for a long minute, finally saying, "You look like hell. Those were some really bad dudes you ran into. We need to get you out of here. If they find out we are hiding you, they'll make trouble for all of us."

Curt asked Wally if he could take them to the nearest airport. "It is only about an hour away," the elder said, "but the airport does not open every day. It is better I take you to a nearby town where you can rent a car."

"At this time of night?" Curt asked, doubtful.

"Yes, anytime I want. I will call on the way. It is owned by a tribal member. He will have a car ready for you."

They loaded into the back of a pickup, about the same vintage as Wally, and he took off, gravel flying in his wake. The ride was rough on the non- maintained road, but no one complained. It was better than dying in a propane explosion.

"What about Richard?" Rick asked.

"I heard some of the other men talking at the village. They're taking him back to the shed. They'll hit him a few times and tie him up. It'll look like we overpowered him," Curt said.

"Wow, he really saved our ass!"

"Yeah," Bob said. "Let's hope they let him go."

The ride was cool as the temperature continued to drop. The four were huddled deep in the pickup bed for warmth. They had no gear, only the clothes on their backs. About an hour and a half later, the pickup came to a stop. They piled out and Curt pulled his wallet. He gave Wally several of his Canadian bills, grinning as he said, "Now, don't spend all that on whiskey." The elder smiled a toothless grin, and gunned the truck back toward the village.

The rental car agency was closed, but a man appeared on the porch. "Wally said you need a car tonight."

"Yeah," Curt said, "we do."

"Let's get the rental agreement signed, the car gassed up, and I'll give you a map. You're a four hour drive from the border, so it won't be long until you're back in the states." The paperwork done, the Indian took them around back. They were greeted by a 1980s Subaru hatchback, looking like it was just retrieved from the junkyard.

"It just keeps on getting better," Bob said with a grin. The Indian said, "Oh, that's my car. Your car is in the garage. You would never clear customs in that piece of shit."

He pulled the garage door open and they were looking at a fairly new Honda Civic. "This will get you over the border, along with your passports and some gear Richard will meet you with. You don't want to try to go across with an empty car."

"Do any of you get the feeling this isn't the first time they've done this?" James asked. The mood was almost giddy as they all grinned and gave nods of assent.

"It's a little scary," Rick said, but "not as scary as getting killed in a propane explosion."

They took the map and headed for the rendezvous point.

Lenny and Abe returned just before dawn to find the scene just as Richard had staged it. They were mad as hell. They checked every public spot in the camp, but there was no sign of the four men they had locked in the shed.

"This doesn't make sense," Lenny said. "Why wouldn't they just take the van and get out of here?"

Abe reached in his pocket and pulled out the key to the van. "Remember? I took the keys."

"Shit!" Lenny exclaimed, "that's right! So where are they?"

They hadn't untied Richard yet, pissed that he'd been stupid enough to be overpowered when the hunters escaped, and pissed that he hadn't heard them kicking out the shed wall and stopped them before they got out. Just to make sure he knew how they felt, Abe kicked him in the stomach. They stormed off to the office and roused Dutch from his bed, cussing Dutch because he had been paid well to keep hunters away from the mine, and demanding to know just how the hunters escaped, how long ago did they get out, and where did they go. Abe was punching Dutch with each question when Lenny said, "Enough, Abe. We're wasting time. Let's check the village. That would be the closest place they could hide." Abe hit Dutch one last time and they left.

The village was quiet, with most people still asleep. A couple of homes had lights on, but could provide no information about four men. The sun was just breaking the horizon. They drove the perimeter of the village for a while, looking for sign of the four men. Finally they gave up. They dreaded telling their boss what had happened.

Abe was driving away from the village, still pissed that their captives had gotten away. He saw a pickup coming toward him on the narrow dirt road. It swerved a little and he had to run into the ditch to avoid it. He slammed his hand on the steering wheel, cussed, and gunned the truck, throwing dirt as he spun around on the road.

"What're you doing Abe?" Lenny growled.

"Going to teach that son of a bitch a lesson. He ran me off the road!"

"Let it go Abe. He's just a drunk Indian coming home to sleep it off. He didn't hit us or anything."

Abe kept going and caught up to the pickup when it stopped. He jumped out, ran to the pickup, and jerked the door open. A startled older man practically fell out the open door.

"You ran me off the road, you stupid old goat," Abe roared.

Wally stumbled out of the pickup, lost his balance and fell onto the road. The half-empty Whiskey bottle tumbled out after him.

Abe looked in the pickup and saw a sack with another bottle on the seat.

"Where'd you get the money to buy that Whiskey, old man?"

Wally just mumbled something indiscernible.

"You got it from four hunters, right?"

Wally didn't answer, and Abe kicked him in the side.

They were just outside the village café and grocery, and an Indian woman came out the door with a grocery bag in her hand. The woman saw Abe kick Wally and ran to help him. "Leave Wally alone!" she shouted, trying to help him up.

Abe reached over and shoved her to the dirt. When she fell, her skirt rode up, exposing her bare legs.

"Okay old man. Don't talk to us," Abe said. "Maybe we'll just have some fun with your lady friend here and that will loosen your tongue."

That got Wally's attention. "Wait, don't hurt her. I'll tell you what you want to know."

Abe heard the story in slurred speech from Wally, and growled, "How long ago?"

Wally mumbled, "maybe two or three hours."

"Damn!" Abe said kicking the dirt. No way we can catch them now, and gave Wally another kick in frustration.

Lenny spoke up. "To get to the rental place, they had to go north for forty-five minutes or so. They'll have to stick to the main roads. If we go cross country straight east and down, we might be able to head them off."

"Okay, let's go," Abe said jumping in the truck. The truck threw dirt on Wally and the woman as Abe spun it around to try and catch the hunters.

Curt had insisted on driving. He was pushing the speed limit as much as he dared. The rendezvous was still an hour away, and they didn't want to get pulled over for speeding. His adrenaline was on overdrive still, and the fear had been replaced by anger at James and Bob. "I told you guys to stay away from that damned mine! Look at the mess you got all of us in. Not to mention Dutch and Richard. Hell, they could be dead by now!"

James and Bob had little to say. Curt and Rick weren't impressed when James told them he had discovered a drug laboratory.

They were approaching the intersection marked on the map. A parked car flashed its lights two times. "Sure hope that's our gear, and not those two goons," Curt said.

In five minutes they were back on the road with gear and a message from Dutch that he would contact them about getting their bear skins—a welcome bonus that cheered them all up a bit. There was no sign of Abe or Lenny when they cleared customs.

CHAPTER 28

T HEY CALLED THEIR WIVES, ONLY telling them part of the story. They all agreed to share the details after they were safely home. James knew Susan was not going to be happy when she heard the story.

They had raced across the border before daylight, and drove in shifts to put as much distance as possible between them and the camp. James noticed they were well into North Dakota when the first rays of the dawn awakened him. Rick wanted to drop the rental car somewhere, but he got outvoted. "We'll stop to gas up and grab some food, otherwise we keep moving," Curt insisted.

James made one more call. "Sam, this is James. I think I may have found your drug lab."

"I thought you were in Canada!" came the shocked reply.

"It's a long story," James said. "We're back in the states. Somewhere in North Dakota." Anyway, there is an abandoned nickel mine across the lake from where we were hunting. Bob and I checked it out, and they're making drugs there."

"Whoa, slow down, mister. You actually *saw* them making drugs?"

"No, but the machines are there, along with chemicals, and pallets of product. They're hauling them across the border into the states. They caught Bob and me in the building, but we got away. It's quite a story."

Sam looked at his cell phone as if he weren't hearing this conversation. "You know I don't have any jurisdiction in Canada. You need the RCMP, not the FBI."

"Yeah, I know. We'll be back in Grand Island by mid-afternoon. I'll fill you in then, and you can call whoever you need to in Canada."

Sam knew better than to question James. "Okay, I'll be there about five. Where do you want to meet?"

"Let's meet at the Chicken Coop, downtown. Do you remember where it is?"

"Sure, the place with the great wings."

"We can discuss the gory details together, then you can go home with me for support. I have to tell Susan the story, and you may as well be there 'cause she's not gonna be happy!"

The house was eerily quiet when James opened the door. "Hey, guys, I'm home!"

Susan came bounding down the stairs. She gave James a hug and kissed him, and told him JJ was down for his nap.

"So what happened? Why did you come home early?" Susan asked.

"You better sit down, hon. You're not going to like hearing this.

"Oh, God, did someone get hurt?" Susan noticed the bandages on his wrist and clutched her hand to her mouth. "James, what happened? Spit it out!?"

James told her they'd stopped at a drug store in North Dakota for the medicine and bandages they all needed, but assured her they weren't deep cuts. He decided he may as get it over with and tell Susan now. He began to tell her the story. As she listened, her shoulders slumped as the color drained from her cheeks. A mixture of anger, frustration, and relief welled up inside her. She tried to maintain control, but finally lost it.

"My God, James! What the hell are you doing to me? First, you get beaten up and disappear for almost a year with amnesia. And now!"

James started to interject....

"Don't interrupt me!" Susan shouted, bringing one of her clenched fists down in frustration. "Then you go on a *bear* hunting trip with your buddies, get taken prisoner in a foreign country, almost get killed, and now you come home and I'm supposed to welcome you back with open arms? I don't think so! I can't spend my life worrying about whether you're going to come home at night or not! And what about JJ? He spent the first year of his life without a father; will it be permanent one of these times? What *is* it with you?" she practically screamed.

James sat mute, not knowing what to say.

Susan stormed up the stairs and slammed the bedroom door. JJ started crying in his room. James walked upstairs and got him out of his crib. He held him tight, realizing what he'd almost lost.

James carried JJ downstairs and put him in his high chair and gave him a handful of Cheerios and a cup of water. This was not going well. He called Sam and told him to forget the Chicken Coop and come directly to his house.

James gave Susan about ten minutes, then put JJ's Cheerios into a bowl, lifted JJ out of his high chair, and took him and his Cheerios and water with him upstairs. James opened their bedroom door. Susan was lying on the bed, sobbing. He walked over, settled JJ on the floor beside him, and sat on the edge of the bed and put his hand on her shoulder, gently caressing her, knowing better than to say anything. She finally sat up, wiped the tears from her cheeks with the back of her hand, and put her arms around James.

"I have no idea what you must have gone through. Part of me wants to just hold you, and part of me wants to slap you. I hate it when my emotions get all twisted up. I worry about you all the time because I love you and I can't afford to lose you again." She hugged him for a long time, until JJ pulled himself up, crying to be picked up.

James held both of them, crying along with them. He was so relieved to be home with his family, he almost forgot about his ordeal. He and Susan had soothed JJ, and they were playing on the bed, laughing and playing peek-a-boo. Then he remembered Sam would be there at five.

James told Susan he had called Sam, and Sam was coming to Grand Island.

"I'm glad," Susan said. "Maybe he can talk some sense into you about avoiding dangerous situations!"

"Uh, he should be here in about an hour," James said, apprehension showing in his voice.

"An hour?" Susan exclaimed. "Can't it wait until tomorrow?"

"Too late," James said. "He insisted we do it as soon as possible." A little lie, but not significant when one took in the big picture. "The lab we stumbled on is probably the counterfeit drug manufacturer they've been looking for. Probably the counterfeiter responsible for the deaths at the nursing home."

"Well, good for you, detective," Susan said. The venom was coming out again. "I need to clean up and make myself presentable." She turned and headed into the bathroom. "You take JJ downstairs. I'm not done with you yet."

Susan heard the doorbell ring. She finished putting on her makeup and went downstairs. She found James, some woman, and Sam sitting at the kitchen table. Sam was holding JJ. He stood, handed JJ to James, and gave Susan a hug. She held on for dear life, feeling suddenly secure with Sam there. Sam finally broke off, and introduced her to his partner, Agent Johannsen.

After some appropriate pleasantries, Susan turned her attention to Sam. "I'm really glad you're here, Sam. Every time I turn my head, James goes and falls into a bucket of shit!"

Sam forced himself to suppress a smile.

"Talk to him, Sam. Tell him he has to learn to stay away from trouble. He'll listen to you...unlike his wife!"

Sam was silent. He knew how tenacious Susan could be. The first time James had gone missing, she was relentless in her efforts to find him. She had posters all over town, news conferences, and damned near put out an Amber Alert. *Not a good time to rock her boat. She'll calm down in a little while.* Sensing her mood, Sam said, "Let's you and I go in the other room and talk. Agent Johansson can talk to James."

Sam had a long calming talk with Susan. He had that special gift where he had a mesmerizing influence on people. Sam knew Susan loved and trusted him, and he said all the right things to assure her that he would keep his eye on James and visit with him about staying away from dangerous situations. They both knew that was unlikely to happen, but it gave her some hope. Sam and Susan rejoined James and Katie.

"Do you recognize any of these people?" Agent Johansson was asking, as she placed six pictures on the table. James gave them no more than a quick glance. He pointed at one, saying, "That nerdy-looking one is Lenny, and this one is Abe. They're the guys that tied us up. I've never seen the other ones."

Katie Johansson looked up at Sam. "Positive ID," she said. "Names match, too. They are the same guys working the lab in Jersey."

"Good job, James!" Sam said. "You may have just busted this case wide open!" Realizing what he had just said to Susan, he quickly added, "Now you need to stay home with your family and let us take over from here."

Katie told Sam she'd gotten the highlights of the experience, but thought he should hear the story also. They listened to James walk them through the entire harrowing experience. When he was finished, Sam said, "I really appreciate your information, James, but you're my friend, not my partner. You need to learn to obey 'No trespassing' signs, mind your own business, and stay out of trouble. What you did is Agent Johansson's and my job. Let us do it. Okay?"

As James nodded his assent, Sam realized he hadn't said that for Susan's benefit. He said it because he cared about James, and didn't want to lose his friend. Susan knew it too. She teared up, knowing how special Sam was to them, too.

CHAPTER 29

D ENVER HAD HIS RADIO TUNED to Willie's Roadhouse as he
cruised south along I-29. He adjusted the ball cap on his head
while he sang along with the music, oblivious to the sound of
the tires splashing water onto his undercarriage. The light rain hadn't
slowed his progress. He always kept the radio loud, as the hum of the
tires from his Freightliner tended to lull him to sleep. Denver was a
handsome man. Thin face with a little stubble, perpetual smile, and
piercing blue eyes. His cap hid his short-cropped graying hair, giving
him the appearance of a man ten years younger than his sixty years.

Denver liked this job. He drove a delivery truck for a pharmaceutical
wholesale house in Kansas City, Missouri, from Monday through
Friday. It paid well, but not nearly as well as his weekend gig. He had
no idea what he was hauling, and really didn't care. All he knew was
that it was a piece of cake. He drove his car to Fargo, North Dakota,
on Saturday, where the eighteen-wheeler awaited him in a designated
parking lot. He fired up the semi, and headed back to Kansas City.
Seventeen hours round trip if he didn't stop to eat. He dropped the
semi off at a parking lot on the north end of Kansas City where his
car was already waiting. He didn't unload the truck. In fact, in the year
he'd been driving this route, he had never once opened the trailer. If
he left at six in the morning he was home by midnight. That left all
day Sunday to tend to his wife.

Denver's wife had cancer. The doctor had given her a year to live.
That was three years ago. Even with their insurance, the bills had
mounted up, more than he could possibly afford. A year ago a former
friend called him. He had moved to the Omaha area several years

prior, and knowing Denver's plight, offered him a job. The money was unbelievable. Denver asked what he would be hauling, but his friend told him he didn't want to know. Denver didn't care. He knew it was probably illegal, but it enabled him to pay for his wife's medical bills. They had one son who was an attorney in St. Louis, but he never offered to help financially. He seldom made the trip home to see his mother. She was all Denver had, and he wanted to hold onto her as long as he could, and their time together to be good, without bills hanging over them—so to hell with whatever he was hauling. Shit, if he didn't take the job, some other schmuck would take the job and spend the money on women, drugs, or both.

Denver checked his watch. 8:45 PM. He was skirting Council Bluffs, Iowa. It was less than three hours to home. He looked and saw the lights of the casinos as he rolled by. He wished he could bring his wife to the casinos there, but he had to keep her out of busy places. Too much danger of catching an infection. That could be fatal with her chemotherapy and compromised immune system. He had taken her to a casino in Kansas City early in her treatment and learned a hard lesson. She spent two weeks in the hospital with pneumonia. He would take her out for a nice drive tomorrow. His spirits renewed, he pushed on, anxious to see the lights of his own city.

The burgundy 2003 Honda van drove carefully along the curving street. Savana strained to see the house numbers in the dark. All the houses appeared to be very similar in style and difficult to distinguish in the dark. Frankie raised his head from between the captain's chairs in the back and ventured a peek. He had already checked out Agent Washington's house. He saw the street sign marking the cul-de-sac that meandered off the main street. All the streets in this neighborhood were curved and seemed to lead to nowhere. Frankie knew Sam's house was the third house down from the cul-de-sac on the left. He had been here before.

Frankie had Savana drive past slowly and go about a quarter mile before making a U-turn and driving back past Sam's house. There were lights glowing from two upstairs rooms. Frankie had Savana kill the lights and park in a neighboring driveway. They watched as one of the lights went out. A half hour later, the other light went out leaving the house in darkness. That told Frankie which bedroom belonged to Sam and his wife. Always be prepared, and plan your moves well in advance. Frankie's deviousness made up for his stupidity. Frankie smiled when he saw there was no police surveillance. This was a good sign. Apparently the cops figured Frankie was no longer a threat. *Stupid cops. You're dealing with Frankie Colter, not some average felon.* Frankie continued to congratulate himself as he returned to his former position kneeling on the floor between the seats. No sense taking a chance on someone seeing his face. Savana drove back to her house in silence, pleased that Frankie had trusted her to drive past the FBI agent's house. She would be more pleased if Frankie gave her money to buy more drugs.

CHAPTER 30

J AMES FELT UNCOMFORTABLE IN HIS tuxedo. Sam and Iris had invited James and Susan to a formal cocktail event in Omaha, to celebrate the opening of a new art center. After all that had happened, he was glad to get Susan away from home, and keep her mind off of the events of the past few weeks. Iris had actually extended the invitation a couple of months earlier, and Susan had made arrangements for her parents to stay in Grand Island with JJ. Her dad and mom came from Minnesota three or four times a year so that she and James could have some time for a "date" by themselves. It also gave her folks some alone time with JJ. The cocktail party was good timing for their visit.

James fell in love with Susan all over again when she dressed for the event. She had selected a royal blue floor length dress, cut a little too low in front by James's standards, but she was striking in it. It emphasized her deep blue eyes and trim figure, and her blonde hair completed the package.

Iris wore a long black gown, more modest, with lots of bling on the top. She and Sam made a beautiful couple and looked happy.

Susan and Iris had to "walk the runway" for Molly and Maddy in their evening gowns so the girls could *ooh* and *aah*, and tell them how beautiful they looked. The women strutted their stuff and bowed to the applause of the girls. There were smiles and chuckles all around as the four adults finally left the girls with their teenage babysitter and headed to the event.

James and Susan were in awe, as everyone who was anyone in Omaha or Lincoln seemed to be in attendance. Iris seemed to know everyone by their first name. Sam, being somewhat of a local celebrity, was known by most of the dignitaries attending. Not long after they arrived, James and Susan were introduced to the mayor of Omaha, the governor of the State of Nebraska, and one of their national senators, Senator Joseph Mellen.

Senator Mellen seemed quite smitten with Susan, telling her that he too was in the medical profession prior to his election. In fact, he bragged, he was on the board of directors of Trae Pharmaceuticals. "I'm sure you are familiar with our pharmaceuticals." As the senator rambled on, a man approached and patted him on the back. "Sorry to interrupt, Senator, but I want you to meet someone."

James was grateful for the interruption, as Senator Mellen's reputation with the ladies was legendary.

"Harris, I was just wondering where you were," the senator said. "I'd like you to meet Susan Wilson from Grand Island. And this is her husband, uh…James, isn't that right?"

As James turned to acknowledge the introduction, his face turned ashen. He felt dizzy, weak, and was afraid he would throw up. He meekly extended his hand and gave a limp handshake. Harris Strang held onto his hand a little too long.

Harris said, "I'm sorry to take you away from Susan, Joe, but we have a client who insists on a picture with the senator."

Senator Mellen took Susan's hand, apologized, and left with Harris Strang.

Susan chuckled. "Looks like the senator's reputation may be well founded." She winked at James. "Let's get another drink."

When James stood still, his face still ashen, Susan asked him if he was really that jealous of the attention she received from the senator.

James regained his composure. "No, it just reaffirms my thoughts that you are indeed the most beautiful woman in the world, desired not only by me, but kings and princes, and now a national senator." He looked Susan in the eye. "You really are beautiful, you know."

"Maybe you don't need another drink," she chuckled.

"Oh, yeah," James said, "I definitely need another drink…and we better make this one a double." James extended his arm to escort

Susan to the bar. Susan gave him a quizzical look and took his arm, thinking that her tête-à-tête with Senator Mellen had indeed made James jealous.

James and Susan found Sam and Iris, and Iris directed them to their table. James was uncomfortable to see they were only two tables away from the table where Harris Strang and Senator Mellen were seated. Sam was quick to notice Audrey Landry was seated at the table with the two. *But then, Audrey is at every social function in Omaha. Probably just coincidence. Or is she with the senator?* Both couples noticed an animated conversation between Strang and the senator, with occasional glances toward their table.

Sam assumed the senator was explaining the relationship between himself and James, and how it had come about.

Susan assumed the senator was thinking of her as his next conquest, which firmed her resolution not to vote for him again.

James simply hoped one of them was right.

CHAPTER 31

I RIS AND SUSAN WERE STILL animated on the ride back to Sam and Iris's house. They discussed the people who made the biggest impression on them, both good and bad. The conversation went from the evening gowns to the obvious comb-overs. James was exceptionally quiet and Sam asked him if he was okay.

"Sure," James said, "just trying to get a word in edgewise between the ladies."

When they arrived home, Sam ran the babysitter home, three doors down. He arrived back home with the announcement he was making Colorado Bulldogs for a nightcap. James volunteered to help.

Sam grabbed the Kahlua and James put his hand on his arm. "We need to talk."

"What's going on with you tonight? You hardly said a word during dinner."

"Maybe you better put the Kahlua back and have a shot of whiskey," James said. "Remember I told you that there were three men at the nickel mine the first day we were there?"

"Yeah?"

"The third man was Harris Strang, the president of Trae Pharmaceuticals."

"What?" Sam stared at him. "You've got to be kidding!"

"I'm not kidding Sam. Same face, same walk, same voice. I only hope I didn't give myself away. I was totally stunned."

"Yeah, but there's no way he could know you were in Canada, let alone at the same place."

"Not true. The senator told Susan he had just returned from a hunting trip, and Susan told him I had been hunting bear in Canada a couple of weeks ago...I'm concerned, Sam. Somebody gave those two Neanderthals the okay to kill us, and I'm betting it was good old Harris. Think about it, Sam. All this time I've been wracking my brain to figure out why anyone in their right mind would manufacture and distribute Warfarin tablets."

"And your answer, Sherlock?"

"Quixtenone."

"What's Quixtenone?"

"Where are those Colorado Bulldogs?" a voice came from the other room. "Did you boys forget about us?"

"No, dear," Sam called, "just putting the finishing touches on them. Had to get the Coca-Cola from the fridge in the garage."

Sam hurriedly mixed two drinks and told James to take them to the girls.

James returned and said: "Quixtenone is an anti-coagulant. And? It's manufactured by none other than Trae Pharmaceuticals."

Sam stared at James, his mind struggling to process what his friend was saying. "Okay, James, that's an interesting tidbit, but how does it explain anything?"

"It fits, Sam. Their company put billions in research into this drug. It was to be the golden child. It had some hiccups in the clinical trials, but they finally got FDA approval to market it. The problem was, physicians got scared off by the clinical trial issues, and they continued to prescribe Warfarin for their patients, refusing to change them to Quixtenone. Trae spent millions on promoting their new drug, and no one would prescribe it."

"So why would they manufacture Warfarin if it competed with their product?" Sam asked.

"That's the key, Sam. What if they manufactured Warfarin at two to three times the strength labeled on the bottle?"

"Patients would bleed?"

"Right. And what would the physicians do? They would begin to order Quixtenone."

"Jesus, James. Let me try and get my mind around this. I thought the FDA tested every lot of tablets manufactured for strength and purity. How could they get the fake tablets into the hands of the public?"

"I haven't figured that out yet, Sam. I sent tablets to the FDA for testing, and…" James hesitated before plowing ahead. "Okay, I know this sounds paranoid, Sam, but I don't trust anyone right now, so I also sent some tablets from the same bottle to an independent laboratory. I'm still waiting for results from both of them."

A voice called out from the other room, "Are you boys coming in to join us? If you do, please bring two more of those drinks. They are outstanding!"

Sam chuckled, and he started mixing up four more drinks. He sounded worried, however, as he spoke. "James, this could explain why the plug got pulled on the undercover FBI operation in New Jersey. It had to be someone high up in the government. A senator perhaps? Okay, we don't talk to anyone about this. Keep it to ourselves. I'll check out some things on my end, and you let me know the test results on those tablets. Theories are one thing, James, but proof is another. We can't take on a federal official without a strong case. God only knows how many other people are involved, and at what level. Frankly, I wish the guys in New Jersey had just dropped it. From now on, you and I only talk in person. No emails, no phone conversations. But now, let's get these drinks in there. We can talk a little in the morning."

As James and Sam walked into the living room, they put off their serious thoughts and grinned. "Would you look at that? We just found the two most beautiful ladies in Omaha sitting here all alone. It must be our lucky day…How would you girls feel about two handsome gentlemen joining you for a nightcap?"

Glasses clinked, conversation flowed, and soon everyone retired. Only two of the four slept.

"I'm telling you, Joey, I'm concerned."

"And I'm telling you there's nothing to be concerned about."

"The guy recognized me, Joe. I could tell by the look on his face. He looked like he was about to shit his pants. He must have been at the mine the day before and seen me then. Damned Abe and Lenny! They let him get away, and now here he is, sitting with an FBI agent!"

"As I recall," Senator Mellen said, "the story according to Audrey Landry, is that this James Wilson suffered a very traumatic head injury a while back. Probably suffers from nightmares, hallucinations, and the like. You said you cleared out the lab in New Jersey, so when the authorities arrived, there was nothing to find, correct? So, when the authorities go to the nickel mine, they will find nothing. It will appear as if our Mr. James Wilson is suffering from delusions from his prior trauma. Too bad...his wife is quite lovely, don't you think?"

Is that all you think about, Joe? Your next female conquest? Get your head above your belt. You can sit in your important desk in Washington protected by the federal government and all the power you have. I, on the other hand, am the president/CEO of a company that may fail if this drug doesn't perform for us."

"That's the trouble, Harris; you need to think positive. Look at the polls in my last election. I was running behind my opponent, but managed to pull out and win the election in spite of the polls. You may just have to get creative like I did. In fact, you damned well better get creative or we both have a ton of money to lose. I don't intend to go down with the ship."

"Don't lecture me, Joe. You're in this as deep as I am. Plus, I know how you won that election. Not exactly on the up and up, was it?"

"The past is the past, Harris. This counterfeit drug was your idea. You put all your faith in that damned new drug; now you better make it work. Do whatever you need to do, but keep me out of it. I bailed you out in New Jersey, but I won't do it again!"

CHAPTER 32

"How's my jealous husband this morning?" Susan asked playfully after she and James got in the car to drive home.

"I'm not jealous," James said.

"Not even a little?" Susan asked coyly.

"Well, maybe a little," James confessed.

Susan kissed her finger and pressed it against James's cheek.

They talked about the affair the night before, and Sam and Iris. James finally said, "I need to tell you something, Susan."

"You thought that brunette in the red dress was hot; is that it?"

"No, this is serious. It has to do with the senator's friend, Harris Strang."

"What about him? Other than he appeared a bit odd?"

"He was the third man I saw at the mine in Canada."

"What? Are you out of your mind?"

"I wish I was. Sam and I have agreed not to talk about this to anyone. I probably shouldn't have mentioned it to you, but we don't keep secrets."

"So what happens now?"

"Nothing. Sam will pursue it on his end only. We'll have no contact other than in person. He wants to keep me completely out of it. Besides, Harris never saw Bob or me, so he has no idea I saw him at the mine. My only job would be to testify at a trial if necessary, but since this was on foreign soil, and they don't yet have probable cause to search the nickel mine, a trial is not looking likely. So, my superhero cape is officially retired." James explained their speculations, and the conclusions they were drawing.

"Sounds pretty farfetched to me," she said.

"Yeah, well it's up to Sam to pursue all this. Let's talk about something else. Wonder how spoiled JJ will be when we get home?"

The air conditioner blasted out cold air, while the heat coming off the corn fields made waves above the grain. Center pivots sprayed life-giving water pulled from deep below the ground in the Ogallala Aquifer on the rows of crops. The green corn seemed to go on for miles making a blanket of grain spreading its folds over the landscape.

Susan broke the silence. "Nebraska has its own beauty, doesn't it? In the spring and summer, green plants sway in the wind as far as the eye can see. In the winter, white snow covers the fields with specks of black cattle grazing. I love the change of seasons here."

James was up early on Monday. He had been gone since Friday and figured his work had been piling up. After he poured a cup of coffee, he checked his phone. No important messages, but he saw that the temperature was going to be in the high nineties today. He looked out the kitchen window and admired how pretty a day it was. He knew it was deceptive, because the moment he walked out of his cool house, the humidity was going to hit him in the face and his car would take all the way to the pharmacy before it cooled off.

James entered the pharmacy, still wiping sweat from his brow. Marcia gave him a cheery "Good Morning, Stud," referring to his formal party in Omaha. "Got a pic of you in a tux? We've all been waiting to see it."

James just smiled and went to his office. He no more than sat down when his phone rang. It was Kathy Mason, Gwen Eyelor's daughter. James hadn't talked to her since her mother's funeral a month ago.

"Hi, Kathy."

"Hi, James. Calling to give you a heads up." *Yep, Kathy gets right to the point. I know what's coming.* "I have filed a lawsuit in my mother's death, and unfortunately you and the pharmacy are named in the suit. I wanted to give you the courtesy of telling you in person."

"Thanks, Kathy, I appreciate the call. So, how are you doing?"

"I'm doing okay. I haven't been back since the funeral, and don't know if I will come back. We only had to deal with the items Mom had at the nursing home, so she didn't leave much of an estate. My attorney has enlisted a local attorney, Brad Madlock, so he may be contacting you on our behalf. Anyway, I just wanted you to know. We'll talk later. 'Bye."

"'Bye," James said to a dead phone line. Then said "shit" out loud. James had known it was coming, and rightly so. He would notify his liability insurance company when he got the letter. In the meantime, he had work to do. *Thank God there were no further incidents, and no other deaths!*

CHAPTER 33

SAM CALLED AGENT JOHANSSON INTO his office. "Close the door."
Katie complied. With a worried look, she asked, "What's up?"
"You and me," Sam said. "I need to know what's going on
with you and Williams. Every detail."

"We already talked about this," she said defensively.

"Yes, and I was never satisfied with your answers. I know you have
been following orders, and reporting back to Williams. Right?"

"Yes, I am following his orders. He's my boss."

"Okay, here's the deal. If you want to remain on this case, you
have to choose: Williams or me. No playing one against the other,
no "pleasing the boss," and no communications other than what
I authorize."

"What's going on, Sam?"

"Are you in complete agreement that Williams remains out of
the loop?"

"He's my boss."

"Let me put it to you another way, Katie. Williams is the head
of the Omaha office. He has illusions of grandeur, and wants to take
credit for our work by keeping tabs on you. He is using you, Katie, just
like he uses every other agent in this office. He isn't going anywhere,
especially up. He will never be reassigned to a bigger office, not New
York, Philadelphia, or D.C. He will finish his career right here. You, on
the other hand, are young, bright, and have innumerable opportunities
to move up the ladder. That's why you asked to work with me, and
then agreed to be Williams's "spy," so to speak, right?"

"Well, not exactly "spy.""

"Yes or no, Johansson?"

"Okay, yes."

"Can you drop the communication with Williams and work with me on this case. Just you and me?"

"What's going on?" Katie asked, narrowing her eyes, beginning to think there was much more to this case than she ever imagined.

"I'm only going to ask once again," Sam said. "Yes or no?"

She thought for a minute, and said, "Yes. I will work with you alone. I will not communicate anything to Williams unless you authorize it first."

"Okay, I believe you. Don't let me down, or your career will be in the toilet. Work with me and it may skyrocket, or it could end up in the toilet anyway. Let's go to lunch."

"But it's only ten o'clock," she protested.

"I'm hungry, and there's a lot to talk about away from this office."

Because none of the nearby lunch places were open yet, they ended up at Starbucks. Over a cup of coffee and a breakfast sandwich, Sam filled her in on his findings and watched as her eyes grew wide. "You're joking, right?"

"I wish I were. We have reason to suspect that Trae Pharmaceuticals is involved in this operation. Morris Strang is the President/CEO, and was seen at the illegal drug lab in Canada. We have no jurisdiction in Canada, so we need to wait until they start a lab up again in the states. Now, I have some research for you to do on Trae Pharmaceuticals."

CHAPTER 34

J AMES LAY IN BED, TRYING to fall asleep. A week had gone by and he was impatient, waiting for the lab results on his tablets. These Warfarin poisonings were showing up sporadically across the nation, but not enough to cause a panic. That is, unless you receive your news from social media. He was glad Sam had assumed responsibility for the counterfeit tablets and he could return to a normal life. Sam had a daunting job ahead of him, especially if the senator was involved. But then, that was speculation. The only problem he had now was that damned lawsuit. In the meantime he was determined to devote his time to Susan and JJ. Her parents had left a couple of days ago and life was beginning to return to normal.

James rolled over and kissed a sleeping Susan, then rolled over onto his back and fell sound sleep.

BAM! BAM! BAM! James bolted upright in bed. *What the hell was that?* He saw that Susan wasn't in the bed, and rushed into the hallway. JJ started to wail, and just then James saw movement out of the corner of his eye. Ignoring JJ, he rushed to the railing on the balcony. Susan was standing at the bottom of the stairs, a gun in her hand.

"Susan!" he shouted. She just stood still, holding the gun, not moving. James rushed down the stairs, but she just stood there like she was in shock. He took the gun from her limp hand, then scanned the room. A figure was lying on the floor. A gun lay beside his arm. James gingerly stuck his foot out and kicked the gun away, out of reach.

He turned back to Susan, still standing there in shock. He guided her to the sofa, and sat her down. She began to sob, her hands over her face. James put his arm around her, and held her for what seemed like an eternity. JJ's crying had stopped, and James assumed he'd fallen back to sleep. The man still lay on the floor not moving. James finally said, "Susan, I need to call the police." She nodded.

James grabbed the phone from the base and dialed 911.

As soon as he hung up, Susan said through her sobs, "James, call Sam right now."

"This doesn't involve Sam, Susan."

"Call him!" she screamed.

James called Sam's cell. It was obvious he'd been sound asleep. James quickly told Sam the situation.

Sam said, "There's no time to talk if you called the police. Tell them nothing. It's probably a break-in gone bad, but the gun bothers me. Maybe Harris did realize you saw him and decided to take care of a witness. You take care of Susan and JJ and call me as soon as you can. Oh, and James, if it was one of the men from the mine, do not indicate you recognize him!"

The sirens wailed in the night, volume increasing as they neared. Soon the blue and red lights were strobing off the windows and walls of the house. James opened the front door to see police officers rushing to the house, guns drawn. James instinctively raised his hands, saying, "Everyone's okay." He led the officers into the house. The man was still on the floor, but Susan was gone.

The officer approached the man on the floor, checking for a pulse before exclaiming, "He's still alive! Get the paramedics in here!" Blue clad figures rushed through the door, pushing James aside, and kneeling over the bleeding man. James watched them open medical kits and grab supplies. He saw Susan come down the stairs. She had put on a robe and was carrying JJ; he had apparently not fallen back to sleep, or perhaps the commotion had awakened him again. The officer asked the family to go to the kitchen while the paramedics worked. He asked James what had happened. Susan interjected, reading aloud from a small card in her shaking hand. She turned and put her head on James's chest and began to sob again.

The card Susan had read from was the one she received when she took her "Conceal and Carry" gun class, which told the officer she was threatened, in fear for her life, and was defending herself and her family, and would make no further statement until her lawyer was present.

The officer insisted he needed to make a report.

Susan took a deep breath and looked the policeman in the eye. "I may have just killed a man, Officer, and I don't give a damn about your report. A blind man could figure out what happened, and you will get a full statement with my lawyer present." James was amazed at Susan's calm demeanor when she talked to the officer. She looked at James, who still had his arm around her, and said, "Call John Montag. He took the course with me; tell him what happened." The police officer let out a sigh. John Montag was a criminal defense lawyer, a damned good one, and not a friend of the police department.

James returned. "John will be right over." He looked at Susan. "Say nothing until he gets here." Susan began to sob again, but asked James to call Nancy, their next door neighbor and assure her that everyone was okay. "I'm sure everyone in the neighborhood is curious and worried." James thought, *That's Susan, always concerned about others as well as herself.*

James glanced around, and could see where the lock had been broken on the back door to gain entry. It was then that the thought occurred to him: *This was no burglary. This was an attempt on my life.* He felt his knees start to buckle, but managed to regain his composure.

James didn't see JJ. "Where's JJ?" he asked, fear in his voice. James heard a familiar voice say, "Susan asked me to take him to the neighbor." James looked up to see Detective Larry Malone, a friendly face. "Worthy and I will take over from here." Worthy was Malone's partner. They had worked with Susan in an effort to find James when he had disappeared over two years ago.

CHAPTER 35

S AM SETTLED INTO HIS CHAIR, pleased that Agent Johansson appeared to be staying away from their boss, John Williams. She had thoroughly researched Trae Pharmaceutical Corporation, and had cataloged its progress since its inception in 1983 by none other than Harris Strang, and his long-time friend, Joseph Mellen, and was giving Sam a report.

Katie continued, "Trae began as a generic manufacturer, based in New Jersey, producing medications on which the patent had expired. Once a patent expires, anyone can manufacture a drug under its chemical, or generic, name."

"The company grew, and soon hired pharmacologists to do research on new drugs. They developed a few "me too" drugs, mostly slight chemical variations of drugs already on the market. They used heavy sampling, unique advertising, and huge physician incentives to prescribe Trae products. It was a success, and both Harris and Joe Mellen became multi-millionaires.

"Joe had other ambitions. He always had a flair for politics and ran for senator from his home state, here in Nebraska. He was handsome, and garnered the women's vote due to his looks and charisma. They apparently didn't believe the rumors about his carousing, or simply didn't care.

"Things continued to go well, and then along came Quixtenone. It was the first revolutionary drug Trae had developed. It had a few problems during clinical trials, but was soon approved by the FDA. It presented a new option for the patient with atrial fibrillation. These patients are controlled by daily doses of Warfarin, an anticoagulant.

The problem is, monthly blood tests are required for patients taking Warfarin. This is a pain in the rear for patients. Quixtenone, however, acted in a different manner to prevent blood clotting than Warfarin, and Trae claimed that no monthly blood tests were required. The company felt this would revolutionize anticoagulant therapy, and soon every doctor would switch their patients from Warfarin to Quixtenone. In fact, they felt patients would demand to be changed to Quixtenone.

"The marketing campaign began as soon as Quixtenone garnered FDA approval. Stock in Trae jumped 20 percent right after they announced release of the drug. It seemed to be doing well, when some side effects surfaced creating a question as to its safety. Several patients suffered severe liver damage within months of starting Quixtenone, and the drug was being blamed for the problem.

"As a result, sales began to slump, and physicians either continued patients on Warfarin, or changed patients on Quixtenone back to Warfarin. Stock dropped back to its pre-release levels. Trae had put billions of dollars of research into this drug, and they stood to lose more billions if it was recalled by the FDA. They have to make this product a success or they face bankruptcy.

"Now, Sam, put all this together, and what better scenario if suddenly Warfarin is posing a threat to patients. The only option is to switch patients to Quixtenone, which may or may not cause liver problems. In essence, bleed to death, or take Quixtenone.

"This is speculation, Sam, and no more than that. However, why would someone manufacture Warfarin illegally? It's not a high profit drug, very common, and anyone can make it. Unless, of course, the tablets were labeled with the wrong strength, and when a patient took a 5mg tablet, it actually had, say, 10 mg in it.

"To add fuel to the fire, there are increased reports of Warfarin poisoning— severe bleeds leading to hospitalization and even death. I have some excerpts from medical professional magazines expressing concerns. This is an unprecedented occurrence.

"We are on this case because Agent Leeds had a similar case in New Jersey, which was shut down—-presumably by someone high in Washington. I know I'm sticking my neck out, but Senator Mellen would have a vested interest in allowing illicit Warfarin production to continue. It would only serve to save the company in which he still owns forty percent of the stock. Which, I might add, has dropped another five percent in the last thirty days."

"Okay, so much for the *Reader's Digest* version," Sam said, rolling his eyes. Katie tended to draw out her stories and theories *ad infinitum*. Sam remembered James drawing the same conclusions Katie had just presented. "That's one hell of an accusation, Johansson."

"You're right Sam," Katie replied. "Proving it is going to be difficult with the information we have. What do you think about following the drugs from their origin in Canada? They had to ship them through North and South Dakota, and that means motels, gas stations, and restaurants. All of these businesses leave a trail. There has to be someone who can identify these guys, and possibly Strang himself."

"Good idea Katie. Pack your bags. You're going to North Dakota."

CHAPTER 36

FRANKIE WAS GETTING TIRED OF waiting. Savana was getting on his nerves. The sex was good, but he was tiring of that too. The worst part was that she was a shitty cook. There was no point in having her buy groceries, but Frankie was tired of delivery from various neighborhood restaurants. Besides, that was getting expensive. He had to do something soon. He paced the floor like a caged gorilla, rage building by the minute.

Frankie had used Savana's car to watch Sam in an effort to find a way to catch him alone. Sam didn't give him much of a chance. He was either at home, at work, or driving between them. Worse, he varied his routes to and from work, always using busy streets. Frankie had to admit Sam was showing his smarts to do that, to lessen the chance of being caught alone on some quiet side street. Sam had also installed a sophisticated security system in his home, making undetected entry impossible. *There has to be a way. Think, Frankie, think. You're smarter than Washington.*

Sam's cell rang. He saw it was Agent Johansson. "What's up?"

"I have a ton of information, but don't want to share it over the phone. Let's meet first thing in the morning. How about that coffee shop in Dundee?"

"Sounds good, it's far away enough from the office and the booths will give us privacy. Eight o'clock okay?"

"See you then."

Denver was up early on Saturday. He had been concerned that no one had contacted him the past several weeks. His wife was still undergoing treatment, but slowly losing her battle. The bills continued to pile up, and he was grateful for the phone call he had received the evening before.

Denver drove to an empty lot in a run-down industrial section of Kansas City. The Freightliner he usually drove was in the lot, with two trailers sitting beside it. Abe and Lenny were waiting in the lot, Lenny sitting on the hood of their car smoking a cigarette.

"Morning, gents," Denver said.

Lenny grunted, and Abe said, "We have two runs for you. One today and one tomorrow."

"That's gonna be a lotta miles." Denver spat at the ground. "You have a way to add hours to a day?"

"We're not going that far," Abe said. "Get yourself hooked up. We'll gas up on the way out of town. You come back home tonight while we unload, and bring the other trailer up tomorrow."

"Where we goin'?"

"Sioux City, Iowa."

"Why the change?" Denver asked.

"None of your business," Abe said curtly. "Let's go."

Denver nodded and hitched the trailer to his cab. He hoped this didn't mean less time on the road and therefore less money. He followed Abe and Lenny north along I-29, thinking of his wife as he passed the casinos in Council Bluffs, Iowa. He knew the chances were slim that she would last long enough so he could bring her for one last visit. Tears welled up in his eyes. He drove on, drumming the wheel to the sound of Garth Brooks.

James and Susan were back in their home after a week in a hotel waiting for the yellow crime scene tape to be removed from their house. It had been a rough ordeal. Susan was having the worst time, knowing she had actually killed a man. Well, not yet. He was in critical condition, but not expected to live.

Susan had taken the conceal and carry course when James went missing. She'd had no idea what had happened to James, she was pregnant, and she was alone in her house. She was a Type A personality, and took charge easily, protecting herself and her baby, just in case what happened to James happened to her. It didn't, but the course had prepared her for the situation that actually did occur.

Both Susan and James had been to see Tony Baldwin, a local psychologist, to help get them through the events of a week ago. Detective Malone had assured them there would be no charges filed, as she had clearly shot in self-defense. There were three shots, and only two rounds were absent from Susan's gun. Although she didn't remember it, the intruder had fired one shot at Susan, and the bullet lodged in the woodwork matched the intruder's gun.

James was still shook up, but glad to be back in their own home, and Tony Baldwin assured them any second thoughts or nightmares would fade with time. James understood better than anyone, after his experiences. JJ proved the resilience of children, grabbing his toys and moving on with his life as if nothing had happened.

In his office in New Jersey, Harris Strang was livid. He found out from his sources that Bob Martin, the man he had sent to kill James Wilson, was in the hospital and not expected to live. Wilson was alive and well. He should have sent Abe or Lenny. Abe and Lenny were still pissed that James had gotten away from them in Canada and would have done the job right. Even though the problem started when they messed up in Canada, they were his best men.

Strang thought it through. He wasn't sure James Wilson had even seen him at the mine. That James *had* seen him was just a hunch, based on James's reaction when they met. It was what it was. He would wait his time out. He hadn't gotten this far by over-reacting. Play it cool. His illicit laboratory would be up and running in less than a week at a new location, and it was important he get the tainted Warfarin back on the pharmacy shelves. It was life or death for Trae Laboratories. *Who the hell expected Wilson's wife to be Wyatt Earp?*

CHAPTER 37

T HE BRIGHTLY FLOWERED WALLPAPER GREETED Sam as he
inhaled the Dark Columbian scent. He got his coffee, and spotted
Katie sitting in the back booth.

"You're here early, Johansson."

"Yep," she replied, taking a bite of her bagel. She chewed her bite
as Sam slid into the booth across from her, spilling a little coffee from
his cup.

Sam waited. His hands were clasped around his cup, as if attempting
to warm them. "Well?"

"Well, Canada is really a beautiful place. I think I would like to go
back sometime."

"Canada? I thought you were in North Dakota!"

"Officially, I was," Katie said. "I have no authority in Canada, nor
any reason to step on law enforcement toes there, so I took a side trip
on my own time. Proved to be very interesting."

"I'm listening," Sam said.

"Good," Katie said, "because John Williams has called me the
last two days wanting to know why we haven't made any headway in
the case."

"And you told him what?"

"Nothing. I didn't have cell coverage in Canada, so I didn't return
his calls. To prove my loyalty I'm going to let you give him the report."

Sam nodded. "Thanks a lot."

"My pleasure," Katie said with a wide grin on her face. "Anyway, I
figured that if that abandoned mine was the source of the drugs, then
that's where I should begin. The camp owner, Dutch, was very kind

and helpful, and agreed to have Richard, his guide, give me a ride across the lake. Richard took me to the abandoned mine, but remained in the boat. Technically I was trespassing, but he and Dutch didn't care after their last encounter with Abe and Lenny. He confirmed what Wilson said."

"That was in the report shared with us by the Canadian authorities," Sam said flatly.

"Yes, but what wasn't in the report were the powder samples I took from the walls of the lab. Everyone looks at the floor, but only a woman thinks about wiping the walls. The powder has been sent to our lab to confirm it is Warfarin."

"Shouldn't we assume that, since James saw the drums labeled 'Warfarin'?"

"Probably, but this is evidence, not hearsay."

"Point taken, Johansson."

"Okay, now I also went down to the sandy area on the lakeshore and found shell casings from an automatic weapon. More specifically, 5.56mm, probably from a Steyr AUG. Most guys would be satisfied with a handgun, but a Steyr auto does serious damage. Anyway, the casings are also at the FBI lab getting tested for prints. I doubt they will find anything, but best to be thorough."

Ignoring the lesson in ballistics, Sam raised his palms and asked, "So what about the reason you went there in the first place? Or did you forget about North Dakota?"

"Patience, Sam. Isn't that what you told me a short time ago?" she said raising her eyebrows. The more impatient Sam became, the more Katie was enjoying herself. He had to admit to himself that she was being as thorough as he himself would be.

Katie continued. "Richard, the First Nation guide—they don't call them Indians in Canada—told me there were logging roads on the north side of the lake and it would be easy to sneak across the border. So...I crossed back into the States, and began to look at routes leading back to the Omaha area."

Sam made a circular motion with his hand signaling to move it along. It irritated him that Katie had some good information, but was dragging her story out.

"I spent two days stopping at every motel from the border to Fargo, North Dakota. I had the pictures from the New Jersey stakeout, and finally, in Minot, North Dakota, I found a desk clerk who recognized both Abe and Lenny. I now have last names for them, and an address that I imagine is false. They apparently stayed there every couple of weeks, just a one-night stay."

"What about Strang?"

"I took his picture from the latest Trae Pharmaceutical Brochure to show them, but got no hits."

"So we're right back to square one, other than we know the last names of the two perps?"

"Well, not exactly," Katie said with a sly grin.

Sam rolled his eyes. "Please, you have my undivided attention."

"Okay, I had some time to kill, so decided to check out motels in Fargo. A bigger place for Strang to fly into. I met this nice guy at the Super 8 along the interstate. He identified Abe and Lenny, and thought Strang looked familiar, but couldn't give me a positive ID. Anyway, he was about to get off work, and asked me to join him for a drink. I mean, what the hell? Most guys run the other way when they see my credentials. He had this gorgeous curly brown hair, green eyes, and obviously worked out...he was from Wisconsin, close to where I grew up in Minnesota. We talked about growing up in the Midwest, had a burger and a couple of beers, and I told him I needed to write a report, and get an early start the next morning."

"I'm not interested that you had a sort-of date with green eyes, Katie. What you do on your own time is your business."

"No, this is the good part. I had booked a room at the Super 8 for the night. I went up to my room and pretty soon there's a knock on the door."

"Do I really want to hear this?" Sam said seriously.

"Yes! Scott, did I tell you his name was Scott? Anyway, he said he remembered another guy who stayed at the motel occasionally, and had dinner with Abe and Lenny. He had his name and address written on a piece of paper and left it with me. I checked it out the next morning. Name is Denver Long. He drives a truck for Medical Associates, a drug wholesaler in Kansas City. I did a little research on him. Turns out he's been with the company for over thirty years, and is a model employee. It also turns out his wife has terminal lung cancer. I did some digging, and he's flown her to some research institutions in Dallas, Phoenix, and San Diego. His insurance won't cover these treatment options or treatment at these clinics."

"Maybe he has another insurance like Aflac or something? A rich uncle?"

"Nope. Only a son in St. Louis who is an attorney. But here's the stickler, Sam. He pays by check or cash. And I'm talking five to eight thousand dollars a week, sometimes up to eight weeks at a time.

"I checked his accounts, Sam. No deposits over $10,000, but several between $5,000 and $9,000. He only carries an average balance of $4,200. It looks like his involvement with Abe and Lenny is paying the bills for his wife's cancer treatment."

"Okay, let's talk to him first thing Monday."

CHAPTER 38

S AM AND KATIE WERE WAITING for Denver beside the driver's
door of his rig on Monday morning.

"Morning, beautiful day. Can I do something for you?" Denver
asked, his smile a mile wide.

Sam showed him his credentials. Denver's smile faded. "We need
you to look at some pictures, see if you can identify some people."

Denver showed up at the agreed-upon diner promptly at noon. He was
pretty sure he knew who was going to be in the pictures. He identified
Abe and Lenny, but had only seen a third man once, and while his
description matched Strang, he couldn't be sure when he looked at
Strang's picture. Denver was, of course, truthful when he said he didn't
know what he was hauling. The trailer was always locked. He never
saw the inside of it.

"Look, I knew it was probably something illegal, or something like
that," Denver said. "But I would never do anything to hurt anyone. "
He lowered his head along with his voice. "I swear, I never knew what
was in those trailers. I just knew that driving for them paid my wife's
medical bills. She's all I have, and probably not for much longer."
Tears welled up in his eyes.

Denver heaved a sigh and wiped his eyes. "You can arrest me now,
if you like. I would like to go home and see my wife first, though."

Sam looked at Katie and there was an awkward silence. Each knew
what the other was thinking. Denver was telling the truth. Katie told
Denver she and Sam needed to talk.

They returned five minutes later and sat back down.

"Okay," Katie said, "here's the deal. You finish out your day today, go on about your business, but you contact us the minute they contact you. We need to find out more information. You don't need to know any more than that."

"So you're not going to arrest me?" Denver said gratefully.

Sam said, "Not today, Denver. But you have been an accomplice in a federal crime. While we believe your involvement was unknowing, we also know that you had to understand something illegal was going on to be paid that kind of money. For now, we're going to consider you a confidential informant as long as you cooperate. When the time comes for charges to be filed, it will look very much in your favor."

"In the meantime," Katie added, "You can share this with your wife, or not. Personally, I see no need to share in light of her condition."

Denver buried his head in his hands and started to weep. "It might be better if she goes not knowin'," he said between sobs.

Sam gave Denver their numbers, and they paid for Denver's lunch. There was silence in the car for almost an hour as they drove north from Kansas City. Sam finally spoke. "Sometimes it feels good to find a witness and possibly break a case open. And sometimes..."

Agent Johansson finished the sentence for him. "And sometimes it feels like crap!"

"It's out of our hands anyway," Sam added. "The federal prosecutor will make the final call."

"Only after he hears my version of the story," Katie said fiercely.

"Okay with me," Sam said. "We know the address Denver delivered to in Sioux City. Let's drive up there, do a drive by, get a feel for the building and the area, and wait for Denver to call. You remember what happened in New Jersey the minute they suspected the FBI was on to them. They split. We don't want that to happen again."

"If we can trust Denver," Katie said. "I can see a scenario where he'd be afraid to contact us, for fear of what Lenny and Abe would do, or even for fear of losing the money. Do you think we're wrong to trust him?"

"No," said Sam. "I think Denver is basically a good man...plus, he's not going to do anything to upset his wife. He just wants her to live as long as she can."

That Saturday, Denver backed his rig up to the loading dock at the back of the warehouse. The dock door opened and Abe drove the forklift out onto the loading platform. He and Lenny loaded the trailer and Denver headed back to Kansas City.

Denver was relieved when he pulled his rig onto Interstate 29 heading south to Kansas City. He had been a bundle of nerves when he arrived at the warehouse. He had done as Agents Johansson and Washington asked. He called Agent Johansson and told her about the run to Sioux City. She had told him to make the run as instructed and call her again when another was scheduled. He was glad Lenny and Abe weren't talkers. All the while he was waiting for them to load, he was afraid they knew he was talking with the FBI, and would kill him. Nothing had been said and they went about business as usual. Apparently they didn't suspect him of talking to the authorities. His worry had been for nothing. Now he was on his way back to his beloved wife He also had more money to continue her treatments. He turned up his radio volume and began to sing along: "Country Roads, take me home..."

The jake brakes shattered the silence as Denver pulled the eighteen-wheeler off of I-29. Jake brakes were illegal, but Denver just liked the sound. Reminded him of the good old days. He arrived at the parking lot, shut down his rig, got in his car and drove home. He wondered just what was in the boxes they had loaded into the trailer. *Oh well, best I don't know. Keep me honest that way.* He smiled at the irony of his thoughts.

"Denver is back in KC," Katie said over her phone. "He parked the truck in the lot and left in his car, presumably to go home. Eleven and a half hours—not bad time. He's supposed to call me when he returns, so I imagine he'll call soon, before he gets home, so his wife won't hear anything. He was pretty nervous about this trip, and concerned about them somehow finding out he was talking to us."

"It was good you suggested we not follow him," Sam said. "It left him to fend for himself if something went wrong, but it also didn't do anything to raise suspicion. Good call, Katie."

"Speaking of good call, that's Denver beeping in the background. I'll take his call, and stay here watching the semi to see what develops."

"Okay."

"Hello, Agent Johansson here."

"This is Denver. Things went all right, thank the Lord. I was so scared when I pulled up to the dock, I almost messed my pants! But they acted pretty normal, so I guess it went okay."

"You did good, Denver. Did they talk about another run?"

"Nope, just loaded me and closed the garage door. They ain't much for talking anyway. Guess they don't suspect nothin'."

"Good. We're going to keep a low profile, Denver. We need to see what happens next. Don't worry, we'll be around. Just contact us when they call you for another run."

CHAPTER 39

K ATIE LOOKED AT THE EMPTY peanut wrappers and Diet Coke bottles, and realized she was hungry. It was going on seven, and she hadn't eaten any real food all day. There was an Arby's back a mile or so from the parking lot. Katie started the engine and edged the car away from the curb. If someone came to unload the semi, he would have to drive past the Arby's and she would see him. She slathered Arby's sauce on both sides of her sandwich, and took the first gratifying bite. She loved Arby's sauce. It was just the ticket after a long day sitting in the car. Only two cars passed going in the direction of the parking lot. She was picking at the remnants of her curly fries when a small white delivery truck went by headed in the direction of the lot. *Wake up, girl. Showtime!*

Katie drove past the lot and saw that the white truck was parked near the semi. She drove past, not wanting to raise suspicion. She turned right, went to the next intersection, made a U-turn, and parked where she could see what was happening on the lot. She took out her binoculars, and got the license plate number on the truck.

Katie waited an hour. Two more trucks, small like the white one, pulled in the lot, followed by a gray Honda sedan. She took license numbers and pulled out her camera. The lot was well lit, but she wasn't sure she could get good images with her long range lens. *Damn! These automatic cameras are great for daytime shots, but no good in low light. Damn Bureau, too cheap to buy a camera that can be changed to manual operation.* Frustrated, she took the pictures anyway, not wanting to move and be spotted. The men were making progress unloading the semi, and she didn't want to jeopardize her plan to follow the last truck.

166

The men finished loading the trucks in about twenty minutes, and they began to leave…all except the man driving the Honda. Katie drummed her fingers on the steering wheel with aggravated impatience. *C'mon, Honda, get the semi closed and locked, and get out of there so I can get a move on! You're messing with my ability to follow those trucks!* The man closed up the back, reached in his shirt pocket, and pulled out a cigarette. *Aargh! No!* He took a couple of drags, then walked to his car. *Thank God! Finally!*

As soon as the Honda was out of sight, Katie rolled forward with no lights. She let him get two blocks ahead before turning onto the street and flipping on her headlights. She remained two blocks behind and followed him until he turned left. It looked like he was headed for the drive-thru lane at Arby's. She was in the clear. *Get to Medical Associates and see if one of the trucks has gone there.* She began to speed up, but noticed headlights behind her. Slowing again, she could see that it was the Honda behind her. She took a right at the next street and watched him drive past the intersection in her rearview.

Katie waited three minutes then ventured back onto the street the trucks had taken. No taillights were ahead of her. She speeded up a little in hopes she might still catch the trucks before they hit I-29.

Bright lights suddenly blinded her from behind. *Where did that car come from?* She slowed to let him pass her. He stayed behind. Katie glanced at the next street sign: Hickory Street. She braked and pulled to the curb, expecting the car to go on past. Instead, it pulled in behind her. *Shit! It's the Honda. Thank God this is a rental and doesn't have government license plates.* Katie pulled her service weapon and put it in her lap.

She watched a man exit the Honda and walk toward her door. She lowered the window and prepared for the worst. He put his hand on the top of the car, leaned close and said, "What are you doing in this area?"

Katie was ready. Her gun was trained at the door, ready to fire right through it if necessary. "I'm looking for a friend. She lives on Hickory Street, and I see I just missed her street. Is this a bad area to be in or something?"

Her reply disarmed the man. He was expecting a reply which would give her away as following the trucks. "I don't know," he finally replied.

"Well, I'm late, so I better go back to Hickory Street and find Mary's house." She pulled away quickly and the man almost lost his balance, as she made a U-turn in the middle of the street and headed back to Hickory. She turned and drove slowly down the street as if looking for a house number. She drove about three blocks and parked her car. She picked out a house, walked up to the door and waited for the Honda to drive past. It never came by. Katie waited a few minutes, returned to her car and decided at this point the best thing she could do was check Medical Associates and see if one of the trucks was unloading there.

Bingo! When she arrived, one of the white trucks was there, unloading. She took pictures of the driver and headed back to her motel.

CHAPTER 40

FRANKIE CONTINUED TO OBSESS ABOUT Sam, lapsing at times into a state of depression. Things weren't working out for him. He was beginning to hate the floral print wallpaper left from the 1960s. The sofa was a piece of crap, smelling of some strange substance, and Savana was a lousy housekeeper. He was stuck in this damned small house with her day and night. She was starting to drive him nuts. It was time to move on. He didn't need her to drive anymore. Enough time had lapsed since his attempt to kill Sam Washington, and he imagined the cops had long ago taken his picture off their list. It was time to get it over with. He packed the money, the clothes Savana had gotten for him at the Salvation Army, and gave Savana enough money to buy drugs. She left, and Frankie knew she would come back high, and spend the next few days stoned. Frankie took a last look at the bleak room and wallpaper, took the keys to her van, and walked out the door.

Frankie cursed. "What the hell?" The van was gone. "Where did that stupid bitch go? She's gonna be collateral damage when she comes back!" and he stomped back into the house.

Agent Katie Johansson glanced at the cheap painting above the bed that put a splash of color in the drab motel room. She set her holstered gun on the nightstand, kicked off her "cop shoes" and rubbed her feet.

There hadn't been much to do on Sunday, so she'd played tourist a bit, exploring Kansas City's Crown Center and just relaxing. Today, however, had been a long day on her feet. After watching the man unload the drugs Denver had delivered, she decided to find out just what went on inside Medical Associates. She thought about her day while the whirlpool tub in her hotel room was filling.

Katie had gone to the front office of Medical Associates this morning and flashed her credentials. Katie always marveled at the reaction they caused. The secretary nervously referred her to the warehouse manager who passed her off to Mike Murphy, the shipping department manager. She explained to Mike that she wanted to spend a little time in the warehouse, and if anyone asked about her, he was to tell them she represented a potential customer. He would walk her through the building, and explain how they received medications, how they were stored, and ultimately shipped. He nervously agreed. She was emphatic that her identity as an FBI agent could not be disclosed to anyone, and assured Mike that neither he nor the company was the target of her investigation. She allowed him to infer that her investigation was of another company, but she didn't want to arouse suspicion at that operation, so chose Medical Associates to do her research.

Katie took the tour, taking special note of the door where the truck had unloaded the boxes the previous night. She asked a million questions. Mike gladly answered them, and she left with a good knowledge of their procedures. She also left knowing that when the man unloaded the drugs last night, it would be difficult not to arouse suspicion. He had to have an accomplice inside, or at least someone who wouldn't question his load arriving at that time of night.

Katie was walking back with Mike when she passed the time clock. Denver was just clocking out. He looked up at her in surprise, but she walked past him staring straight ahead. Denver left work feeling nervous.

Katie called Denver as soon as she left the warehouse. "Denver, sorry you were startled by seeing me today. I sent you a text last night. You never replied."

"Yeah, I was busy with Virginia. She was having a bad night."

"How is she today?"

"About the same. The hospice nurse was here and she wants her to take more pills. Says she shouldn't wait for the pain to get too bad. Kind of keep ahead of it, I guess. Virginia hates it because she sleeps so much. I think the Hospice nurse is right. I hate for her to sleep so much, especially since we don't have much time left. But then, I don't want her to have more pain either. I don't know what to do, Agent Johansson."

Poor man has no one to talk to. "I can't tell you what to do, Denver. I would suggest you take the advice of your medical people."

Katie felt sorry for Denver, but time was running out to keep the latest delivery of illicit drugs from getting out.

"Who is the man in the photo I texted, Denver?"

"Well, the picture was kind of dark and it was out of focus. I can't be sure."

"I really am sorry for your situation, Denver. But I don't have time for bullshit. My feet are killing me, I'm tired, and the people you work for are hurting people just like your wife. Now tell me who you *think* it is in the picture."

There was silence on the line for a long moment. "I'm pretty sure it's Jake Kaminski."

"What's Jake's job with Medical Associates?"

"He works in the warehouse. Unloads trucks on the night shift."

"Thanks, Denver." *So it wouldn't appear unusual to other employees.*

"We still got a deal?" Denver asked, worried about not returning her call.

"As long as you keep your part of the bargain," Katie replied.

"Okay. I gotta fix Virginia some supper."

Katie checked her watch. Medical Associates was still open. Katie immediately called Mike Murphy. "Mike, this is Agent Johansson. I need to know what Jake Kaminski delivered last night. And I want you to find out personally, with no communication to anyone."

"I thought you were investigating another wholesaler. Is Jake involved in something?"

"Like I said, Mike, get me the information, and tell no one. If I don't hear from you in thirty minutes, I'll get a subpoena."

"I'll call you right back."

Good call, Mike.

Katie waited impatiently. Her phone rang. "Agent Johansson, this is Mike Murphy with Medical Associates. Jake delivered medications from DC Generics."

"What drugs were in the shipment?" Katie asked.

"Aah…Warfarin. That's about all we buy from them. Their price is about the same as the other manufacturers, but they give us free goods with each purchase of Warfarin, so we can pass on the savings to our pharmacies."

"Thanks, Mike. You have been a great help. And you tell no one. Understand?"

"Yes, Agent Johansson."

"Oh, and Mike. Email me copies of the invoice for the original shipment from DC Generics and the invoice listing the free goods delivered last night. I need to compare lot numbers." She gave him her email address. "And I need them as soon as possible, Mike."

CHAPTER 41

THE SMELL OF HOT DOGS and buttered popcorn drifted through the gymnasium, and the noise level was overwhelming with all the laughing children and chatting adults.

The big moment had arrived. Maddy and Molly had spent the evening throwing darts at balloons, fishing for prizes, and playing games. It was the Summer Carnival at St. Andrew's school, an annual fundraiser. The big prizes for the night were a laptop, a tablet, and a bicycle. Molly was sure she had won the bicycle because her dad had given her five dollars and she had put ten tickets in the raffle. Her mouth was agape when another girl's name was announced as the winner.

Molly was holding back tears after the drawing; Maddy had left her alone to go talk with her friends. A smiling lady approached the stunned and disappointed Molly.

"Hi, Molly. My name is Patty Stokley, and I work at the bike shop." She handed Molly a card that said FITCH BIKE SHOP with her name on it. "There's been an embarrassing mistake. There were accidently two names drawn for the bicycle, and yours was the other one. I called the bike shop, and Mr. Fitch, the owner, said he would donate another bicycle. In fact, he was just closing the shop, and he's bringing it right over for you."

Molly's eyes lit up. "I knew it! I knew it!" She jumped up and down. "I've got to tell my mom and dad!"

"Oh, wait," the lady said, putting her cell to her ear and nodding. She put her phone in her back pocket. "That was Mr. Fitch. He's outside now. Let's go get your bike, and then you can actually *show* them your new bicycle."

She and Molly headed for the door, when Maddy spotted them. Maddy came running over. "Where are you going?" she asked, wondering why Molly was suddenly happy again and who the woman was.

"Going to get my bike," Molly squealed. "This is Patty from the bike shop. There were two bicycles and I won the other one. See?" She held up the card with Patty's name on it.

"I think we should wait for Mom and Dad," Maddy said, but Molly was already running out the door. Maddy didn't think it was a good idea. She looked around for her parents, and not seeing them, decided she shouldn't let Molly go out alone. She ran after Molly and got there just as Patty said, "Okay, Molly, come on over to the van and you can get your new bike. I hope you like blue."

Patty had removed the second row seats and folded down the third row seats of the van. She also turned off the interior lights so it would remain dark when the door was opened.

"Where is it?" Molly asked, leaning in, Maddy close behind her.

"Let me turn the light on," Savana said, as she pushed Molly inside, and grabbed Maddy, catching her off-balance, and shoving her inside also. Savana jumped inside the van with them, and grabbed Maddy by the wrists, twisting her arms behind her, and tied them together with an electrical cord. Molly froze, disappointment and disbelief reflecting from her face. Savana threw Maddy down, put her knee in her back, and quickly bound her feet. She turned to Molly, still in shock, and bound her also. Maddy was yelling, but Savana slapped her and put duct tape over their mouths. She got behind the wheel and the van sped away from the school.

Molly and Maddy bounced in the back of the van as it ran over speed bumps, potholes, and dips in the pavement. They were both bound with their hands behind their backs, ankles together; and duct tape covered their mouths. Molly was on the verge of hyperventilating; with duct tape blocking her mouth, snot ran from her nose mixed with tears, further constricting her breathing. Maddy tried to see around the inside of the van. *Who is this woman? What does she want with us? She's got to be crazy!*

Lights of oncoming cars flashed by, momentarily illuminating the inside of the van. Maddy rolled close to Molly in an effort to calm her down, but to no avail. The sobbing just escalated. The woman driving turned her head and shouted, "SHUT UP!" Molly finally settled down, and the ride lasted about twenty minutes. The van finally stopped, and the woman got out, locking the doors behind her.

Maddy twisted herself upright. She couldn't see anything in the dark. She needed to keep calm, remembering how her mother had told her to take deep slow breaths when she was at the doctor's office and had to get a shot.

She took long deep breaths through her nose, and eventually began to calm herself. As her eyes adjusted to the darkness she saw the van was parked in a garage. There was no sign of the woman…and she had left the garage door open. *If I can get into the front seat, I may be able to get out and get help.*

Savana had been planning something like this for weeks. When she wasn't too high to function, she watched the news and read the newspaper to kill her time. She wouldn't invest her own money in newspaper delivery, but the old lady who lived in her house until she died, had paid a year in advance for the newspaper, so Savana continued to get the paper for now.

She saw a notice in the paper that St. Andrew's was having their annual Summer Carnival tonight at the school. She and Frankie had driven past the Washingtons' house often enough and she'd seen the St. Andrews bumper sticker on Iris's car. She deduced that's where the girls attended school. The prizes were listed along with their donors. She knew the bicycle would be a much desired prize. A quick trip to the bike shop, which was only two miles away, revealed the business cards on the counter. This was her last chance. She sensed Frankie was ready to split. *If I do something really nice for him, maybe he will take me with him.*

Maddy wanted to communicate her idea with Molly, but it was useless with the tape over their mouths. She twisted onto her knees, and launched her torso at the opening between the front seats, hitting her face on the console. She shook off the pain, pushed herself forward, then twisted onto her back. She pulled her feet toward her bottom, then pushed her back onto the front seat. *Almost there.* She swung her legs and feet over the passenger seat back, and used her feet to lever her head up and tried to grab the door lock by her teeth. Her face was pressed against the glass when she suddenly saw two eyes set in an ugly face peer in the window. She froze in terror. The door jerked open and she spilled out onto the garage floor.

Frankie Colter laughed a spine-chilling laugh. Maddy recognized him from his picture on the news. She twisted around his feet and tried to roll out of the garage. She rolled right into the legs of the woman who had kidnapped them. Maddy stared at the two of them with wild eyes.

"Well, well, what do we have here? " Frankie said. "Could Sam Washington possibly be your daddy? I wonder what Daddy would say if he knew where you were right now?"

Maddy twisted and heaved her body around in an effort to yell back at him, and free herself. The ties just cut deeper into her wrists, and the duct tape smothered her voice. She finally settled down as she felt the cold of the floor seep into her bones. She watched with horror as Frankie stuck his head into the van and grabbed Molly to drag her out. Molly fought like a demon, kicking him, twisting, and finally giving him a head butt that hit his nose. He yelled, grabbed his nose, and backed out of the door, hitting his head in the process. He was in a rage now. He reached in and slapped her. Hard. The blow stunned her, and he dragged her limp body out of the van by her feet. Maddy watched in horror as Molly's head bounced onto the concrete floor.

"God, Frankie," Savana said. "No one said anything about hurting them."

"The little brat head-butted me right in the nose. It's bleeding."

"Big fucking deal, Frankie. Big bad man gets bloody nose from little girl. Now, what are we going to do with them?"

"I haven't had time to figure that out. This wasn't exactly my idea, you, know," Frankie said with disdain.

"You've been obsessing about that FBI agent for weeks. You think you're so smart. You messed up the first time you tried to kill him. Now I do something to help you out, and you don't know what to do. All this time you've been telling me how fucking smart you are, and now you say you can't figure it out, and you don't even thank me! You're a loser, Frankie. I should have just taken your money and let you go fend for yourself. You could spend the rest of your life wallowing in your self-pity!" Savana was livid.

"Shut up!" Frankie yelled back, as he walked toward her. Savana cowered and put her arms across her face to ward of the blow.

"DAMMIT" Frankie shouted. Frankie was backing away. The girl at Savana's feet had kicked him in the leg. "What the hell is it with these kids?" Frankie stepped back and prepared to kick Maddy back. Savana stepped between them and said, "Frankie, stop it! Think about this. You have this guy's daughters. He will have to come to you to get them back. Then you can kill him or do whatever you want. The girls don't have to get hurt." She had her hands on his shoulders, trying to calm him and hold him back at the same time.

Frankie stared at her for about thirty seconds, then said, "You're right. He won't dare call in his FBI buddies if I tell him I'll kill the girls if he doesn't come alone."

"We can't do it here," Savana said.

"So where in the hell are we gonna do it?" Frankie scowled. "It's not like we have anyplace besides your house."

"Yes, we do," Savana said. "I have a friend who moved out of her house a couple of weeks ago. They haven't rented it yet, and it's not far from here."

He stared at her and narrowed his eyes as he thought it over for a moment. "Okay." He shoved Savana toward the doorway as he said, "My things are packed inside by the front door. Go in the house and get them. I'll get these brats back in the van."

Molly was not a problem; her sobbing had subsided, and she was still stunned from the blow to her head. But by the time Frankie had literally tossed Molly back in the van, Maddy had twisted and rolled about twenty feet down the driveway. Frankie caught up with her, and her writhing and kicking stopped when he pulled out his knife and held it in front of her face.

"You know, I only need one of you alive to get your daddy to rescue you. Now get up and walk into the van," he said, cutting the ties binding her ankles together. She scrambled to her feet, losing her balance and falling once, but finally stumbling to the van. Frankie gave her a shove and she fell inside. He turned and found an electrical cord, and bound her ankles.

Savana returned with Frankie's stuff. It consisted of two duffel bags. She knew one of them held the money from the robbery, but was afraid to take any of it. Frankie threw the bags in the back, hitting the girls in the process.

CHAPTER 42

"**H**EY, JJ, LET'S GO UPSTAIRS and take a bath. You can bring Goofy." JJ scooped up his favorite friend, Goofy, and headed up the stairs. He loved his bath, and Goofy never left his side, even in the tub. Goofy was actually a rubber pig, and JJ had named him. James and Susan never found out where he had come up with the name. Another one of the great mysteries of life. James followed JJ up the stairs to ensure he didn't take a tumble. Susan was working a late shift to fill in for a nurse who was recovering from a car accident, and James was in charge. James regularly helped with JJ, but seldom had him alone for long periods. And as much as James enjoyed his father/son time with JJ, he was exhausted. *How much energy can a an eighteen month old have? This kid is wearing me out!*

James filled the tub, tested the water, stripped JJ's clothes off, and hoisted him into the tub. JJ reached his arm out and said "Goofy." James grabbed Goofy and handed him to JJ.

JJ was snug in his bed after a story from his dad. James seldom read books to JJ at bedtime, preferring to make up stories for him. Sort of a *James's Fairy Tale* edition. James tried to combine happy endings with some life lessons, and he never seemed to be at loss for a good tale. After draining the tub and wiping up, he went downstairs to watch a little television.

He settled in and his phone chirped an unknown ringtone. He had ringtones programed into his phone for frequent contacts. He waited for the next commercial then eased out of his recliner and checked the phone. Voicemail. "James, this is Katie Johansson. I interviewed you after your bad experience in Canada. Please call me back when you get this message."

Katie had finished her bath. Feeling refreshed, she settled into her pajamas and called James Wilson. No answer. She left a message and pulled her Kindle from her suitcase, plopped onto her bed, and began to read.

The phone surprised her when it rang, interrupting her story.

"Hello."

"Agent Johansson, this is James Wilson."

"Thanks for calling back, James. Sam gave me your cell number. And by the way, the name is Katie. Anyway, I'm in Kansas City and visited Medical Associates today. What I need from you is the name of the manufacturer of the Warfarin you purchase for your pharmacy.

"DC Generics," James said. "What's up?"

"You found the illicit lab in Canada. I think Sam and I just found their new location in Iowa."

"You have to be kidding me."

"You wouldn't think so if I sent you a picture of the two guys loading the truck. Do the names Abe and Lenny ring a bell?"

"Holy shit!"

"Yeah. I normally wouldn't talk to you about it, but you and Sam broke this thing wide open when you recognized Strang."

"So you've busted this illicit drug manufacturer?"

"Far from it. But we're getting close. I'm sure Sam will fill you in after I talk to him tomorrow, but I wanted to give you a heads up, knowing it would be welcome news. Anyway, thanks for your help. Goodnight."

Wait, I have a question...Okay, thanks...Goodbye. James hit the red telephone button, his head spinning. *She's not much of a talker. At least she didn't make me miss much of my TV program.* James returned to his recliner.

CHAPTER 43

IRIS WAS FRANTIC. SHE AND Sam had been visiting with other parents, and let their guard down; after all, this was an all-school event, and the children were having fun. She hurried through the crowd, looking for the girls. She saw Sam across the room and rushed over and interrupted his conversation. "Sam, have you seen the girls? I've been looking for them and can't find them." The worry was obvious in her voice.

"I'm sure they're here somewhere," Vern Duggan, the man Sam was visiting with, said. "I haven't seen Dustin for a while, but he's safe in the school. Probably just running around with friends. I'm sure you'll find them."

"Thanks, Iris," Sam said, walking away with her, "that guy never stops talking. Now, let's find the girls and get them home so they won't be too tired for tomorrow's orientation."

Iris had calmed down a little, and she went left and Sam went right to walk the halls of the school.

They walked all the halls of the school, checked the rooms with the games in them, and finally met in the middle. "No sign of them," Sam said, the panic rising in his throat. "Let's work our way back. We may have just missed them."

Sam saw Sierra, Maddy's friend. She told Sam that Maddy and Molly were with some lady a little earlier. Sam asked her the lady's name. "I never saw her before," Sierra said. "They were walking toward the front door."

Sam took off on a dead run toward the front entrance. He looked frantically, then ran out the door. No sign of them.

Sam ran back inside. There were a lot of kids milling around and several leaving with their parents. Sam yelled over the commotion, "Did any of you kids see Maddy or Molly Washington?" Iris came to the lobby just in time to hear. She ran to Sam and whispered, "Oh God, Sam, can't you find them?"

April Martin, a girl in Maddy's grade, came up to Sam. "I saw them go outside with some lady. They were looking inside a van, but it's gone now."

Sam grabbed Iris by the arm. "Come with me." Sam found the principal and asked him to make an announcement over the PA system, telling the girls to come to the office immediately.

The announcement came, but no girls. The principal then announced that anyone who saw the Washington girls leave the building to come to the office immediately. Iris and Sam waited impatiently. Iris sobbed and Sam paced. A couple of kids came and said they saw them with a lady earlier. Sam had Iris sit down beside Amy Hansen, their neighbor, while he called 911. He explained the situation, asked for an Amber Alert. He relayed the information that it was a dark van, maybe blue or red. Sam remembered the maroon van he'd seen outside his house several times in the past and asked April, who was standing close, "Could it have been maroon?"

"Maybe," the girl said. "It was dark and I didn't pay much attention. I'm sorry, Mr. Washington."

"That's okay, April. You've been a great help. Thank you."

Sam told the operator it may have been maroon. He waited impatiently while she got all the information she needed. Five minutes later Sam and Iris were explaining the situation to two Omaha police officers.

Sam decided to wait at the school, and sent Iris home with Amy Hansen, just in case the girls were home, or if someone called. *Damned maroon van! I knew there was something weird going on!*

Sam paced back and forth in the principal's office. *How could this have happened? What did I do to deserve this? I no sooner than get my life back and now this! Dear God, don't let anything happen to my girls.* Sam wrung his hands and wiped the tears from his eyes. A couple of friends stayed with him, while others continued to canvass the school and surrounding area.

Sam looked at the scene around him. The principal's office had about ten people in it, mostly parents. He could see the lobby and front doors to the school through the glass partition. Four police officers were conducting interviews. People, parents and children filled the lobby, milling around, talking and gesturing. Some were wiping their eyes, others were crying openly. It was like watching a scene from a movie, but he wasn't watching a scene. This was real. And he was the lead actor, only he didn't know what the next scene would be. It scared the hell out of him.

An eternity passed and Vern Duggen entered the office and put his hand on Sam's shoulder. "We've covered the entire school and surrounding block, but there was no sign of the girls," he said. "Several parents are driving the neighborhood, looking. I'm so sorry."

Sam nodded, and said, "Thank you, Vern," and turned his head to hold back the tears.

Sam's cell rang. He looked at the caller ID. It was John Williams. "Hi, John," Sam said.

"Sam, I just heard. Are you sure your daughters have been abducted?"

Sam drew in a deep breath. He wanted to tell Williams *Yes, I am goddamned sure and I have better things to do than listen to your bullshit!* Sam quelled his anger and said, "One of the kids saw them go to a van outside the school with an unknown woman. I can't believe they would do anything that stupid. If I told them once, I've told them a million times to be wary of strangers. And now they're missing. Jesus, John, I don't know what I'm going to do."

"You are going to do nothing, Sam. Assuming this is an abduction, it falls under the Bureau's jurisdiction and I am personally leading the case. I just wanted to talk to you before I turn the dogs loose. I have spoken to the Omaha Police Department, the Douglas County Sheriff's Office, and the Nebraska State Patrol, and we are meeting in fifteen minutes to get a task force dedicated to the situation. I want to assure you that we will get your girls back safe and sound."

Sam listened with mixed emotions. His instinct told him he should be thankful Williams didn't put him off, but his gut told him Williams was showboating. *This could be his big break. Find the missing children of a fellow FBI agent. Be the hero he always wanted to be. Maybe get that promotion he thinks he deserves...*

Sam's silence must have un-nerved Williams. "Sam, are you listening?"

"Yes, John, I'm listening. I want you to keep a line dedicated to me and keep me up to speed on everything as it develops. Have you gotten an Amber Alert out yet?"

"No, the rules say we need a description of the vehicle and a license plate number. I'll have to talk to the other agencies about that." *Dumb shit can't make a decision on his own!* "That will be our first priority. Now, I want you to go home and wait for a call. I'll send Morgan and Sedlacek to your home to set up a call trace. I'm in route to the sheriff's department right now. I'll keep you informed."

"John, get that Amber Alert out, goddammit!"

"Mr. Washington! Let me see Mr. Washington, it's important!" the young boy said, trying to twist away from an adult attempting to keep him from the office.

"Just a minute, John," Sam said, "hold on." Sam held his phone away and looked down at the insistent boy trying to get into the office. "Let him in," Sam said. The boy ran to Sam. "What do you need to tell me, Danny?" Sam asked. Danny was a boy in Maddy's class. He was labeled as a slow learner, and sometimes would stutter. Danny took a deep breath to get his wind.

"I s-s-saw the van, Mr. Washington. It was a Honda, just like my mom's. And it had a s-s-s-sticker in b-back."

"You mean a bumper sticker?" Sam asked.

"No, a st-t-ticker in the back window. It looked like a st..." Danny took a deep breath. "*Star.*"

"Did you see the color of the van?" Sam asked.

"Yeah, it was dark red," Danny said.

"Could it have been maroon?" Sam asked.

"If maroon is dark red, y-yes," Danny said.

"What about a license number?"

"I only remember the first three letters," Danny said, "Cuz they are the same as my mom's. *SVN*...I'm sorry I don't remember the rest.

"But you are sure about the star-shaped sticker on the rear window?"

"Uh-huh," Danny nodded,

Sam put his hand on Danny's shoulder. "Good work Danny. Thank you very much for the information. I'll pass the information on to the police. I think you just helped find Maddy and Molly."

Sam put his phone back to his ear. "Did you hear that John? We just got a more definite ID on the van. It is a Honda, maroon, late model, and the first three letters of the license are SVN. It has a star-shaped sticker on the rear window. That will give you enough information for an Amber Alert. And I'm coming to the task force meeting. Will it be in our offices?"

"No, we'll have better communications if we use the sheriff's office. But I want you to stay home with Iris. You are not part of this case, Sam. You are the victim, and I can't risk your involvement over-riding your judgement. Now go home. That's an order. Oh, and text me pictures of the girls. The phone went dead.

Sam realized that Williams was right. His place *was* at home with Iris. *Bet he had to look her name up in his file. Asshole!*

Sam clenched his fist and banged it on the counter. He wanted to be there. Wanted to know what was going on. Wanted to know when they found his girls. Wanted to know they were safe. Wanted to be there for his girls. Wanted to hold them and tell them how glad he was they were safe, to calm their fears and tell them it was all right. *But they aren't safe. They are with some stranger and God only knows what she is going to do to them. I need to see Iris. She must be as frantic as I am.*

"Agent Washington?" The voice startled Sam out of his trance. He turned to see Officer Kelly Garrity, wearing jeans and a teeshirt.

"I don't know if you remember me?" he began, "I'm Kelly Garrity. We met a while back at the stabbing in the mall parking lot."

"I remember," Sam said.

"Sorry to bother you, Sir, but my partner called me at home and told me the situation. I live about ten minutes from here and stopped by to let you know every cop in this city, on duty or off, is going to help find your girls."

Sam was overwhelmed with emotion. He reached out, shook Officer Garrity's hand, and thanked him. "I can't tell you how much this means to me."

"Anything for a fellow officer, Sir. Is there anything I can do for you right now?"

"Could you give me a ride home? I'm a little shaky and would appreciate your company."

CHAPTER 44

"**K**ATIE," SAM ANSWERED THE PHONE.

"Hi, Sam. How was the school carnival? While you were playing I was—"

"Katie, stop. The girls have been abducted."

"*WHAT?*"

"Last time we saw them they were with a bunch of girls at the school. Iris and I were getting ready to go and couldn't find the girls. We were told they were seen with an unknown woman approaching a van outside the school. The van is gone and so are the girls." Sam's voice cracked, and he fought back tears.

"Sam, I'll leave now. I can be there in less then three hours!"

"No, Katie. Stay where you are. If this van heads south, I want you to be around when they intercept it."

"Who's handling the case, Sam?"

The silence told Katie what she feared. "Please don't tell me it's Williams."

"Yes, dammit!"

"Sam, don't worry. Everybody in the office knows Williams is in over his head. In fact, the local PD and sheriff know it too. Williams may think he's in charge, but the others are good officers. Just hang in there, Sam. They'll get the girls back safe and sound. You be there for Iris; we'll be there for you, okay?"

"Thanks, Katie. I know you will." Sam clicked off. He realized he hadn't heard Katie's news. He shrugged; he really didn't care right now.

Sam went back into the living room to be with Iris. She sat on the sofa, silently wringing her hands. Marcus Sedlacek and Bruce Morgan were in the dining room checking their equipment. Morgan, a man of about fifty with graying hair, was a fellow agent in the Omaha office. Sam didn't know Sedlacek well. He was in his early twenties, had long hair and a wimpy beard, and was wearing a Zac Brown Band tee shirt. Guns and badges weren't his thing. He was a techie for the Bureau. Right now his job was to tap into Sam's cell and home phones, in hopes of tracing a call when one came from the kidnapper. He had computer screens set up with maps of the Omaha area to trace calls through cell towers, in case the caller didn't have a GPS in his or her phone.

Sam held Iris's hand. Iris put her head on his shoulder, and began to sob. "Why would anyone do this, Sam? Why do they want our girls? God knows, we don't have any money."

"I don't know, Iris. It doesn't make any sense. I just can't believe the girls would leave the building with a strange woman. Unless they know her from somewhere...? They have the woman's description, a good description of the van, make and model, a partial plate number plus a star-shaped sticker in the rear window. Every cop in the area is looking for it, and John Williams has gotten out an Amber Alert. They'll never get out of the city."

"Did you say John Williams? Your boss? You told me he's an idiot! And he's in charge of finding our girls? Oh God, we'll never see them again!" Her wailing began again.

The doorbell rang.

Special Agent Morgan went to the door. An elderly lady rushed past him. "Iris, honey. An FBI man came and picked me up. What's this about Maddy and Molly? He said they've been abducted!"

"Oh, Mom," Iris said, rising from the couch and going straight to her mom. Her words were muffled. "I'm so glad to see you." She held on for a long, long time, both women sobbing in each other's arms.

Sam took the opportunity to go into the dining room and visit with Sedlacek.

"What's happening, Marcus?"

"Not much to report, Sam. I just got off the phone with the dispatch officer from the task force. The whole police community has

FOLLOW THE BLOOD TRAIL

rallied to help out. We have our entire staff on it, and every cop and deputy in the area is helping out, on duty or off. They have roadblocks and check points set up all around the city. We figure it's less than an hour since the abduction, so they have calculated maximum driving distance, and concentrated black and whites in the surrounding area. We'll get her, Sam."

Sam paced for a few minutes, went back into the living room and joined Iris and her mother.

"Grace," he said, giving her a hug. "Thanks for coming. Iris and I are grateful for your support."

"Sam, they're my granddaughters. Besides you and Iris, they're all I have. No way I'm not going to be here when they come home." Her speech was brave, but Sam could feel the worry in her voice. "We need to pray together," Grace said, taking Sam by one hand, and Iris by the other. They held hands while Grace said a prayer.

CHAPTER 45

SUSAN HAD ARRIVED HOME ABOUT ten from her extra shift. She was soaking in the tub when James's pager buzzed. He took the order from the nurse at Mayflower Nursing Home and called the courier, alerting him to be at the pharmacy when he arrived. James knocked on the bathroom door. "Susan, I just got paged. I checked on JJ and he's sound asleep. Enjoy your bath. I'll be back in twenty or thirty minutes."

The voice from the tub answered, "I'll be asleep by then. Be sure and lock the door."

"Okay. I'll try not to wake you."

James left, and she was left alone with her thoughts.

Susan was still paranoid after the shooting incident. She hadn't slept well since then. Ever since she'd heard the intruder had died of his gunshot wounds, the slightest noise would awaken her, and sleep would elude her like a shadow dancing across the wall. At times she wondered if it was worth having a concealed handgun permit. It had empowered her to take the life of a human being.

On the other side of things, she knew James wouldn't be alive if she hadn't learned to handle a firearm. The training she had undergone to earn her permit had taught her how to store the gun safely, handle it with confidence, and use it only if her life or the lives of others were threatened. The course had also taught her to aim for the middle of the target, thus ensuring a fatal hit. She had done exactly as she was taught and trained to do.

What the course did not teach her was how to deal with the burden of having taken a human life. She was a nurse, and her life had been devoted to saving lives, not taking them. Susan would forever have the image of that man lying in a pool of his darkened blood, a scarlet stain creeping across the wooden floor as his breathing stopped. She washed her hands incessantly ever since that night, trying to remove the blood which had long disappeared. She looked at her hands while in the tub. The skin of her fingers was already clean and soft, but she took the bar of soap and scrubbed them again.

She finally reached over the edge of the tub, grabbed a towel, stood, and wrapped it around herself. The time of reconciliation was over for today. She instructed herself to get on with her life. After all, she might not have a husband if she hadn't acted. The thought consoled her for the moment. James had never said that the intruder must have been there to kill him, but she'd put two and two together, and realized it had to be a result of his discovering the illegal drug lab on his trip to Canada. *I need to go see Monsignor Kelly.* Monsignor Mike Kelly was the parish priest at her church, St. John's, and a friend. He always had a listening ear, and good Irish whiskey.

James took the bottle of Warfarin from the shelf. He studied it before packaging the tablets. *DC Generics. That's the brand Agent Johansson said was involved in the counterfeiting. I sure hope these are the real thing. Guess there's nothing I can do now.* James placed the clear plastic lid on the cassette, affixed the label, packaged it, and handed it to the courier. He wished this was over and he didn't have to worry about the safety of the medications he dispensed.

As James locked up, his cell jingled. He looked at the screen and saw it was Susan. "Hey, babe, thought you were going to bed."

"James," Susan was sobbing and he had trouble understanding her, "Maddy and Molly have been kidnapped."

It took James a moment to make sense of what she'd said. "*What?*"

"Iris just called, James. She wanted us to know before we saw anything on the news."

"What happened?"

"I don't know for sure. Iris said they were taken from a school carnival or something. They have an Amber Alert out and everything. Oh God, James. I can't believe this has happened."

"Should we go to Omaha tonight?"

"I offered to go right away, but Iris said her mother is there, and all we can do is pray. She will let us know when they find the girls."

"I'm just leaving, Suz. I'll be home in ten minutes." James got in his car and started to drive away, when he thought, *Geez, did I lock the door?* He turned his car around, got out and shook the door to make sure it was locked. He got back in his car and hurried home.

James and Susan stayed up until midnight talking about Sam and his family.

"James, does this have anything to do with Canada, or the attempt on your life?"

"I don't know, Suz. I've come to the conclusion that a man who would manufacture drugs in the wrong strength just to put money in his own pocket will stop at nothing. He has absolutely no regard for human life. Would he take Sam's kids? Sure, but why? He has nothing to gain by ordering one of his men to take Sam's girls. I honestly don't think it's related to the drugs."

"What then?" Susan asked.

"I don't know. I'm sure Sam has made enemies over the years. I'm still trying to wrap my mind around this thing. Meanwhile, let's bring JJ in here with us tonight."

Susan nodded in agreement, got up, walked down the hall, took JJ from his bed, and carried him into their bedroom. He stirred, then promptly rolled over next to James and fell back asleep. Susan stroked his fine blond hair, and smiled as he slept in his Buzz Lightyear pajamas. He reminded her of James, and seeing the two of them lying together gave her a warm feeling.

Before settling down to sleep, Susan went to the top drawer of her dresser and withdrew the handgun. She placed it in the nightstand next to her bed, and pulled a chair back next to it so JJ couldn't open the drawer if he awakened.

"I thought the police had your gun," James said.

"They do. They said they have to do ballistic tests and other stuff on my weapon. Larry stopped by the day we moved back from the motel and gave me this gun."

"Detective Larry Malone? Is that legal?"

"Yes, and I don't know. Now, you left lights on downstairs, right?"

"Yep, and the doors and windows are locked."

"Good." She leaned across JJ and gave James a soft kiss. "Now let's get some sleep." Susan pulled the sheets and blue comforter up around her neck, reached up and turned out the light. She lifted her head and looked at James in the light provided by the streetlights through their curtains. "And say a prayer for Sam, Iris, and those poor girls."

"Yeah. Don't think I'm going to sleep anyway." He told Susan he loved her and pulled the covers up over himself and JJ.

CHAPTER 46

S AM AND IRIS SAT IN the captain's chairs in the back of the Suburban. Sam reached across the space and held Iris's hand. He could see her trembling, and her hands shaking. She looked straight ahead, and finally said, "O God Sam? Do the girls have a chance of coming home?" She was pleading with him to reassure her, while underneath she thought she knew the answer.

The siren wailed as they approached a busy intersection. They were traveling much too fast to rely on the red lights alone. Iris looked out and saw the red lights reflecting off the cars stopped beside the intersection. A black and white OPD cruiser pulled out in front of the Suburban and it turned on its red, white, and blues to escort them. Iris felt slightly dizzy. It was like a sick disco experience: the pulsating lights, the fear welling up inside, Agent Morgan weaving the car through traffic, swaying and throwing her side to side. At one point her head hit the window. She held tightly onto Sam.

Sam finally spoke. "I think there's a very good chance," he said. "I have no idea what this woman wants, but women seldom take hostages. In all likelihood she can be talked down."

"So we just have to sit idle and wait?" It wasn't really a question.

"I don't know yet. From the chatter coming over the radio, it sounds like the entire OPD, Sheriff's Department, State Patrol, and FBI have the place surrounded. They're trained to handle these hostage situations, honey. Trust me, they will get the girls out alive and unharmed." As an FBI agent, Sam hesitated to promise anything to the mother of girls being held hostage, but as a husband, he could see Iris needed that promise. He prayed that he was right, and that the girls would be returned to them, safe and sound.

Iris stared and looked at the lights of the police car leading them through traffic. Soon they turned off Center Street and headed south. As they reached a residential area, the cars turned left. Everything slowed down and all that was left was the lights; the sirens had gone silent. Sam saw the pulsating glow of red, blue, and yellow lights a mile or so ahead. He knew they were close.

Sam and Iris had been waiting for a call from the kidnapper. It never came. Instead, the 911 center was alerted by an off-duty Omaha police officer. Officer Vicki Martinez was driving the area looking for the van described on the Amber Alert. She met a van that matched the description, turned around and caught up to it. SVN license, star-shaped sticker on the back window, maroon van. *I've got it!*

She called 911, told them she had the van in her sights and would follow at a safe distance. Vicki relayed the last three numbers of the plate to the dispatcher, then followed the van and watched it turn off Center Street. She went on past the intersection and made a U-turn. She raced back to the intersection and turned right. She saw the taillights ahead and slowed to a crawl, keeping the van in sight. The 911 operator kept her on the line, and directed police units to the area. Vicki Martinez was to keep her distance, and the units in the area, although converging, were not to approach the van. They didn't want to risk alarming the driver. The command center would set up a moving perimeter until the van reached its destination, and all units were to stay away from the immediate area. This situation was likely to escalate into a hostage situation, and had to be handled with caution. It was risky to allow the van to proceed; but not as risky as a confrontation on a residential street. Besides, they felt they were moving units strategically and had the neighborhood cordoned off.

Officer Martinez kept her distance and informed dispatch that either the van occupants had spotted him, or were taking evasive action as a precaution. "They've gone around the same block twice, and heading east again on Corning. I parked and watched them go by, so I don't think they made me. Resuming pursuit. Left turn signal blinking now, will give you the street name when I get there."

"Goddamn it, Savana! I thought you knew how to find this place."

"I do, Frankie. It's just that I've never tried to find it in the dark. Just keep going east; I'll know it when I see it. It sits on a block all by itself, just on the edge of these other homes."

"I can't drive around all night. You're sure no one saw you?"

"No, honest, Frankie, it was dark. No one saw me. I was careful."

Frankie continued to drive, getting angrier by the minute. "This was a dumb fucking idea, Savana. *Your* dumb, fucking idea!" A moment passed. "In fact, maybe we better just dump the kids and get the hell out of town. Or better yet, maybe I should just kill them. That would settle the score with Washington."

"Wait a minute, I recognize that Dollar Store!" Savana was relieved. "Turn left at the next corner. We're almost there."

"You better hope so," Frankie hissed. "If you're wrong, you might just end up like those damned kids!"

"Just one more block, I think," Savana said. "Yeah, there it is."

"I don't see nothin'," Frankie snarled.

"Right there," Savana said, pointing. "Turn down this road."

Frankie grumbled, but turned down the gravel path. His lights shone on a small house at the end of the drive. It looked run down, deserted, and even in the dark, it was obvious it hadn't been rubbed elbows with a paint brush for a long time. It was old, and the large trees on both sides confirmed its age and suggested cool shade from the summer heat.

Frankie saw a single car garage to the right of the house. He made Savana get out and open the door. Safely inside, he opened the back door of the van.

"Okay, girls, here's where you get out." He reached in and grabbed Molly. She kicked at him with her bound feet. Frankie crawled in the van over the top of her, and grabbed Maddy by the hair. His face was so close to hers she could smell his fetid breath and body odor. Her eyes widened with fear when she saw the knife in his hand.

Frankie looked at Molly and said, "You either settle down, or I use this knife on your sister. She's not going to be very pretty with her nose cut off." He pressed the blade of the knife alongside the side of her nose. Seeing them recoil with fear, he said, "I'm going to cut the cords from your ankles and you're going to walk in the house. If either of you tries to run, I kill your sister. Understand?"

Maddy nodded in assent toward her sister. She could see the defiance in Molly's eyes, and was afraid she would do something stupid.

The house stank and the summer heat was stifling. A combination of who-knows-what lodged in the horrid green shag carpeting, so filthy it was difficult to determine if green was its original color. The closed-up air held the stench close to their nostrils. Maddy thought she was going to puke. She was afraid if she did she would asphyxiate herself with the duct tape over her mouth. She willed herself to keep the bile in her stomach. She was sure she could smell dead mice in the walls.

Frankie said, "Put them in the bedroom and lock the door."

Savana herded them into the bedroom, and yelled at Frankie, "There's a window in here. They might get out."

Frankie walked in, the dim light from the single bulb barely casting a glow. "Duct tape their ankles, put them in the closet, and push that dresser in front of the door." He looked at the girls. "And you keep your mouths shut!"

Maddy had to stifle a smile, if that were possible with tape over her mouth. *He's so dumb he thinks we can talk with our mouths taped shut.*

Frankie sat down on a rickety chair and began to make his plans to lure Sam into the trap.

Yeah, that's it. Savana will call Sam's house, and tell him she has the girls. If he comes alone, she will trade the girls for him. If the cops show up, Frankie will kill the girls. Frankie rehearsed this with her.

"Will you kill the girls?" Savana asked, fearing for the worst.

"Not if he comes alone." Frankie had just started to dial the number when the house was bathed in flashing lights. Frankie ran to the window and looked out to see more cars rushing onto the lawn with red lights flashing.

Frankie was livid. He whirled around and hit Savana in the face, knocking her to the floor. "You said you weren't followed, his venomous voice hissed."

"Frankie, I swear…"

"Get up and lock the doors!" Frankie growled.

CHAPTER 47

THE SUBURBAN PULLED IN BEHIND what looked like half of the area's police cruisers, sheriff department vehicles, SWAT teams, the state patrol mobile command van, and at least fifty officers. Both Sam's and Iris's eyes went wide.

They were ushered to the state patrol command center, where they were met by John Williams. "Good to see you, Sam. I've got the situation under control. This is Sheriff Watkins. I'm going to let him brief you on the situation."

Watkins was tall, maybe six foot two—about Sam's height. He was graying, but looked lean, mean, and serious. Sam knew he had a stellar reputation, but had never met the man in person. He emitted an aura of quiet confidence.

Sheriff Watkins extended his hand. "Sam, Mrs. Washington. I'm sorry about your situation. Let me fill you in. The perpetrators, one Savana Zeis, and an ex-con named Frank—"

"Frankie Colter," Sam said, fury and venom in his voice, as the pieces fell in place.

"You know him?" Sheriff Watkins asked.

"Yeah, we have a history of sorts. He's the guy that tried to shoot me last spring after a bank robbery."

Sheriff Watkins nodded, "I remember that incident now. Anyway, we've ascertained that your daughters are alive and safe for the time being."

For the time being, sent a shiver down Sam's spine.

"We have snipers on trucks behind the house, SWAT teams ready to move on a moment's notice, and damned near every cop in the city around the perimeter. Our biggest problem is the trees on either side of the house. We can only see inside the front and back."

"How do you know my daughters are safe?"

"The woman brought them to the window. They had duct tape over their mouths, but they looked okay. We haven't heard any shots fired, so assume they are safe for the time being."

Sam took another look at the dilapidated house. It was bathed in bright light from the spotlights attached to tall poles rising to the sky from the emergency vehicles. It was dimly lit on the inside, but there was no sign of movement. The surrounding block was as dark and foreboding as Satan himself.

"Pardon me, Sheriff Watkins, but his nickname is 'Frankie the Knife' because of his preferred way of killing. Now tell me again how you are sure my daughters are safe."

"You have a point, Agent Washington. But you know he will keep them safe in an effort to free himself."

"All I know, Sheriff, is that this psycho will stop at nothing until he has my head. He vowed to get even with me after my testimony sent his brother to prison. He tried once and failed. If push comes to shove, and I think with all this manpower, we're very close to that point, the next best thing to killing me is to kill my daughters. He's going to extract his revenge in any way he can."

"So what do you suggest?"

"A trade. Me for my girls."

"I can't do that. Agent Williams who, I might remind you, is in charge—said he will not negotiate under any circumstances."

"Agent Williams couldn't negotiate with a five-year-old. He couldn't find his ass in a dark room if he had a flashlight. And you want me to put my family's lives in his hands? Sorry, Sheriff, this conversation is over."

"I can have you arrested if you attempt to interfere, Agent Washington."

"Yes, you can. But can you imagine the press you will get when my daughters are dead, and you are the one who had the grieving father arrested? They will crucify you, Sheriff. Your career in law enforcement will be over. Plus, you will have to live with blood on your hands the rest of your life."

Sam paused to let it sink in. "Do what's right, Sheriff. Why do you think Williams is allowing you to talk to me? If things go wrong, it won't be on his head. He has someone else to blame. He knows how to end this thing. He just doesn't have the balls to do it...do you?"

"Give me a few minutes, okay?"

As Sheriff Watkins walked away, Sam reached over the console and grabbed the mike for the loudspeaker.

"FRANKIE COLTER, THIS IS SAM WASHINGTON. I'M GOING TO MAKE A TRADE. I WILL WALK IN UNARMED, BUT YOU LET MY DAUGHTERS GO FREE."

One of the deputies grabbed the mike from Sam's hand. Sam didn't resist. The sheriff rushed over, grabbing his handcuffs from his belt.

Sam raised his hands in surrender. "No need to cuff me, Sheriff. We're wasting time my girls don't have. I'm going in that house, and I don't think you or any of the other officers here will put up a hand to stop me."

The sheriff backed off. He knew Sam was right. Put any one of his own officers' kids in danger, and the officer would have the backing of the entire department.

Sam opened the door of the command center. Agent John Williams was striding toward him, his face red with anger.

"Washington, what the hell do you think you're doing? I am ordering you to stand down right now, Agent."

"You want my badge, you can have it," Sam said. "You already told me I can't have anything to do with this case. As an FBI agent, I complied with your order. Now, as the father of the victims, I'm going to do what I have to do. This is personal between Colter and myself, and if I can do anything to save my daughters, I'm going to do it. And my advice to you, John, is to stay the hell out of my way."

Williams was completely taken aback. Sam hadn't slowed his pace as he walked to the car where Iris was crying. Iris had felt compelled to leave the command center. It was crowded and she felt she was in the way.

"I heard what you said, Sam. That's crazy! Am I going to lose my entire family in one night? I can't take this much longer." Iris was in a state of shock, and trembling with fear. She had already lost so much, having to endure four years without her husband; the thought of losing her beloved daughters was unfathomable.

Sam stroked her trembling arm, calming her. "Iris," he said, "Please trust me. All three of us are going to walk out of that house alive. I promise I will get our girls back."

Iris gulped and squeezed his arm. "Sam, do whatever you have to do. But you end this thing now!"

Sam looked into her eyes and repeated, "Whatever I have to do. This ends now." Sam tenderly stroked her cheek and walked to the command center.

"I want earbuds on you so we can communicate," Williams said.

"No argument," Sam replied. "Let's hurry up before he does something drastic."

"We have him on the phone, Sam," the sheriff said. "He wants you to approach unarmed and he will release one of the girls."

"Tell him no deal," Sam said. "It's both girls or he doesn't get me."

"Are you sure about this, Sam?" Sheriff Watkins asked.

"Yes. Frankie Colter is a psycho, but he's also stupid. His hatred for me has been consuming him for years. He won't do anything to lose the opportunity to finally kill me."

The sheriff returned to the phone connection. After a few minutes, he said; "He agreed. He will release both girls as soon as you enter the house."

"We'll work that out when I get up there," Sam said as he slowly walked to the house.

There were five steps leading up to what had once been a screened-in porch. The screens, or rather what was left of them, hung loosely from their frames. Sam climbed the steps slowly, hearing every creak in the wood, wary that Frankie might have a gun and shoot him before he got to the door.

Sam said into the mike, "sheriff, tell him to bring the girls to the door and let them step onto the porch. When they are outside, I will step in."

"He said he will release one of the girls to the porch. He will release the other girl as soon as you are inside," the sheriff replied.

"Fair enough, but tell him I want both girls in my sight as soon as that door opens."

It was somewhere between a minute and eternity before he got a response. He could hear arguing or shouting from inside the house. He heard Frankie say, "Get both of the girls out here. I want to get this over with!"

More shouting and yelling. Sam decided to take matters into his own hands. He threw his shoulder into the door, breaking the molding around the lock. He heard the word "Abort!" as he hurled himself into the front room, losing his earbud, and the rest of the communication vanished into the night air.

CHAPTER 48

IT WAS NEARLY MIDNIGHT. THE quiet of the room when the air conditioner wasn't running kept James awake like a scream in the night.

James couldn't sleep. He had been downstairs to the kitchen twice to get a drink of milk, but sleep just wouldn't come. His mind raced thinking about Sam, Iris, and the girls. *What must they be going through? This has to be hell for them. Those sweet little girls…how JJ loves them.*

His mind kept racing. James never had a real family. His parents were killed in a car accident when he was young, and he had been raised by an uncle. He had a good childhood, went to good schools, had friends, and his uncle gave him shelter and love. But…it wasn't the same as a real family: mom, dad, a brother or sister.

James had been envious of his friends as a teenager. He was sometimes invited over for dinner or a sleepover, and marveled at the laughter and stories told around their tables at meals. He would watch parents joke with their children, and brothers and sisters show both affection and animosity toward each other. These were normal families, not a family marred by tragedy like his own.

Most of the time James was content. His uncle was company, and eventually his memories of his parents began to fade. He went away to college and met Susan. James fell in love and, while his past was still tragic, James learned to live in the present and for the future. Susan brought purpose into his life, and he loved her for it.

After James's beating and while he was suffering from amnesia, Sam became his first real friend since his and Susan's marriage. After his ordeal was over, contrary to the warning his psychologist had given him, the bond with Sam remained, and Iris, Sam, and the girls were as much a part of his family as Susan and JJ.

James reached over and started to shake Susan awake. He saw that she too was awake, deep in thought. She looked James in the eye and said, "We need to go to Omaha now."

They held each other and cried. Ten minutes later JJ was in his car seat and they were headed for I-80. They spent most of the trip crying, worrying, and praying everyone was going to be all right.

CHAPTER 49

THE CLOSET WAS DARK AND cramped. And it smelled. There were a few clothes hanging in there and some boxes on the floor. The girls could make them out as their eyes adjusted to the dark.

Maddy kicked at the door. She tried to push it with her shoulder. It wouldn't budge. They were trapped. Molly was whimpering again.

Maddy got on her knees and placed her face against Molly's hands which were still bound behind her back. Molly finally figured out she could grab the tape over Maddy's mouth. It took two tries, but Maddy finally twisted her face to loosen the tape as Molly held the corner. It hurt, but she didn't care. "Now you, Molly."

Molly got on her knees, and Maddy grabbed the tape while her sister twisted away and tore the tape loose. Maddy said, "Good job, Molly. Now let's figure how to untie ourselves."

"I want Dad," Molly said. "He's going to rescue us, isn't he? I think that was him I heard in that really loud voice."

"I don't know, Molly. I couldn't make out what the man said, and I don't know if it was Dad or not. But we can't wait for Dad. We need to get away before that horrible man hurts us."

Maddy knew she need to bolster Molly's courage. "You've been really brave, Molly. Now let's look around and see how we can get out of here." It was then that Maddy saw it. The opening to the attic was located in the closet ceiling above their heads. But how could they get to it?

Maddy could see a coat hook on the back of the door. With her teeth, she grabbed one of the coat hangers hanging there, and dropped it on the floor. She sat down, and after a few tries managed to grab it.

She held the top in her hand, and used her foot to push the bottom side down. Turning it upside down, she finally succeeded in hanging it upside down from the coat hook.

"What are you doing?" Molly asked. "We need to get out of here."

"We can't do it with our hands tied," Maddy replied. Her wrists were raw from trying to work her bonds loose. She used the coat hanger to try and work her knots loose. It cut her already-raw wrists. She fought through the pain and kept trying. Soon the coat hanger bent and was useless. "Okay, Molly. Turn around and see if you can untie my knots." She could feel Molly's fingers working. "Use your fingernails."

"I'll break them," Molly whined. Iris had allowed the girls to get their nails done before the school carnival.

"Just do it!" Maddy said. "If you hadn't gone with that stupid lady, we wouldn't be here right now."

"Oh yeah, blame me! You came along, too. It's just as much your fault."

Maddy could feel her bonds loosen. It was working. She finally slipped one hand free. Her wrist hurt when she tried to move it. But it was free! She said, "Way to go, Molly. Turn around and I'll untie you."

"But how will we get out?" Molly asked.

"Look up," Maddy said. "Remember when Dad had to go up in the attic? He went through a hole just like that one." She pointed to the ceiling.

"How do we get there?" Molly asked. Her hands were untied by then.

Maddy looked around her. The boxes were too flimsy to be any use. She squatted down. "Sit on my shoulders." Molly climbed on.

"I can't reach it," Molly said. "Will the shelf hold me?"

Maddy looked at the shelf and tried to wiggle it. It was loose, but looked sturdy.

"Okay, Molly, here's what you'll do. Move yourself from my shoulders onto the shelf. Once you're there, carefully stand up, and push up the board in the hole there. Be sure you're quiet with it." Once Molly got herself pulled onto the shelf, Maddy watched her progress and coached her, step by step. "Good job, Molly!" she whispered. "Now, go up through the hole. And be sure you only step on the narrow boards up there! If you step between them, your foot will go through the ceiling."

Maddy watched Molly's progress, and flashed her sister a smile when she made it. "Now, stay there and don't move," Maddy whispered.

"How will you get up here? I'm scared."

"I don't know yet."

Maddy could reach the shelf, but she couldn't pull herself up. She stood and studied the situation and finally realized she could take the shelf down and turn it front to back inside the closet. It would make a very steep ramp. She pulled on the clothes rod to steady herself, but it started to pull out. She looked at how it was secured to the wall. She tried again. This time it held, and the soles of her tennis shoes gave her enough grip to climb up. It was hard work, but she made it, using the top edge of the now-vertical shelf to get a toe hold. She pulled herself up into the dusty attic.

"We made it," Molly whispered.

"Not yet. Where is that light coming from?" Maddy whispered back.

Molly was holding onto one of the roof braces to keep her balance and stay on the rafter. She pointed to the light streaming in through the attic vent. The spotlights were throwing streams of light into the attic, the dust dancing in the light. Red strobes pierced the white light, throwing the girls' balance off.

"Hold on to these braces," Maddy said. "We have to get over there, and then we can get out."

"Will we have to jump?" Molly asked.

"Let's get there first," Maddy said. "And watch where you step."

The girls slowly worked their way to the vent. They could hear voices coming from below, but couldn't make out any words.

"Okay, you push on the bottom of the vent, and I'll hold the top so it doesn't fall."

The girls worked at the vent but it wouldn't budge. Finally, frustrated and scared, Molly hit it with the palm of her hand. It popped loose, making a dull thud when it fell onto the roof. The girls froze in fear, afraid the man or woman downstairs had heard it.

Molly squinted out the opening into the bright light. "There's a roof outside. We can climb out onto the roof. Look at all the police cars, Maddy."

Maddy looked out the window and the lights blinded her. She saw they were at the back of the house, and finally made out a figure, standing atop a truck, waving at them to come outside.

"Is that Dad?" Molly asked.

"I don't know," Maddy said. "He's waving for us to come outside, though."

The girls wiggled through the opening, landing headfirst on the porch roof. Maddy lost her footing when she tried to turn and sit down, but caught herself before she fell the ten feet to the ground.

The man on top of the truck was waving frantically. He had his palms in the air, pushing toward them.

"He wants us to stay here," Maddy said. "Let's just sit here until he tells us to move."

Molly and Maddy sat with their backs to the siding of the house, shielding their eyes from the blinding beam of the spotlight.

"My feet hurt," Molly whimpered. "This roof is scratching my skin."

Maddy fought the urge to chastise her, and instead reached out and put her arm around her. Molly put her head on Maddy's shoulder, and burrowed her head into her caress.

"Look at all the bugs in the light," Maddy said.

"I hate bugs!" Molly said with disgust.

That statement told Maddy the old Molly was back, and she just held on tight.

They waited. Suddenly a shot shattered the air.

"What was that?" Molly exclaimed, her head snapping up.

"Somebody shot a gun."

"Was it Dad?" Molly asked.

"I don't know."

"I'm scared," Molly said.

"Me, too." Maddy tightened her grip on Molly.

Sheriff Watkins heard the confirmation that one of the perpetrators, the woman, was down. Everyone heard the shot, and he sent a deputy to tell Iris what had happened.

CHAPTER 50

SAM SCRAMBLED TO REGAIN HIS footing after crashing the door in. He stood face to face with a startled Savana and Frankie. Sam's shoulder ached from hitting the door so hard, but the adrenaline was strong enough that he hardly noticed. All he heard in his earbud was "Abort" before his earbud came loose when he hit the door. He never got the rest of the message that his girls were safe.

For a moment, time seemed to hold still. Frankie had been yelling at Savana when Sam had crashed in. Sam remembered he'd heard Frankie calling Savana a stupid bitch. "How could they get away?" With a rush of relief, Sam put two and two together. His girls were safe. *Thank God. Whatever happens now, my girls are safe.* And then time was moving again, and Sam realized the danger he was in.

"I guess things worked out for me after all," Frankie said with a smile on his face, as he leveled the pistol at Sam.

Frankie's phone rang. Figuring Frankie was distracted and wouldn't notice, Sam edged toward a window. Frankie answered and listened for a moment before responding. "Well, here's the deal now. I have Washington. If you want to see him alive, bring that chopper and you are going to take the three of us out of here." He didn't wait for a reply before clicking off.

"Where are my girls?" Sam snarled.

"Ask the stupid bitch over there. She let them get away!"

Sam had seen the snipers with rifles on all sides of the house. If the girls were safe, they would shoot. He shifted a bit more to lure Frankie in front of a window, giving them a shot. Frankie moved with him. *Just a little more*, Sam thought. *Stay out of the line of sight, but get him in it.*

There was a slight "poof" sound. All Sam saw before he heard the gunshot was Savana's head explode, and a spray of fine red mist fill the air where it had been. She had moved into the line of sight of the other front window and they could see the gun in her hand. *One down, just me and Frankie.*

Frankie and Sam dropped to the floor at the same time. Frankie hadn't seen Savana go down, and apparently thought it was a wild shot, because he quickly regained his composure, and hit Sam in the head with his pistol, temporarily stunning him. Just as Sam got his bearing back, he felt the knife at his throat.

"Okay, asshole. Tell them to back off. I want that chopper, or you are going to be Butch's twin." The statement brought back visions of the man with the slashed throat in the Tahoe. Sam knew his earbud was working, even though it was no longer in his ear. The command center could hear every word. Sam figured Frankie didn't know that, so thought of a plan to get Frankie to move his hand.

"Okay, call them," Sam said. As Frankie released his grip on Sam's arm to grab his cell, Sam's forearm shot between his throat and Frankie's arm holding the knife. Sam had been a Ranger in the army, and was trained in hand-to-hand combat. Sam knew, however, that he was a lot slower now than in his youth, and Frankie was a psycho. Psychopaths often have superhuman strength and he might have to deal with that.

They struggled on the floor, Sam holding tightly onto the wrist of the hand holding the knife. Sam knew he needed to get Frankie in front of a window, keep himself out of the line of sight, and away from the knife in Frankie's hand. He got to one knee, and was just standing up when Frankie broke free. Sam started to pursue him, but stopped quickly to avoid wild slashes from Frankie's knife. The steel shone in the dim light, a menacing sharp edge begging Sam to come closer.

Outside in the command center, Williams was yelling, "Take the shot!"

"Can't get a clear shot, sir. Permission to shoot when clear."

"Yes!" Williams said, exasperated. "Got a five thousand dollar scope on that rifle and the idiot can't get a clear shot. I can't believe it. Hell, I can see them in the window from here!"

All the officers in the front of the perimeter could see two shadows struggling in and out of the light provided by the window. "They're too close together," the sheriff said. "One small move and we hit the wrong man," justifying his sniper's decision not to shoot.

Sam and Colter continued to parry and struggle. Colter tried to slash at Sam who managed to grab his wrist as he fell backward and crashed onto a cheap coffee table, still holding the hand gripping the steel blade. The legs of the table broke free and both men fell to the floor. Colter landed on top of him, temporarily knocking the wind out of Sam. Sam managed to push Frankie off, twist around, and regain his footing, all while gripping Frankie's wrist. Colter, who seemed to have figured out he was in danger if he got in front of a window, maneuvered around carefully, staying clear of the windows.

Sam was wet with sweat, his shirt soaked. They were nose to nose now, looking directly into each other's eyes. Sam could feel the evil coupled with rage emanating from Frankie's pupils. They were cold, yet seared with hate. Sam had to end this soon. Colter was younger and stronger. *Got to break his concentration for just a second.*

"Your brother Dave was a wimp," Sam said, struggling for breath. "He cried like a baby when I arrested him. The only bigger loser is you, Frankie."

Sam could see the rage welling up inside Frankie. Now was the time to make his move while Frankie had an image of his brother crying. Sam lunged as hard as he could, taking Frankie by surprise and pushing him against the wall with his shoulder. The air went out of Frankie's lungs from the blow, and Sam banged Frankie's wrist against the wall to free the knife.

Sam felt a sharp pain in his shoulder. Frankie was biting him! Sam shifted his body as he slammed the knife hand harder against the wall, again and again. Frankie wouldn't release his grip. Sam managed to throw his shoulder into Frankie again, crushing the air out of his lungs. Frankie dropped the knife.

Sam kicked the knife across the floor, and hit Frankie several times in the face. Frankie slumped to the floor. Sam backed off a little, catching his breath.

"Don't you ever mess with me or my family again," Sam said. His voice shook with fury and malice. Sam wanted to finish the job and kill Frankie on the spot, but something deep inside him wouldn't allow it. Instead, he turned away, raising his voice for the earbud, and said, "All clear in here. Come in and get this scumbag out of my sight."

Sam could hear voices and footsteps hurrying toward the house, when he heard a noise behind him. He turned just in time to see Frankie pushing himself up, and moving in the direction Sam had kicked the knife. Sam dived for the knife, but Frankie got there first. Sam had slid onto his back when Frankie lunged, the steel blade flashing in the light.

Sam's hand reached out and felt for something to use as a weapon. His hand found the splintered leg of the coffee table that had been destroyed during the fight. He raised it just as Frankie lunged. The knife stopped inches from Sam's throat, shook violently, then dropped to the floor. Frankie had impaled himself on the sharp end of the coffee table leg.

The SWAT team entered the room just in time to hear Sam, looking the dying Frankie in the eyes, say, "Tell Dave hello from me." Sam watched the evil black eyes dim as the life drifted from them.

CHAPTER 51

"SIR, IF YOU WILL COME with me, we're getting your daughters off the roof in the back of the house."

Sam limped as he followed the officer clad in riot gear around the house. On the way, Sam asked, "Does my wife know they are safe?"

"Yes, sir. She knows we will be bringing them around directly. We thought it best to keep them on the roof until the scene was secure. Less chance of collateral damage."

Sam shuddered at the thought of his daughters being collateral damage, but it could have turned out that way if gunfire erupted. He turned the corner just as the officer carried Molly down the ladder, and set her on the ground. Maddy was starting down on her own.

"Dad!" Molly exclaimed, rushing into his arms. Sam had dropped to his knees and held her tight in his arms. "I was so scared," she said, burying her face into his chest. Maddy was right behind her, and Sam opened his arm to pull her into the embrace. He sobbed openly, telling his daughters he loved them, how he couldn't have lived without them. Molly smiled. "I knew you would come and rescue us, Dad."

"I'm very proud of you girls. I think you rescued yourselves. Now, let's find your mother." They all stood up and clung to each other as they walked around the house. As soon as they saw Iris standing in front of the flashing lights, crying with her hand clutched over her mouth, they let go of Sam and went running to their mom.

The SWAT officer was following. Sam turned to him and said, "Do you know where Officer Martinez is?"

"No sir, but I will find her."

Sam ran to Iris and joined in the tearful family reunion.

When the girls had finished telling how they got out onto the roof, Sam glanced around. There was a lot of commotion going on around them. He loaded Iris and the girls into the Suburban and told them he had to thank some people. Iris said, "Tell them thank you from us, too."

Sam went to the command center and stepped inside. Sheriff Watkins had a huge grin on his face. "Nice work, Agent. I have to admit I had my doubts, but all's well when it ends well."

"Thanks for your support, Sheriff. I'll never be able to thank you enough." Sam glanced around. "Where's Williams?"

"He left as soon as we got the all-clear signal. I think he's assembling a team to set up a press conference as soon as possible."

Sam nodded his head and said, "I reckon you're right. I'm going home with my family now, Sheriff. Please tell your guys thanks."

Sam nodded and turned to leave. A young Hispanic woman was waiting outside the trailer. She was short, wearing paint-spattered jeans and a Creighton University sweatshirt. "I was told you wanted to see me. I'm Vicki Martinez."

Sam extended his hand, saying, "I understand you are the off-duty officer who spotted the van and followed it here."

"Yes, sir."

"I can't begin to thank you enough for taking time to help when you could have been spending time at home with your family."

Martinez said, "We all have to help each other, sir." She added with a small smile, "Now we both can spend time at home with our families."

Sam nodded, gave her an answering smile, turned and headed for the Suburban holding his family. It was time to go home.

CHAPTER 52

GRANDMA GRACE, JAMES, SUSAN, AND JJ were waiting for them when they entered the house. There were tight hugs and Grace proudly announced, holding her rosary, that her prayers had brought her girls home. *Not to mention my brave husband and girls,* thought Iris.

James and Susan had gotten a motel, and said they thought it was time to give the Washington family some time to themselves. Iris cried and thanked them over and over for coming. After hugging everyone again, James and Susan left, thankful that Sam and the girls were safe.

It had been a quiet ride home. No one spoke from the time the lights stopped reflecting in the car windows until they reached the house. They just sat in the car looking at each other and exchanging lot of hugs.

While the girls cleaned up, Sam got out of his bloody and torn shirt and sat down to make some necessary phone calls. Iris appeared with a glass of Scotch, and they exchanged smiles as she handed it to him. He called his parents, Katie, Amy Hansen, and the school principal, sharing the good news. He figured they would spread the word.

The girls came down from their baths and Iris attempted to put lotion on their faces where the duct tape had been, but they both cringed when it stung the abraded area even more. She finally settled for some antibiotic ointment for their other small injuries. The girls asked for some hot cocoa. Iris raised her eyebrows. "In the summer, you want hot cocoa?" They giggled and nodded. "All right," she smiled. "And I suppose I should add some whipped cream on top?"

As Maddy and Molly settled down with their mugs of cocoa, they came to life. They were clean, had their jammies on, felt safe and relaxed. Three in the morning or not, their account of the night had to be told. They excitedly told details, often talking over one another, each giving their version of what had happened. Iris was stunned. Sam was pleased that they had endured it so well, stayed calm, and found a way to escape.

By four, the praises of bravery for each other had diminished to calling each other stupid. Iris decided this was enough for one night, and decreed it was time for everyone to go to bed. Teeth were brushed in record time, and it wasn't long before Iris was curled up next to Sam, and they could finally talk in private. They talked about how brave the girls were, how horrible it had been, and how Sam had saved the day. Iris finally asked Sam what had happened in the house.

Sam was silent for a long moment. "I'll elaborate another time. For now, let's just say I took your advice. 'I ended it forever.'"

They finally drifted off, exhausted, into a fitful sleep.

CHAPTER 53

THE NEXT DAY SAM MADE arrangements for Iris and the girls to see Kim, his therapist. He spent the balance of the day giving statements to the task force and other law enforcement agencies involved about his role in the incident. The FBI interviewed the girls individually at home with Iris present. It was a grueling day.

Due to the media attention, Williams asked Sam to make a statement to the press. Sam videotaped a statement on behalf of his family to be shown on the news. "On behalf of my family, my wife Iris and daughters Maddy and Molly, I want to publicly thank all the law enforcement agencies involved with apprehending the perpetrators who abducted my children. In particular, Agent John Williams of the FBI, head of the task force, Sheriff Watkins of the Douglas County Sheriff's Department, the Nebraska State Patrol, and the Omaha Police Department. In addition, I want to thank Officer Vicki Martinez, who volunteered to help in her off-duty hours, and spotted the van used in the abduction. Also to Danny Lemanowski, a classmate of my daughter's, who provided a description and license plate number of the van. And last, a thank you to everyone, friends and neighbors, who supported us in any way during this ordeal."

It was against Sam's nature to do the videotape, but felt he owed something to the overwhelming number of people who had come to his support. Sam bit his tongue when he mentioned John Williams, but the situation had ended well for all. Sam had his family back and Williams got his glory on several press conferences. More than a fair trade. *Maybe this will get him a promotion to another office.*

PART III

CHAPTER 54

A WEEK LATER SAM RETURNED TO the office. He was tired of answering questions. He was usually on the other side of the fence. He understood it was necessary to justify his actions, but that didn't make it fun.

Sam settled into his chair. It seemed different somehow. He looked around the office and everything was in place. Perhaps it was just a reaction to the trauma of the last week. *This scheme all started with Frankie Colter being released from prison last March. First, the attempt on my life. Then the abduction of my girls. It's finally over; I don't have to live every day wondering when it will happen.* Sam closed his eyes and let out a sigh of relief.

Lost in thought, Sam rubbed his left shoulder. It was still sore and numb at times. The entire family had undergone physical exams and been given clean bills of health. Frankie hadn't broken the skin when he bit him, and Sam's shoulder was just bruised from hitting the door. The doctor merely said. "Take some Naproxen, You'll be fine." That comment bruised his ego.

"Sam! You're back!" The sound of the voice startled Sam out of his reverie. He looked up to see Special Agent Johansson charging at him. She bounded behind his desk and hugged him in his chair. "I'm so happy to see you! I know you said you were going to attempt to make the joint meeting, but I didn't dare hope you'd actually feel up to it."

Sam was a little embarrassed, but recovered quickly. "You're in a good mood today," he said, smiling.

"You bet!" Katie said. "I'm confident we're going to wrap this thing up in the next week or so."

"And you did it without me?" Sam asked.

"Well, you were a little help initially," Katie said, grinning. "Now, if you behave in this meeting today, I might just keep you for a partner."

Sam groaned and shook his head. Katie had called him every day this past week as he recovered from his shoulder injury and waited out the Bureau-mandated time off because of the mental stress the abduction had caused. He was touched by her show of support.

"Ten o'clock sharp in the conference room." Katie turned to leave, but looked back at Sam and added, "Oh, and we have some guests. Williams has called in ATF and Homeland Security." She rolled her eyes and walked out the door.

Sam closed his eyes and shook his head with a chuckle. He sure had misread Katie Johansson initially. Or perhaps, he had just brought out the best in her. He had to admit she was as good as anyone he had worked with.

Sam strolled into the conference room. He found representatives from ATF, Homeland Security, and Special Agents Leeds, Kopeck, Johansson, and Williams already seated. Introductions were made. Leeds and Kopeck expressed their sympathy for the ordeal Sam and his family had undergone, but Sam assured them everyone was fine. Katie introduced Kelly Standage from Homeland Security and Bruce Whaley with the ATF.

Katie didn't waste any time. "Well, gentlemen, shall we begin?"

She went back in time to the illicit drug laboratory which was discovered in New Jersey, and the subsequent act of removing the FBI from the case. She explained that the case was taken over by the Omaha FBI office, as it was thought the illicit drug laboratory was being moved to the Midwest.

"A pharmacist in Grand Island, several hours west of here, is a friend of Agent Washington, and expressed his concern over several of his patients experiencing Warfarin poisoning. We have two deaths directly attributable to Warfarin poisoning in the Grand Island area, and social media postings of similar events attributed to Warfarin poisoning across the nation.

Katie went on. "While on a hunting trip in Canada, the same pharmacist inadvertently stumbled onto the location where the drug laboratory was now located, just north of the Canadian border in Saskatchewan.

"Agent Washington and I then traced the movement of the drugs across the border into the United States. This trail led us to the truck driver who hauled the illicit drugs to a warehouse in Kansas City. We approached him, and he agreed to cooperate with the Bureau."

"The same scenario happened in Saskatchewan as happened in New Jersey. As soon as the lab was compromised, it was moved to another location. This time we had a man on the inside, and the truck driver informed us the lab has been moved to Sioux City, Iowa. So it would appear we are right back to where we started in New Jersey."

Heads nodded.

"So how do we play it?" Williams asked.

"Number one," Katie said, "we have to stop the distribution of the drugs. We have enough to arrest the goons making and distributing the illicit drugs, and we have enough to arrest Harris Strang, President and CEO of Trae Pharmaceuticals, who is behind them."

Sam spoke up. "Our big question was, why would anyone manufacture counterfeit Warfarin? It's common, not unusually expensive, and certainly not very profitable...Our answer came from James Wilson, the same pharmacist, when he realized Harris Strang was involved. The answer is Quixtenone."

Katie nodded at him to continue.

"Trae spent billions developing this drug, but after the FDA had approved it for human consumption, questions surfaced about liver failure in some patients. Physicians were afraid to change patients to Quixtenone, and sales suffered. This is all about money, pure and simple. Strang knew that Trae was so deeply in debt, Quixtenone sales had to pull them out of it. When sales didn't rise, he took it upon himself to find a way to make it happen."

Sam looked at Katie. "By poisoning people with Warfarin," she said. "It's an ingenious, yet heinous, scheme to force physicians to order Quixtenone. They would lose confidence in Warfarin, and switch patients to Quixtenone, driving Trae's sales through the roof, and saving the company."

"We have to stop this right here and now," Williams spoke up for the first time. "Why haven't we raided the plant and confiscated the drugs?"

"Katie and I discussed this very problem John," Sam said. "Do we sacrifice more lives while we wait until we can catch the Washington bureaucrat who is undermining our operation? The answer is no. But Katie has a plan to accomplish both objectives: Get the drugs off the market and take the Washington connection down at the same time." He nodded to Katie.

"Okay," Katie said. "It took me almost two weeks to figure out why the counterfeit drugs were poisoning people, and also how they were getting them mixed in with the legally manufactured product. It's quite ingenious, really. Let's see if I can bring you up to speed."

"DC Generics, owned by Trae Pharmaceuticals, manufactures the Warfarin tablets in Delaware, packages them in twenty-pound drums, and ships them to a re-packager. The re-packager puts the bulk tablets into bottles of 100 or 500, and ships them to the wholesaler. The wholesaler then sells them to the pharmacies.

"The problem is, the re-packager is manufacturing their own tablets, *and the tablets they manufacture contain 10 mg of Warfarin, not 5 mg*. The re-packager then mixes their 10 mg tablets in with the original tablets when they bottle them, say twenty counterfeit tablets in every bottle of a hundred.

"The end result is that some patients who take a Warfarin 5mg tablet are actually getting 10mg of Warfarin, causing the bleeds we are seeing."

"But I thought all Warfarin tablets were color-coded, plus have the strength embossed on them," Williams said.

"They are," Katie said. "But think about it. It's simple to match the color of the tablet, and to have a tool and die maker duplicate the tablet mold. Or, perhaps they just took a mold from DC Generics. Anyway, gentlemen, that is how the illicit tablets are getting into the pharmacies. The pharmacies dispense the tablets to their patient, and some of those patients get sick, even die. Not every tablet, not every bottle, but just enough to steer patients and physicians away from Warfarin. And the obvious drug of choice now becomes Quixtenone.

"Okay," Leeds said. "What's your plan to stop it?"

"We have an informant in place, the semi driver. He will call us and tell us when the next shipment is due to be shipped. He'll haul the shipment back to Kansas City and it will be distributed from there."

"So how do we keep the drugs from going on the market?" Williams asked.

"We have two options, depending on the timing involved. The semi-trailer is left in the lot overnight. Either the next morning or the next evening they unload the drugs into three smaller trucks for distribution. Only this time, we break into the semi-trailer, confiscate the counterfeit drugs as evidence, and replace them with the correct tablets. The perps will unknowingly be delivering the correct drugs."

"Why aren't we going to arrest the drivers?" Williams interrupted, obviously irritated.

"Bigger fish, John," Katie said. "But that's the second option— we certainly can arrest them once we have the evidence we need to get the senator. It's just an issue of when the next batch is delivered and when we get what we need so that everyone involved can be prosecuted. We already set up surveillance this morning in Sioux City, but told our guys to be sloppy about staying hidden. Strang's two main people, names Abe and Lenny, will spot our agents and report back to Strang. It's our hope he will try and get the Bureau to back off our operation long enough to move his lab. When Strang calls his contact in Washington, D.C., Senator Mellen, who we're certain is involved, we'll have them both."

Williams shook his head and scowled in vehement disagreement. "Personally, I think this is a hare-brained scheme," he said, "and I won't go along with it."

CHAPTER 55

HE DISCUSSION GOT HEATED. WILLIAMS was adamant that everyone involved be arrested immediately when the transfer was made. The ATF and Homeland Security representatives thought Katie's idea sounded good, but weren't jumping into the argument. Agents Leed and Kopeck were on board with Katie's plan; they wanted to nail whoever had pulled the plug on them in New Jersey.

"John, if we have someone crooked in Washington, we owe it to the public to expose him."

"Hell, everyone in Washington is crooked," Williams snorted.

Sam could see that this conversation was going nowhere, and sensed Williams needed a cooling off time. "John, can you and I have a word in private?"

"Why?" Despite his defensive tone, Williams had already risen to leave the room.

When they were outside, Sam said, "John, I can sense that you don't want to be part of Agent Johansson's idea. What would you suggest?"

This took Williams by surprise. He thought for a minute. "I will not be part of tapping a senator's phone. And I will not ask the director of the FBI to put a tap on a senator's phone. If we're wrong, my head will roll right along with his."

Sam knew Williams wouldn't jeopardize his job by sticking his neck out. "Okay, John. I will go back in there and tell them we are not going to tap a senator's phone, even if it blows the case."

Williams was taken aback. "You'd do that—take my side?"

"I will," Sam said. "Just give me a few minutes to convince them, okay?"

"All right guys, here's the deal," Sam said when he returned to the room. "We can't tap a senator's phone."

There were loud protestations and Katie was livid. "That damned Williams is going to blow this whole thing up just to cover his own ass. And he's the one who got us involved, Sam."

"Actually, it was Agent Leeds and I," Agent Kopeck said. "We thought he would back us up."

"Let's not get ahead of ourselves," Sam said. "I promised him we wouldn't tap a senator's phone. We don't have to."

Katie's eyes lit up. "You're right, Sam! All we have to do is tap Strang's phone. If he calls a U.S. senator, that's not our problem. All legal, and his involvement would be a surprise to us." Katie gave Sam a high five.

Agents Leeds and Kopeck were on board, and Kelly Standage and Bruce Whaley also agreed the plan was solid. Williams re-entered the meeting and agreed to put the tap on Strang's phone.

After the meeting, Leeds said to Sam. "Looks like Williams left his balls at the academy. I had hoped for a little more from him."

Sam merely smiled. "Let's just hope we can pull this off."

"This is worse than a stakeout," Katie said, "except at least we get to drink coffee and eat our meals." Two days had gone by, and Strang still hadn't made any calls about moving the lab.

"Are you sure they know we have the lab under surveillance?" Williams asked. "Maybe they didn't see any of our agents?"

"Trust me, they saw our Suburban sitting outside the facility for two days," Sam said. "These guys aren't stupid. Well, not exactly smart either, but very street smart. We need to give it time." Sam was seasoned enough to know the decision would be made in Strang's time frame, not the FBI's. He told Williams and Katie to just be patient.

Abe and Lenny had indeed spotted the black Suburban sitting outside the fence surrounding the warehouse parking lot. They had called Strang within a few hours—and before the the wiretap was in place—and he told them he needed to make another shipment before moving the lab again. Abe and Lenny continued to repackage the rest of the counterfeit Warfarin they had on hand. It took almost three days.

Abe called Strang to inform him the repackaging was completed. Strang told them to make the shipment of Warfarin, and then start packing up the tableting equipment. He wanted to get the machines out of the lab the day after the shipment.

"Harris, what the hell is going on?"

"Joe, the FBI has discovered our lab in Sioux City."

"Your problem, not mine."

"*Our* problem, Joey. You're in this as deep as I am. You got involved when our lab in New Jersey was compromised."

"All I did was make a phone call. I was only aware of the lab because you told me of its existence. I told you to close the lab, and called a contact in the Department of Justice who owed me a favor. He convinced the Bureau to drop the investigation. It's called a quid pro quo, Harris. Not corruption, just politics. Happens every day. Goodbye, Harris." The line went dead.

Strang slammed the receiver down, furious. "That bastard's not going to put this all on me. Not if I can help it."

The taped conversation was passed on to Sam, Katie, and the rest of the team.

"Do we have him or not?" Agent Leeds asked.

"I think so," Katie said. "Did I mention that the deed to the land where the lab was located in Canada is in the name of none other than the Honorable Joseph Mellen? Dutch will testify that Mellen had visited the camp in early spring."

"Thanks for telling me about this before," Sam said. "Some partner you are!"

"I started to tell you, but that was the night the girls were abducted, remember?"

"Oh, yeah...your phone call. I remember. Okay, I'll give you this one." Sam smiled even as pain at the memory of that night covered his face.

Williams jumped into the conversation. "Okay, I've heard enough. Get warrants out on Strang and his men, and those delivery drivers also,"—he gave Katie a firm stare—"and let's button this thing up. We have lives to save."

"Agent Johansson, this is Denver. I just got a call. I'm supposed to make two runs. Tomorrow I pick up a shipment of drugs in Sioux City, Iowa and bring it back to Kansas City. Then they're going to unload it tomorrow night, and I'm going back to Sioux City the next morning and pick up some equipment. I'm supposed to bring it back to Kansas City."

"Make the first run as instructed, Denver. Park the trailer in the lot, and make the second run the next day."

Denver parked the trailer in the lot as Katie had instructed. After he left, FBI agents watched the lot. About midnight, three trucks showed up and loaded up the Warfarin. They closed the doors on the trailer, and each was followed by a black Suburban. They were arrested *en route* to their respective destinations, and the counterfeit Warfarin confiscated.

Katie was anxious to wrap up this case. She had spent countless hours putting it all together, and here she was still waiting. The operation had to be coordinated so that they could take the entire operation down in twenty-four hours. Stopping the delivery trucks and confiscating the counterfeit drugs was the first step. Now came the hard part. They had to arrest Abe and Lenny along with Strang at the same time. Katie spelled out her plan to the other agents.

Abe and Lenny watched the Freightliner pull away from the empty warehouse in Sioux City, the tableting machines safely stored inside. Denver had seemed nervous, but they figured he was worried about his sick wife. Abe went into pack up their personal things while Lenny finished his cigarette.

CHAPTER 56

LENNY WAS OUT HAVING ANOTHER smoke when he saw the tactical van pull into the parking lot of the warehouse, followed by at least four other vehicles. He threw his cigarette aside and rushed back into the warehouse, shouting the alarm to Abe.

Abe grabbed his Steyr A3 Carbine and raced to the window next to the front door of the warehouse. "Cover the dock door," he yelled at Lenny.

The FBI SWAT Team had their hands full. There was nothing but open space between them and the warehouse. Sam and Katie stayed with the SWAT Team in the tactical van as it pulled into position at the front of the warehouse. The SWAT Team was using the heavily armored van as cover from gunfire. Four agents jumped from the van in full tactical gear, as Abe fired a burst through the front window. They sought cover behind the van and waited for Abe to reload.

Williams could hear automatic weapon fire from the front of the warehouse. Williams asked if the assault team needed more agents.

"No sir," came the reply. "We have this under control."

Abe was not going down without a fight. It was short-lived. One flashbang grenade through the window was enough to temporarily disorient Abe, allowing three FBI agents in full tactical gear to breach the front door.

Abe raised his Steyr, but before he could fire, a hail of bullets cut him down. Lenny wasn't far away, lying on the floor, curled up into a ball, crying, "Don't shoot, don't shoot me!"

Denver Long heard about the arrests on the news. He waited at home for the knock on his door. It never came.

Special Agent Leeds and Kopeck had flown back to New Jersey. They had started this investigation and wanted to be part of the arrest at Trae Pharmaceuticals.

Harris Strang sat at his desk, looking over the sales reports. Sales of Quixtenone were rising rapidly. The Warfarin scare was generating thousands of new orders for Quixtenone, as physicians were becoming concerned about the Warfarin deaths. He smiled to himself. Harris owned fifty-five percent of the stock in the company, stock prices were at an all-time low, and now was the time to act before the markets picked up on the latest sales figures. He called his broker and told him to buy every possible share of Trae stock, offering a price ten percent above market. *That ought to force some of the minority shareholders to get out before their stock drops even more. Maybe even Joey. With all his involvement he may see this as a way to get out of this mess and avoid a scandal. I'd be okay with owning all the stock!*

Harris sat back in his comfortable desk chair, looked out the window at the city, and rose to do something he never did during working hours. Have a drink. He plucked the outlandishly priced Scotch from the cabinet and poured it over ice. He raised the glass in a toast to himself, and moved it to his lips as the door to his office burst open.

"What the hell is this? You can't barge in here like this!"

Special Agents Leeds and Kopeck flashed their credentials and told him he was under arrest. Kopeck began to read the warrant, when Harris made a mistake. He flung the glass at Leeds, hitting him in the chest.

In seconds, Strang lay on his stomach, hands being cuffed behind his back, while he was given the Miranda warning. As Special Agent Leeds roughly pulled him to his feet, angry that he had thrown the glass of scotch at him, he managed to bump the bottle off the desk, spilling it all over the carpet.

"Hey, that's a $500 bottle of scotch!" Strang yelled.

"Maybe your friends can bring you some in jail," Leeds said, marching him out the door.

Down the hall, agents showed a court order to Kevin Curtsman, the Chief of Operations and second in charge at Trae Pharmaceuticals. The order instructed Trae to contact the FDA and issue a recall of all Warfarin manufactured by DC Generics. The recall went all the way to the consumer, and Trae was further instructed to issue warnings to the public that patients should not consume any Warfarin in their possession, but take the tablets back to the pharmacy.

Stunned, Curtsman demanded to see Strang. The agent pulled his handcuffs, and said, "Comply with the order immediately, or you can visit with Strang in his cell." Curtsman complied.

Sam and Katie were notified that the arrests had gone well in New Jersey. They were glad the case was finally solved and decided to call it a day. Williams, however interrupted their celebration with the news that he was to hold a press conference in a half hour, and wanted them in attendance.

"So much for an afternoon off," Katie sighed,

Special Agent Williams held a briefing at the Omaha office of the Federal Bureau of Investigation. He went over how his team had apprehended the illicit drug manufacturers and Special Agents Kopeck, an academy classmate of his, and Special Agent Leeds apprehended Harris Strang, the president/CEO of Trae pharmaceuticals in New Jersey. After the briefing he smiled and said, "I think we can put this case to rest. Good job, everyone."

"What about Mellen?" Katie asked.

"I'll talk to the director," Williams said. "That's a very touchy subject. He may consider it off limits. Politics and all. Besides, we got the trafficking stopped."

Katie sighed. She knew Williams was stonewalling. She smiled to herself. *If the mountain won't come to Mohammed...*

CHAPTER 57

S AM HAD ONE PHONE CALL to make before he left for the day. "James, this is Sam. Just wanted you to know that Strang, Lenny and several others are now in the custody of the authorities. We had raids this morning and rounded everyone up. It looks like your Warfarin woes are over. Oh, and your old friend, Abe, is dead. He made the mistake of trying to shoot it out with the bureau's SWAT team."

"That's great, Sam! I can dispense my new Warfarin without worrying about who's going to be the next victim. Thank God you got this stopped. Unfortunately, not soon enough for my friend Gwen Eyelor. Thanks for calling."

"Least I could do. If it hadn't been for that hunting trip we might still be trying to solve the case, so a good portion of the thanks goes to you."

"So I can schedule another trip soon?"

"Aaah—-not going there. That, my friend, is between you and Susan. Take care and we'll talk soon,

James hung up the receiver and rushed to tell Marcia and Jennifer the news.

James, along with the rest of the country watched the day's events unfold on the six o'clock news. James groaned when he thought about the recall of all the Warfarin tablets.

Patients flocked to their pharmacies to exchange their Warfarin tablets, getting only a week's supply to tide them over, as the recall created a massive shortage. The Warfarin poisonings finally subsided and life returned to normal for James and the rest of the medical profession.

James and friends went to lunch the next day. Dutch had emailed Curt, and told him he had taken the bearskins to a taxidermist in Winnipeg. The hunters were to call the taxidermist and he would make arrangements to begin making their rugs. James had forgotten all about the rugs. He cringed; *Now I have to tell Susan about the rug...*

Trae declared bankruptcy the following week.

Her firearm and black suit replaced by black three-inch heels, Katie moved to the sounds of *Y.M.C.A.!* She was stunning in a simple white sleeveless top and a short skirt, showing off her long slim legs. Katie was having a blast, letting herself go, and enjoying the moment. It was the most fun she had had in a long time. Most of the people there would never guess she was deadly with a Glock in her real life.

The band finally took a break. Katie was grateful as she needed to extend her best wishes to the bride and groom. "Congratulations, Sheila! You are the most beautiful bride," she gushed, giving her cousin a hug. "And Greg, you are one lucky man." She asked about honeymoon plans, a bit envious that she wasn't in a position to be leaving on a Jamaican honeymoon. "Well, I'm sure you'll have a wonderful time! Sheila, do you happen to know where your dad is? I thought I'd have a word with him."

It wasn't long before Katie's Uncle John showed up at her table. "Katie! It's so good to see you! You look great! I was just going to find your table and visit with you when I heard you were looking for me. Shall we dance? You can tell me all about being an FBI agent."

"I'd be delighted," she said, with a smile as she rose. "And while we dance, perhaps I can tell you about my dilemma."

A warrant was issued for the arrest of Senator Joseph Mellen two weeks later.

"Well, Sam, are we partners now?"

"We always were, Katie. I knew you had it in you; I just had to push you a little. You're a good agent, and will rise quickly. I'll work with you any day.

Sam gave her a long look. "And, by the way, how did you get Williams to bend on Senator Mellen?"

Katie grinned. "I went over his head... Remember what you told me about doing your homework, Sam? Williams didn't do his. He never dreamed that the Assistant Director of the Bureau is my uncle. When I went to my cousin's wedding a couple of weeks ago, I just asked Uncle John to look at our files, and he came to the same conclusion as you and I."

"I'll be damned," Sam laughed. "I suppose that means there's no chance Williams will get promoted now."

"Afraid not, Sam. Sorry. But I'll tell you what. I'm going to take you and Iris out for dinner...but *you're* getting the tip this time."

OTHER BOOKS

The Black Angel

ACKNOWLEDGEMENTS

FIRST AND FOREMOST, I WOULD like to thank thank Arlene, my wife of fifty years. I could not have accomplished this work without her patience, dedication, and support. Her enthusiasm kept me going when words failed to come, and her praise encouraged me to continue when they did.

To my family and friends: I appreciate your wholehearted support.

Thanks to Ken Lessig, whose newspaper story about his hunt inspired us to join him on this one.

My editor, Carol Weber, kept me on the right track. She was critical when necessary, yet supportive throughout. We shared a few emotions, but I only remember the humorous ones.

My cover designer, Victorine E. Lieske, a *New York Times* best selling author; *How to find Success Selling eBooks.* She once again came up with a dynamite cover.

My formatter, Craig Hansen. Craig always adds some creativity to his formatting, along with lots of flourish.

My physician, Ryan Crouch, D.O. Dr. Crouch assisted with the clinical information for Warfarin overdose and treatment. (Any misstatements are solely on the part of the author.)

My friends who accompanied me on the actual bear hunt: Dave Gilroy, Dick Kittridge, and Ken Staab. I hope you like your new names, and I'm sure the hunt isn't exactly the way you remember it.

My grandchildren, a few of which granted me permission to use their first names.

My readers from my first book, *The Black Angel*, who encouraged me to write this one.

The Nebraska Writers Guild for their dedication to Nebraska authors.

ABOUT THE AUTHOR

Ben is a native of Grand Island, Nebraska, a graduate of the University of Nebraska, College of Pharmacy. He has been a practicing pharmacist since 1967, and now specializes as a pharmacist consultant to long term care facilities. Up until his first book, he joked that his writing had been confined to "one liners" on the labels of prescription bottles.

This is his second novel, and incorporates scenarios which deviate from the usual thriller "chase scenes". He hopes you will enjoy this diversion.

39560988R00139

Made in the USA
San Bernardino, CA
29 September 2016